Encore! Encore!

A Novel

ELÍAS MIGUEL MUÑOZ

RATTLING GOOD YARNS
PRESS

Rattling Good Yarns Press
33490 Date Palm Drive 3065
Cathedral City CA 92235
USA
www.rattlinggoodyarns.com

Cover Design: Rattling Good Yarns Press

Library of Congress Control Number: 2023946005
ISBN: 978-1-955826-51-8

First Edition

To Tracy D. Terrell and John Miller, beloved friends, still alive in my heart.

Ya suben los dos compadres
hacia las altas barandas.

(They are climbing at last, the two friends,
up to the high balconies.)

—Federico García Lorca, "Romance sonámbulo"

First Act
(of many)

Luis

Why does he see his life as a play? Obviously, because he loves the theater, though he hasn't seen that much of it. Luis mostly remembers the shows with songs, and a drama that didn't have singing in it but which blew him away. Of course, he forgot the title. He tends to forget a lot of stuff for some bizarre reason, especially titles and character names. This play sounded like a superhero movie, something to do with spiders. But Mister Paul explained to him beforehand that it wasn't about those creepy critters. The drama told the story of two men who are locked up in the same prison cell, and only one of them is gay, but they end up getting it on. No surprise there. Luis knows how that goes! The faggot loves old Hollywood movies and narrates a horror flick to his cellmate about a panther woman. Not scary at all, and in fact, it made Luis laugh. Most movies suck, anyway. Luis would never go on and on describing them like the character in this play. He wanted to shout at him, Just shut the fuck up and let the other guy talk!

It turns out that the straight prisoner is in the slammer for his revolutionary work and his politics. And the queer guy's doing time for corrupting minors, which means he likes to have sex with very young men. There are so many people like him who vacation here in Santo Domingo! Luis has known a good number of them, his johns. Those tourists could end up in jail too, but no chance of that happening. Lots of Dominicans know what's going on at the Hotel Cristóbal, and they all pretend not to notice. Better for Luis and for his buddies in the biz. If the authorities started to crack down on the corrupters of minors in this city, a bunch of tourist money would stop coming in. So let all the horny foreign assholes keep coming to this tropical paradise!

Only a few of his johns stand out enough for Luis to remember them without having to jot down their names, the ones who stick around longer than a couple of nights and come back, like Mister Paul. It was Paul's idea to take Luis to see his first play at Teatro Las Máscaras. And he tries to get them tickets for new shows whenever he visits. Paul prefers American musicals on tour, even if all the actors are Dominican. He says a lot of gay men love musicals. Come to think of it, so does Luis, but that just means he digs a good story with songs 'cause he ain't queer!

Mister Paul taught him all about theater stuff. Unbelievable that Luis can recall so many big words. It helps that he studies them from time to time, not minding that it's just like doing homework. For example, the main characters can be either the protagonist (the good guy), or the antagonist (the bad guy.) There's also action, what happens in the play. Conflict is the hardest idea to grasp, and it's like a struggle between two characters, a character and the world, or between a character and himself. The turning point, an event that makes everything change for everyone. Resolution, how the conflict gets resolved. And message: what the work wants us to learn. Like in the case of the two prisoners, the fact that a straight man can fall in love with a gay man 'cause true love knows no gender. Or some heavy shit like that.

So, if he, Luis Miranda Ramos, is the protagonist in the story of his life, then who would be the antagonist? Definitely not his mom or his best friend Richard or Mister Paul. Could it be his father, though he's not in the picture? Yeah, that creep is the villain because of what he did to Mamita. Luis has never met him, doesn't even know what he looks like. Does that mean his father can't be the antagonist? Could that bad character be absent during the whole story but still affect the action? Does every work of theater need that type of *adversary* (Paul's word)? Can the antagonist be a place or a job instead of a person? And what about a whole city? A hotel?

Too many questions to ask Paul, and too many words for the parts of a damn play! Yeah, 'cause there are also unities of action, place, and time, and acts, which are like sections. By the way, this play about Luis would need many acts, at least three. You can't pack all his thoughts and dreams into just two measly sections. That's not how real life works. Not for him.

Paul says there are plays called absurd that don't follow any rules and where nothing makes sense. Luis hasn't seen any shows of that type and doesn't think he'd enjoy them. He wants reality to make sense, not like the telenovelas his mom watches, which tell stories that would never happen in the real world. They're not plays 'cause there's no art in them, but they might be the closest thing to absurd that Luis has seen.

He's grateful to Mister Paul for all he's taught him. Paul is an editor for a big textbook company in California, and he loves the theater more than anything. He's seen many plays, read many books, yet he doesn't show off his knowledge like some of the professors Luis has had sex with, johns who are always dropping names and quoting the great writers. Luis is very familiar with the type. Mister Paul can't stand them, says they're full of shit. But those profs buy and use the books he sells, so he has to be nice to them and praise the way they teach, even if they just talk at the students nonstop about themselves and how famous they are. Paul doesn't do that. He likes to share what he knows, which is a lot, with young people. And he's a good listener.

Mister Paul is a huge fan of a Black singer from England named Shirley Bassey. Wow, Luis remembers her full name! Shirley sings big ballads with a deep chest voice, and Paul says she's a gay icon, which means she's popular with faggots. That's the reason Luis didn't know about her 'cause he ain't no fag. Paul gave him a cassette of her music last year, along with a tape player that also had a radio. Luis has enjoyed the gift and Mister Paul's favorite song on the tape, "The Greatest Performance." Paul explained the lyrics to him, and what a fucking sad story they tell! Shirley is singing as if she were an actress who gave the most fantastic performance of her life tonight, but her heart was breaking, and she was crying inside while she performed.

That would definitely not be Luis's case 'cause he never cries, especially not when he's singing or playing the guitar. It makes him feel so happy to play and sing his own songs. And, besides, only women cry. Luis has no reason to be sad, anyway. His life is exciting, full of possibilities, and with an open ending. In that sense, it's not like a play that must end, 'cause he plans to live forever, or at least for as long as people remember his music.

Sometimes, after they're done fucking, Paul pretends to be Shirley and tells Luis that he just gave the greatest performance of his life in bed. And then he sings the damn song instead of letting Luis take care of the singing, which he can do so much better than the Gringo!

Luis wishes he could get to see more plays, at least one a month. And maybe become an actor? Shit, that'd be so fucking amazing! Tough job, though, impersonating other people and having to memorize a ton of words. Could he do it? It's the issue of memorizing stuff that he'd be concerned about. His brain has a tough time retaining information, though Luis does manage to remember the songs he writes, words and melody, and most guitar chords by way of repetition. To become an actor, he'd have to hire a drama coach and practice all the time. Hey, maybe Paul could give him some pointers about this, since he knows so much about the theater.

The theater. Yeah, it's more mind-blowing than movies for sure 'cause a live drama entertains you but also makes you think, even comedies and musicals. Movies don't get inside your head and teach you things, definitely not the ones with lots of action. Luis has enjoyed most of the sci-fi flicks his buddy Richard is into, like *Blade Runner*, the only title he's managed to remember. At the movies, they always sneak in a bag of empanadas made by Luis's mom and eat to their hearts' content while watching androids who look just like humans, Earth colonies thriving all over the galaxy, and spaceships traveling at the speed of light. Those films give you a glimpse of the future, says Richard. Problem is, they typically have shoot-'em-ups, laser gunfire, and lots of explosions. Boring crap! And Luis would just rather see a play. He hasn't managed to get Richard excited about the theater 'cause he says he can't afford the tickets. Neither can Luis, for that matter. Theater is more expensive than movies, especially American musicals.

So, yes, now everything in Luis' life feels like he's acting in a play as the protagonist, and everyone around him is a character. He has no idea what the conflict is and no clue how it's going to end, but he's sure it won't be a sad ending. No, not like the play about the two cellmates, where the gay man dies, and the other one gets tortured. That's why it's a tragedy, says Paul. Because even if you don't get to see the character's death, they mention at the end that he gets shot. Luis will make sure the play of his life isn't tragic. Maybe it'll be a tragicomedy, like Paul has suggested, which is both serious and funny. Or better yet, a comedy 'cause it'd make people happy, though Luis isn't particularly funny. He should learn some jokes!

The info Paul gives him sends his head spinning like a Ferris wheel sometimes. Luis has a hard time filing it all away. School is good for that, says the Gringo, not just to teach you things but also how to remember those things. Luis wishes he'd finished at least *nivel medio* in high school. He was getting good grades and learning a lot. But then, at the end of his second year, he had to quit 'cause his mom was in the hospital, and he had to go to work to pay the bills. Hey, but that's not the story he wants running through his head just now. Too depressing, though it has a happy ending 'cause his mother got better, and Luis found a way to make lots of money and rent a nice house for her. Who cares that he doesn't have a high school diploma. Certainly not his clients, as long as he can communicate with them about the basics.

And speaking of communication, maybe Paul could translate this play about Luis's life into English so it can reach a wide audience. English is an international tongue, says Mister Paul, which means that it's spoken all over the world. Problem is, then Luis wouldn't be able to say typically Dominican things like *tostado*, crazy, or the word you use when you're surprised, *Adió!* He couldn't say *quillarse* either, which means to get mad or angry. Or *pollo*, a handsome man like himself. And *piña*, not just pineapple but also a quarrel or a fight. Or the word *arrechar*, what Luis does to his clients: excite them. And *fundillo*, meaning ass. Oh, and there's his favorite word, *pechú*. He likes that one because it means brave and daring, and it describes Luis perfectly. Yeah, he's definitely a *pechú* kind of stud!

Mister Paul knows all those Dominican words and likes to use them, though they don't sound right coming out of his mouth. Why the hell is that? How can a person who's a linguist and knows Spanish so well, who even uses idioms and colloquialisms (big Paul words!), not be able to pronounce things the way you're supposed to? What happens in that person's brain? He'll have to have Paul explain this issue to him. And he'll be careful not to hurt his feelings, of course. Luis will just say he's referring to some of the dumb Gringos he's known over the years.

Okay, time to get this show started! First, he must mention where and when the action takes place: in the city of Santo Domingo, capital of the Dominican Republic (where Luis was born), during two weeks of May in 1984. Those fourteen days are usually the chunk of time that Mister Paul spends here, and maybe they can represent Luis's life until now.

A lot of people are saying that 1984 is a great year 'cause Dominicans finally have a good president, and there are no corrupt politicians in the government. The president and his people have been declaring all the time lately, on the radio and on TV, that the country is going through a period of stability. Well, so far, so good, but anything could happen between now and December. Like, the country's leader could be assassinated by the military in cahoots with the rich conservatives. Heaven forbid, as Mamita would say. She likes this new dude in power.

What about the characters? He'll start with his mother and himself. Damn, he almost forgot there have to be scenes in a play! Okay, here's the opening scene, where he sees the bright morning light reaching every room and corner of his house. First, he'll show the kitchen, which is welcoming and can work as a dining room, too, with a table and chairs. Some appliances stand out: a gas stove, a big refrigerator with an ice maker, a toaster, and a microwave oven, all stuff he's bought for his mother. There are plants on the table and next to the sink; on the back wall, pictures of Santo Domingo beaches. The kitchen, with its trendy blue-tile floor, leads to a hallway where you'll find the two bedrooms and the bathroom.

He sees his mother entering the kitchen. How can he describe his own mom that he adores without saying mushy stuff? How about keeping it simple: Mamita (Elena Miranda Ramos) is a beautiful, forty-five-year-old mulatta from Santo Domingo. She's wearing a loosely fitting beige cotton dress and is preparing breakfast: fried plantains, scrambled eggs, fresh cheese, buttered pan de agua, white coffee, and lots of fruit. Elena has trouble using her left hand, which hasn't regained its full strength since she had an operation years ago.

In the shower, Luis Miranda Ramos (that's him, of course) is singing a ballad in the style of the Mexican performer Luis Miguel, his idol. And this is where he gets to describe himself. Better not overdo it! Okay: Luis is a handsome young man with a light brown complexion, black curly hair, olive green eyes, and Afro-Caribbean features. He's also a gifted singer-songwriter.

After his shower, he'll offer to help Mamita in the kitchen...

Richard

There's that song again, playing everywhere he goes, in stores and homes and here at the Cristóbal, the latest hit from some New Wave group he hates. Many of his classmates rave about these singers, though to Richard, they sound like all the others. His school friends think something's wrong with his head 'cause he doesn't care for music. But it's just a matter of personal taste, isn't it? For example, he digs sci-fi movies, and his buddy Luis can't stand them. And there's nothing wrong with Luis because of that, is there? Besides, Richard does like Luis's songs, and it's a good thing he does 'cause Luis loves playing his music. It'd be a total bummer if Richard didn't appreciate his buddy's passion! He'd fake it if he didn't, of course, because Luis deserves his support. Because that's what best friends do for each other.

Richard would probably not be working here if it weren't for Luis, who helped him out a lot the first time he walked into this hotel. Richard was so nervous that day! He remembers that he headed for the bar immediately and found it packed with tourists, all men, and some local guys, the "workers." There was so much cigarette smoke everywhere! Disgusting. How were you supposed to breathe in there?! He saw a few old Gringos in shorts and bright (too fucking bright!) color shirts, and a couple of johns who looked kind of young and were snazzily dressed. And he noticed a group of fem nerds in a corner, acting even more awkwardly than Richard and staring out at the terrace where there was no one, possibly because the hotel clients don't want any passers-by to see them. Richard paid little attention to the Dominican guys, but he did note the ones seated at tables with their johns and being lovey-dovey with them, holding hands and letting their clients touch them all over... Revolting!

He thought he could blend in, yet it must've been obvious that he didn't know what to do. Should he sit at the bar counter, at a table, or just stand somewhere? He opted for leaning against the back wall, which was made of cobblestone and had flowerpots hanging across the top, overflowing with coralillo flowers. So pretty. And that's when Luis came up to him, acting like he knew everything. Which he did! Later, much later, Luis said that he'd felt bad for him. Luis knew what it was like to navigate the Cristóbal the first time, how to hook up and who to trust. He'd been watching Richard since the moment he came in and wanted to help him...

Now, when Richard thinks about that day, it all becomes a sort of time loop in a sci-fi movie. He sees it all unfold over and over again, and each time, there are elements that change, or things he remembers that he hadn't noticed before. But some details appear in each replay. For example, the fact that Luis approached him smiling, gave him a pat on the thigh, and said, "Hey, buddy!" Then he leaned against the wall next to Richard to watch the tourists.

That scene recurs in his memory as if projected on a big screen. After a while, Luis started describing some of the tourists, mostly where they all came from, and he asked Richard if he'd met Señor Zamora, the manager. Richard said no, and why should he have to meet him? Luis replied that no one could work at the Cristóbal unless they made arrangements with the boss. He suggested that they go to the malecón, and that's where he explained the biz to Richard as they walked down the waterfront: how to carry yourself and what to say, what parts of the body were off-limits, which acts were not allowed, how much money to ask for, and what percentage of it went to the Cristóbal for providing the locale and the clients.

The only thing Richard didn't like was having to give Señor Zamora a cut of his earnings, and also asking for the same amount as all the other guys. No, Richard would set his own price, the highest price ever paid at the Cristóbal. Yeah! Because he was young, strong, healthy, and big down there. He'd had sex with his girlfriend, Isabel, and a couple of times with a guy, a classmate who'd offered to suck him off. True, Richard didn't have a lot of experience and couldn't imagine how he'd be able to fuck those foreigners, how he'd get turned on if they didn't appeal to him. There wouldn't be a problem getting hard; that was easy, but what if some of his clients repulsed him and made him throw up? A big challenge for sure, having to touch those people, caress them. Though fortunately, kissing wasn't part of the deal, according to Luis.

Richard told himself he was up to the challenge, highly motivated by the rewards. He'd just close his eyes and pretend he was making love to Isabel, or maybe screwing one of the really cute boys at school. In his head, Richard would become a pro, a sought-after and desired whore who swung both ways with ease and know-how. Like a bisexual alien from a planet on the edge of our galaxy, who could be anything and everything for everyone for the right sum of dough. Like a shapeshifter! Or like a member of an android race called *sexoids*. Yeah, the sexoid named Richard was programmed to make people's fantasies come true, no matter how wild!

So, yes, Luis showed him the ropes, asking for nothing in return. He didn't touch him, other than the pat on the thigh, because he said they were real men and good friends, not faggots who got it on with each other. Luis introduced him to Señor Zamora in the manager's office, the only penthouse in the Cristóbal, like no room Richard had ever seen. Zamora's desk was all glass and had a huge computer on it, the new Apple model probably. The office was on the fourth floor, yet it felt like the top of a high mountain. What an amazing view! You could take in the city, the seawall, the cars, the ocean, and even the horizon.

Señor Zamora didn't look like Richard had expected; for one thing, he seemed so young. He was wearing tight blue jeans and a brightly colored guayabera with too many pockets; his hair was long, curly, messy in the style of British pop singers. He didn't speak like a boss, either, with fancy words. The manager took a liking to Richard and invited him to be part of his "brood of chicks." As a welcome present, he gave him a bunch of coupons for the movies, and that gesture won Richard over. He agreed to obey all the rules as one of the hotel's new chicks.

His best friend, the only one Richard could trust with his life, that's what Luis became to him. Too bad he got so bossy. Ordered him to follow his lead and kept repeating the four main rules of the biz. Number One: never show up at the hotel alone. Number Two: never let the johns get near your ass. Number Three: always use a rubber. Number Four: drink but never get drunk.

There are times when Luis acts like he's Richard's big brother, and Richard knows he acts that way because he cares for him. His bossiness is actually kind of amusing, like a game, and Richard always does what he wants anyway. Like being here alone today, breaking Rule Number One. Shit, Luis is going to be so mad!

Richard just said hi to Franklin, the bartender, who's husky and kind of grouchy but has a nice face. The last time he was here, the place was packed. But not today. The indoor patio is sort of empty, in fact, though it won't look that way tonight when it turns into a dance floor. In a corner by the stairs is the stage, big enough to fit two stools and a standing microphone. That's where the guest performers of the Cristóbal play nice background music that makes it easy to talk. Richard likes the current musicians okay, though not as much as he likes Luis's stuff. They're called Los Bachateros, a trio that used to be famous and is known for singing bachatas, boleros, and some pop. Good singers, but they can't belt like Luis. Oh man, it'd be so cool if Luis got to perform with them. He'd make them sound better for sure!

Friday afternoon, too early for live music, and that's too bad 'cause instead, he's being tortured by some loud New Wave. Richard walks to a table by the stage and sits down after ordering a Coke. He catches his reflection in the mirror behind the bar. Fuck, he looks young, which he is. It freaks him out sometimes to imagine himself as an old man, all wrinkled up, with aches and pains and that damn arthritis that's threatening to cripple his father's hands. Bah! No need to worry about that future. Chances are he'll stay strong till the very end, if he takes good care of himself. And maybe by that distant time, they might've developed a drug to make people look youthful their entire lives, although that sounds like sci-fi, not reality.

It's the present that matters, after all, when the mirror shows him a hot young hustler looking back at him. Yeah, he's younger than Luis and with a lighter complexion. Too white! That could be a problem, 'cause the johns tend to go for a darker type. But ain't nothing Richard can do about that. He could work harder on his outfits, though, maybe get some ideas from Luis. Never again will he come to work dressed so formally, wearing his black jeans and his brand-new sky-blue guayabera. And what the fuck did he do to his hair?! Instead of letting the wavy strands fall naturally on his forehead, like his mom says he should, he combed them all back with mousse. So, now he's the spitting image of some fag dancer in a TV variety show.

Wow, an old Gringo at the bar counter is trying to catch his attention. What should he do? Smile but not too much; he doesn't feel ready to start working just yet. And it's a good thing Richard hasn't flirted with the tourist 'cause there's Luis walking in, obviously pissed off.

"What are you doing here?" Luis asks him.

"Nothing," Richard replies. "Just hanging. It's Friday, and I did all my homework already, so I thought I'd check out the scene..."

Luis sits with Richard, lights up a cigarette, says to him, "Didn't I ask you to always wait for me at the malecón? Don't get into this biz alone, Richard. You don't know shit."

"What's there to know? Stick it in and pull it out 'til they come, and that's that."

Luis, sarcastic, "Really? That's all there is to it, Richard?"

"Yes, I have all the experience I need. You know I've done it many times with Isabel. But it's not like I forced her or anything, okay? Don't get the wrong idea; I'd never do that to her. She was the one who said we should go all the way. We'd been making out a lot, and then, one day, we were alone in her house 'cause her dad was at work and her mom and sister had gone shopping, and we got so hot we just couldn't stop ourselves."

"Yes, yes, you've told me that story already. Man, you sure talk a lot!"

"Okay, but what I didn't tell you is that Isabel took her clothes off first, and in a big hurry, saying that she couldn't wait anymore. And I told her she needed to be sure 'cause this was something you couldn't undo, and I asked her if she didn't want to save her virginity for marriage, which is what most girls supposedly want to do, and she just laughed and started taking my pants off, laughing the whole time, and grabbing my prick and putting a rubber on it and placing it between her legs. It was like she knew exactly what to do, how to move and..."

Luis, laughing, "Sounds like you were the virgin, not her!"

"Yeah, and it was amazing, Luis. Incredible. At that moment, when we were doing it, I thought there could be nothing better in the whole universe. It felt like..."

"I know what it feels like the first time, Richard, so spare me the details, okay? Just shut up for a minute and listen to me!" He puts out his cigarette, lights another.

"But I didn't tell you the most important thing, Luis, and that's that I care for Isabel. Though we've never talked about love or made any promises 'cause she says she wants to be free. So, I don't think she's in love with me..."

"And you're not in love with her either, you idiot!"

"I guess you're right about that."

"Damn it, Richard, you're so fucking naïve. You need to be careful working here, okay? This is serious business, not a game or one of those stories you like to read."

"I get that. And I'm being careful, no need for you to worry."

"You'd better! We wouldn't want a john to get you from behind."

Richard, sure of himself, "No one's ever gonna do that to me!"

"Good to know."

Richard walks to the stone wall and leans against it. Luis joins him there seconds later.

"How's your mom doing?" Richard asks his friend.

"Mamita's just fine. Still bugging me about the Cristóbal. What about your folks?"

"Okay, I guess. Papá is working too much, as usual. We hardly ever see him. And all of us kids are in school, which makes my mother happy."

"Your dad's a pharmacist, right? Pharmacists make lots of dough. And your mom has a job as a teacher, no? I know teachers don't get paid that much, but it's still an income."

"It's not enough for a big family like ours, Luis. And Papi has to use his hands so much at the pharmacy that they're starting to hurt him a lot at the end of the day. Poor Papi. I'm glad I'll be able to help out so he can cut back on his long shifts, and so Mami can quit her job. It's hard for her to work and look after all of us without a maid."

"Even so, are you sure you need to be doing this, Richard?"

"Yes, I'm sure. My brothers need lots of school supplies and clothes and shoes and stuff like that, and I want to chip in and get it all for them."

"Okay, you can always quit this joint if it doesn't work out." Silence. "Hey, don't forget that Mister Paul is arriving on Sunday. We're gonna go to the airport with Franklin to welcome him, okay? I want him to meet you. He's coming for the book fair."

"But that fair is in almost two weeks. I heard the announcement on the radio."

"Yeah, but many of the attendees come here several days before to have some fun."

"Are you going to hang out at the fair at all, Luis?"

"No way! I already have the only book I'm interested in, for learning English."

"I've heard it's an exciting event. You get freebies and watch cool videos."

"Nah, just a horde of bookworms shooting the bull. What could be exciting about that?"

"I like books, Luis, especially poetry. It'd be great to get some for free."

"Man, you're weird. Poetry sucks."

"But you write songs, and they're like poems, you know."

"Sure, with easy-to-understand lyrics and catchy melodies, not like those poems I had to read in school, which made no fucking sense."

"They would make sense if you let me explain them to you, Luis. Then you'd see how beautiful they are. A lot of poetry is hard for me to understand, too, but I try to figure things out using a dictionary and picturing the images in my head..."

"Thanks but no thanks! Anyway, you won't have time for that shit. By the time the fair rolls around, you'll be dry as a bone and needing lots of sleep."

"Really, Luis? You think I'll score big?"

"Yes! You're cute and fresh out of the oven, so you'll be in high demand."

Richard feels flattered. "Thank you for saying that I'm cute, Luisi..."

"Shut up! And don't you ever call me *Luisi* again!"

"I'm going to make a fortune off these tourists. Yeah!"

Luis, caressing his friend's face, "I know you will. With that pretty face of yours, they'll offer you the world." Suddenly faking annoyance, he slaps him gently. "Just be careful, okay? And remember that we all charge the same amount."

Richard, defensive, "I know how to fend for myself, okay? I can negotiate all kinds of deals with the tourists. I already have, more than once."

Annoyed, "You shouldn't do any negotiating, Richard. We have a price agreement in this hotel. Didn't Señor Zamora tell you?"

"I haven't agreed to anything."

"Suit yourself. Just don't come crying to me when Zamora kicks you out."

"Men don't cry, buddy."

"Of course not." Luis laughs. "And since you're such a macho man!"

Three of the hotel guys come in, men Richard doesn't care for at all. They're in their mid-twenties and act like they own the place. And they all have American names they can't pronounce, which sound stupid when they say them. That happens a lot in Santo Domingo, parents giving their children English names, like they think that way their kids will be more important. That's not the reason his mother named him *Richard*, no, no. She said it was because of a British actor she liked, Richard Burton. There are other popular American names he likes, Joshua, Evan, and Engelbert, although not as much as he likes *Richard*. He tries to say it right, practicing with his English teacher at school and in front of the mirror. *Reichaardd...*

Something else that turns him off about those guys is that they pretend they're popular and cool, always showing off the latest fashion. Yeah, but if you look closely, you'll notice they're as rough and unpolished as everyone else. The telling details: worn-out shoes on William, one of the two mulattoes of the trio; a stain on George's pants;

a peeling leather belt on Michael, who thinks he's a Gringo because he has light skin and blondish hair.

They go up to Richard, making a racket, and he feels bullied, harassed.

"How is our new baby doing?" says Michael, pinching his cheek. "Still a virgin? Or did you get your bottom broken already?"

William grabs Richard's crotch, yells, "Ain't nuttin' here!"

And George says, "Didn't I tell you? Tweet tweet tweet, little birdie."

Luis shoves them away. "Leave the kid alone, damn it!"

"The hubby!" yells George.

"Look at him showing his spurs!" exclaims Michael.

William, "Defending his chick!"

The three young men sit with Richard and Luis when Juanito, the waiter, shows up. Juanito is playful, effeminate. "Be nice, my loves. Order something and shut up, okay?" George touches his ass. "How dare you? I'll tell Franklin!" To the bartender, "Sweetheart!"

Franklin, from behind the counter, "Careful, boys. Respect my wife or else!"

"You know the temper he has," says the waiter. "Better not make a scene... But, hey, it's too early to start boozing up. So, how about a round of Presidente for everyone and nothing else until you start working tonight?" The young men give the offer their thumbs up. "Good," reacts Juanito. "We'll get that going for you. And I'll just put it on your tabs, okay? Be right back!"

Damn it! Richard hates beer, the taste, the number it does on his head. It's like drinking a toxic potion that makes you feel dizzy and heavy and confused and just fucking sick all over. As if an alien had taken over your mind and forced you to talk too much, say stupid things, and tell secret stuff about yourself. No, thanks. Not worth it. But he must act now! "Excuse me, Juanito! Could you make that a Coke for me instead of a Presidente...? If that's okay?"

"Yes, of course, sweetie. A wise choice. One Coke for you, coming up!"

Michael turns to William, "I haven't seen Amalia in a while. Is she still getting around?"

William grabs Michael by the neck, knocking down his chair. "My girlfriend is none of your fucking business, you son of a bitch!"

George tries to get William to sit back down. And now Franklin is standing beside them, his index finger pointing to the door. "Take your problem outside! Now!"

"Sorry, Franklin," says George. "We were just horsing around, that's all. But it won't happen again. Please let us stay."

Franklin, like a school principal, "Okay. But I'll be watching you!"

"Hey, buddy, what was that all about?" George asks William, who's still fuming and doesn't respond. "Let's get this shit out in the open once and for all, okay? Ain't no secret that Amalia goes with a tourist now and then. She's even been with me and Michael, and she's gone down on my wife a couple of times. Hell, I've even gotten to watch them!"

"Yeah, that's right," adds Michael, chuckling. "She likes to get nailed by men but won't suck them off, never ever. When it comes to tongue action, she prefers a juicy pussy."

"It takes all kinds!" Luis remarks.

George, "Listen to our very own philosopher!"

Richard is feeling bad for William, whose heavy breathing reminds him of a large, caged animal, or a raging bull at a bullfight. Why are his friends doing this to him?

"Fuck you all!" William cries out, and he sits at the counter with the old Gringo.

The tourist greets him in Spanish with a British accent and asks, "How big?"

William, leaning back, "Huge."

The tourist fondles him, says, "Let's go!" But he has trouble standing. William holds him by the waist, shows his friends the middle finger as he and the john leave.

"He's got it made!" Michael exclaims.

"Let's hope he doesn't beat the crap out of that Gringo, as mad as he is," says Luis. "Or maybe that's just what the john's looking for, a good thrashing."

George, "I wish he'd use the dough to buy himself some new shoes."

"Yeah, man," adds Luis, "he's been wearing those boots to death."

"A present from his Italian Papi last year," George explains.

Luis, "Man, they must stink!"

Richard can't stop thinking that William didn't get to have his beer. Sure, his client will buy him another Presidente, even some expensive cocktail. But it won't be the drink he was meant to have here and now with his friends, as himself, not as a worker with an old john.

There's that music again, louder this time, exploding in his head. Richard can't hear what the guys are saying anymore, only the music, yet another techno song with a catchy refrain. His next earworm! A sign that the night shift is starting? Yeah, it's finally dark out, and he's ready...

Luis

Mamita is right outside the bathroom door, talking to him like she does sometimes when he takes a shower. "I don't understand how you can feel like singing first thing in the morning," she says. "They can hear you all the way to the malecón!"

She doesn't get that she's louder than Luis could ever be. Mamita has a big voice! Deep, thunderous, yet there's something mellow and sweet about it, especially when she sings.

Luis comes out humming a ballad, his hair wet, a towel around his waist. He kisses his mother. "It's a good way to start the day, singing! You know that, Mamita." He sings the last line of the song, which culminates in a crescendo.

"That's enough, mijo! Or they'll drag us out of town for disturbing the peace."

"Drag us out?!" he says in jest. "That's what you say to a son who serenades you?"

"Sorry, baby. I know I'm lucky."

Luis gets dressed in his room while listening to mellow pop music on the radio. Today he'll wear high-waisted, acid-wash blue jeans; a white T-shirt that fits snugly on his lean frame; and an oversized denim blazer for just the right look, not to actually put it on during the day.

"The manager of the Cristóbal likes my voice," he tells his mother, who is standing at the bedroom door. "He's going to let me sing in the hotel one of these days, with Los Bachateros."

She looks surprised. "Los Bachateros are playing there? But they used to be so famous."

"They still are," he remarks, combing his hair. "And I'd love to sing with them!"

She is obviously skeptical. "Yes, I'm sure you would."

"Just you wait and see. You're gonna be proud of your son."

"I already am, Luisi."

"Yeah, but even more so."

All dressed, Luis heads to the kitchen, serves himself a cup of coffee, and sits at the table. His mother follows him, resuming her breakfast preparation.

"Can I help, Mamita?"

"No, mijo, thanks. You'll get your clothes all dirty. Besides, I'm almost done."

"Okay, but you should let me give you a hand once in a while. I miss cooking."

"Yes, yes, maybe tomorrow, when Richard comes to eat with us. Did you invite him like I told you to? If he wants to join us for lunch instead of dinner, I can go to the early Mass and be home by eight, so I can start cooking right away. I'm going to make sancocho, which he likes a lot. And mofongo, your favorite. But I'm not sure about dessert, maybe coconut cream...?"

"Tomorrow? He won't be able to, Mamita." Silence. "He's going to the airport with me to welcome Mister Paul. You remember him, no?"

"Yes, the Gringo who gives you nice presents."

"And then Richard and I have some errands to run..."

Sarcastic, "Yes, of course. *Errands.*" She serves him breakfast. "But tomorrow is Sunday, and Sundays are for me, Luisi, for us. That's the agreement."

"I'm sorry." Luis digs in eagerly. "The biz is important."

Disdainful, "The biz? Is that what you're calling it now?"

"There you go with that shit again!"

"People are saying things, Luis, and I can't just cover my ears when they talk."

"Fucking busy bodies! Don't they have anything better to do? Fat old hags!"

"Are you saying I'm an old hag?"

"If you pay attention to all that gossip, then, yes."

"Ay, Luisi, I'd give anything for you to quit that *biz*."

"Enough with your harangue, Mamita. We have to make a living, don't we? And better if it's a good living, I'd say. Like, we've been able to afford this big, nice house in Arboleda, with two bedrooms, and we have a new television..."

"The price for all those things is just too high, mijo. Let the tourists find someone else for their filthy vices." Caressing his face, "Not you. You are my baby."

"Yeah!" He grabs his crotch. "A baby with a horse's dick!"

"Bad boy!" She laughs. "That is so vulgar, Luisi. I raised you better than that." She sits to have a cup of coffee with her son. "I want you to go back to school, Luis. You have a good head for learning. The Autónoma is taking applications from students who didn't finish *nivel medio*, and the government is giving out scholarships. Could you at least try to...?"

"Those scholarships are hard to get. Besides, I don't have time for school. Maybe later."

"Later when?"

"When we have enough money saved up."

"We have substantial savings already, Luis."

"Okay, fine, I'll take classes in the States."

"Yes, of course you will." She prepares a plate of food for herself. They eat in silence. "You never talk about your girlfriend anymore," she remarks minutes later. "The most beautiful girl in Santo Domingo, as you used to say."

"You mean María Eugenia? She left me for another guy."

"She must've found out..."

"María Eugenia didn't love me, that's all."

"Did you love her?"

"I don't know. Anyway, I have other girlfriends now."

"Yes, women you sleep with. But that's not what I'm talking about." Worried, stressed, "Please, listen to me, mijo. Stop servicing those tourists."

"Yeah, so we can be poor again."

"We were doing okay before you started working at that hotel. I had a job."

"You're not going to be anyone's servant anymore!"

"We're always someone's servant."

"Not you and me. I swear. One day we're gonna go to the North, and we'll have our own business." Daydreaming, "A restaurant! You'll be the chef or better yet the one who thinks up the menu, sitting comfortably and ordering everyone around. And I'll sing to our customers."

"It's a big dream, mijo. I hope you can make it come true..."

"I will! That's why I'm learning English." He runs to his room and comes back with a textbook. "This book Mister Paul gave me last year is helping me a lot." He hands it to Mamita, who flips through it indifferently. "It's one of the books he publishes. The best one!"

Returning the textbook to her son, "Yes, it looks good. I like the photos and drawings."

Excited, "This is the only thing I'm interested in learning, Mamita. English! You'll see, I'm going to get famous in America." He sings part of one of his favorite American ballads. "By the way, you're going to design all my cool clothes for the stage."

Laughing, "I am?"

"Yes, Mamita, you'll make my personal outfits and basically create my look."

"Okay, sure, but what if you don't like the look I create? What if I'm no good at it?"

"You'll be great, I'm sure. My success will inspire you."

Luis can tell she's on board with the idea. It's her laughter. He loves her laughter!

"That would be fantastic, Luisi," she says. "Except that I'm going to be awfully busy, not just running an upscale restaurant but also designing your clothes."

"You're right. Forget the restaurant! You'll just be the mother of a superstar. 'Cause I'm not just going to sing, no. I'll be an actor, too, and make movies in Hollywood. Good movies with believable stories and great characters, not the sci-fi action crap Richard likes so much. And not telenovelas either! I must go far, Mamita, and take you with me wherever I go."

"Thank you, baby. Such beautiful dreams. Of course I'll go with you anywhere you want to take me, as long as I get to die in my country. Hopefully in this house."

Kissing his mother, "When you're about to kick the bucket, I'll sing you a bachata and you'll feel like living again. Remember how the saying goes...a bad bug never dies!"

Suddenly, Mamita is too quiet. "Yes, of course I remember that saying," she comments seconds later. "But it should be a *stupid* bug that never dies, in my case. Because that's how I feel sometimes, like a stupid bug, unable to understand what is happening in the world."

"What do you mean?"

"Things were simpler in my youth, mijo." Silence. "The world has gotten so strange..."

Done eating, Luis clears the table. Mamita gives him a hand. He feels annoyed by her last comment, can't help wanting to confront his mom, to make her tell him, once and for all, about his goddamn father. It angers him that she tries to avoid this topic, that she has so few details to share with him regarding that man. Even if Luis would rather not hear a single word about him!

He lights up a cigarette and asks her, "What about what my father did to you 'in your youth,' Mamita? Was that... *simpler*?"

"You need to know what actually happened, Luis."

"Yeah, finally, the truth about that story." The weird thing is, he doesn't really want the facts, not now, maybe never. "Just forget it, okay? I'm sure it's just a typical telenovela plot."

"But there are no telenovela plots in the real world, mijo." Silence. "Anyway, we'll talk about this some other time, when you feel ready." She looks at him lovingly and takes his hand. "I want you to know I'm grateful for everything you've given me, Luisi. Never think I don't value all you do for us, on the contrary. I am a lucky mom."

He hugs her. "And I'm a very lucky son."

"Forgive me for watching over you so much, baby." She smiles. "Like a damn hawk, right?" Silence. "The thing is, if I don't give you advice and guidance, who's going to, Luisi?"

"Nobody." Acting macho, in jest, "Don't nobody tell me what to do!"

"Yes, sir! I will make sure nobody does," she says, and they both laugh.

Paul

He really isn't the person he presents here most of the time, or not just that person. What people see is a performance. This one in Santo Domingo is the Bitch, a cutting, sarcastic queen who is partial to big dark dicks. But he's also several other people: the domestic partner who's made his marital nest in San Francisco with Vincent, a Napa Valley hunk so madly in love with Paul that he's willing to turn a blind eye to his many infidelities. And there's the loyal friend, a role Paul doesn't have to try hard to perform. He does value and nurtures his friendship with a handful of gay men and especially with the Spanish writer Antonio Fernando Luján Saavedra. He could never have imagined that he'd end up with a conceited Spaniard from Madrid for a friend. How the fuck did that happen?! Certain circumstances brought them together and, over the years, provided a context for their bond to grow and strengthen. He does love Tony (what he likes to call him) dearly, though he'd never tell the egocentric Gallego. No way!

Oh, and there's the serious role he plays as a textbook editor, provider of innovative teaching materials and promoter of the latest theories on language acquisition. Blah blah blah, says the Bitch. Primarily, when he's vacationing here, Mr. Paul G. Edwards is a blonde, tall, slim, forty-something Gringo from Dallas who speaks Spanish fluently, having fine-tuned it in DR, but who hasn't been able to master the pronunciation and thus comes across as a hick in his second language. The Texas drawl he's been able to lose, yet no speech coach in the fucking world could make him sound like a native *caribeño*. Paul keeps trying. He mimics the Cristóbal guys and gets away with it occasionally, with certain words. But it ain't happening.

His most hateful performance is the one he used to have to put on around his Texas compatriots and relatives, many of them Republican bigots who think Reagan (the hack actor running the U.S. government these days) is too soft and liberal. Empty-headed, big-hair mammas (his

27

aunts) and larger-than-life white men (his father and brother.) All of them stereotypes, yes, but also scarily real, definitely when it comes to their obsession with guns. His father and brother love to collect them and display them, clean and polish them, and even caress them!

Paul is such an aberration among those people. He's never fit the mold. He didn't, for instance, want to learn the names and types of all the different weapons his father owned, their parts, or how they functioned. He would only manage to remember one word from that belligerent lexicon, *magazine*, for obvious reasons. How did the same word end up describing both a periodical publication and the ammunition storage and feeding device of a firearm?

He was ten when his dad first had him hold a gun, determined to turn him into a real man like his sibling. Little Paul was shaking, his whole being averse to the feeling of that horrific object in his trembling hand. He started sobbing and threw the gun on the ground. His father picked it up and had him grab it again, asking him to fire at a tree in the backyard. Paul couldn't even hear the demeaning words Dad was screaming at him because his own voice resounded in his head, deafeningly repeating a phrase like a mantra, *I hate you! I hate you! I hate you!* At some point, he took off running. His father caught up with him in his jeep down the street, shoved him into the vehicle, and drove him back, cussing the entire time.

There were more failed attempts after that. And there was a forced visit to a shooting gallery (his brother's favorite hangout) two years later, where Paul stood against a wall, refusing to do what he was supposed to. Everyone there was laughing at him, pitying his father for having such a sissy son. Losing his patience and his temper, Dad whacked him in the face, making him bleed from the mouth (the disgusting taste of blood!) But Paul didn't budge.

Following that incident, he started getting bullied at school, mostly by his brother (two years older) and his brother's friends. Paul just had to endure the abuse since no one would come to his defense. He survived it all by telling himself that someday he'd be able to leave that hell and never return to his home and family, to their fucking Stepford neighborhood—a gated community where the cops towed away any vehicle whose license plate number wasn't listed on the homeowners database; where pedestrians were harassed by the police if they didn't fit a certain type; and where males, even young boys, were expected to be fearless and racist.

Shooting. The Christian thing to do, right? How ironic that so many gun-toting Americans regard firearm ownership and usage as their God-given right. His father and brother, for instance, like to invoke God to justify their macho brutality, their racism, and their sense of entitlement. It's typical of many religious people, especially in Dallas, advocating the right to do harm in the name of their deity. And no wonder, since they've heard it from the horse's mouth in this case: the pastor of the quote-unquote Christian megachurch Paul's family attends.

That so-called minister invokes the Second Amendment in his sermons and proclaims the American citizen's right to bear arms. He doesn't get that the amendment refers to firearms from the 1700s, when the Constitution was written, not the lethal weapons of today! If only those people, including his relatives and the church minister, could all be sent to another planet so they can have their Anglo Cowboy Utopia there. They'd surely end up killing each other off!

Paul eventually stopped going to that worship house of violence (more cursing from his dad, more shoves and smacking and humiliating Paul.) And he'd rather not even mention what happened when he started hooking up with men—not very secretly, on purpose. No. Too hard to revisit that phase. No need for it. He knows exactly where his family stands regarding his sexuality. He spent too many years trying to pass for straight, pretending to be for his society what he couldn't be for himself. Until he tried no more. Until he moved to San Francisco, gay capital of the country, and said goodbye to his infernal home state forever.

Don't mess with the Republic of Texas, right? Sure, as long as Texas doesn't mess with Paul Edwards! And it *will not* because he won't let it. He'll stay away from there and go back only to see his mom, to whom he's devoted. She does have the big hair and the annoying Texas accent, but she's also the only kind, accepting, nonviolent member of his clan. He tries to call her every other day and has her visit in San Francisco at least once a year. He loves that sweet woman!

Yes, different people named Paul Edwards inhabit his psyche. But isn't that how most folks go through life, wearing various masks? Or, in theatrical terms (which Luis would love), memorizing and performing scripts. He's tried to integrate all his *characters* into one single identity, instead of having to suppress his gay feathers in some situations and downplay his intellectual self in others. Or having to claim, in certain contexts, that he only reads gay pulp. Or not admitting that his most celebrated performance isn't in bed but behind the podium, commanding the attention of hundreds of profs with his lively presentations. Yes, he could be all those people at once (except for the native speaker, sadly.) Yet what would be the fun in that?

Last but certainly not least, one of his favorite personae: Luis's lover. Here they are, Paul and Luis, in this "lovely" old suite at the Cristóbal. Paul would rather stay at the Hilton, but all the action is here. On a brighter note, the rooms are spacious, and the hotel boasts about offering great comfort and valuable antiques. Like this room, which has a high-end TV set with remote control and cable, a queen bed with immaculate linens and a wooden headboard that was carved to simulate a garden, two bedside tables, crystal lamps, a nightstand that doubles as a desk, and a comfy recliner. It also features a dresser framed in ornamented imitation bronze. Their idea of an antique? Tacky!

The moonlight filters through the window: the only light Paul allows in when he's making love. He and Luis are lounging in bed, both naked. Luis has been obsessing a lot about the idea of his life being like a play, though not a tragedy, he says. Paul suggested to him that he think of it as a tragicomedy, which would be both dramatic and comical, and Luis was immediately excited about the suggestion. It all started after they went to see Manuel Puig's *Kiss of the Spider Woman* last year. Unfortunately, Paul won't be taking Luis to the theater during this visit. The pickings are too slim. Hackneyed melodramas and no American touring shows. Most local theater sucks. One of the few exceptions: Puig's play, a brilliant Dominican production, the best mise en scène Paul has seen yet. No wonder it blew Luis's mind!

That kid has so much potential, despite his memory issue. He refuses to go to school, so Paul has decided to teach him English and a bit about theater arts (Paul's passion) when he visits and in letters he writes to the young man periodically. No doubt he'd be able to do a lot more for Luis if the kid lived in the States, but that's not a project Paul is willing to take on just yet. Too complicated. Too much responsibility. Sure, it would be possible with some effort and a good amount of money. But what about Vincent? Surely he'd end up feeling neglected (betrayed?) having Paul's young boyfriend around. No, Paul can't do that to him, although that wonderful man would put up with anything to humor him...

Paul gets today's theater lesson out of the way—this time about Pirandello's magnum opus, which Luis finds fascinating. "Characters searching for an author?! Wow!" he exclaims. "Just like me, since I'm trying to figure out who the hell is writing the play of my life!" He displays his mischievous smile, insinuating that Paul might be his author.

Paul reacts at once, "Don't look at me! I'm not *that* wicked and definitely not that creative, babe. Have you considered that you might be your own playwright?"

Luis ponders the question as he lights up one of his long, filtered cigarettes.

"Get rid of it after your next drag, please," Paul tells him. "You know I can't stand it."

"You got it!" Luis puts out his cigarette in a frilly clay ashtray by the bed. "It's not good for the voice, anyway. Not for people who want to be singers, like me."

"And take the ashtray away, too. Maybe put in the bathroom for now. It stinks! God, one can't escape the fucking cigarette smoke in this country!"

"Sorry, Mister Paul. It's just that smoking is a thing men do."

Laughing, "That's why I don't!" Silence. "And speaking of men, tell me about Richard."

"Richard doesn't know anything, definitely not about the biz."

"While you, on the other hand..."

"I know what's important."

"What, for example?"

"Like, like... the way you have to make your prick go in at first, slowly, so it doesn't hurt the client too much. And like... the words you must use."

"But most tourists don't even understand you, babe!"

"If you talk to them in a strong voice, not loud but forceful, you know, then they get the message. And it helps if you can speak a little English, too, 'cause it seems that everyone in the whole world speaks your language, Mister Paul. So, for example, I tell them, 'You turn me on!' Or 'I dig your tight ass.' Or 'Want to take a ride on the wild side?'"

"I taught you those phrases!"

"Yes, you did, and I'm so grateful. By the way, I'm learning a lot with the book you gave me." Caressing Paul, "Thank you so much."

"What else does one have to know in your 'biz'?"

"You must lean back when you're sitting down so the john can easily note your boner. And you have to put your hands on his ass like this, see? It turns you on when I do this to you, doesn't it, Mister Paul?"

"Yes, but not right now. Please, stop."

"And then you start pushing your fingers between their butt cheeks..."

"Stop it, I said!" Laughing, "What if they don't like to be touched that way?"

"Then you teach them to like it. You're always the man, in command, even if they make all the decisions 'cause they got the dough."

"So, what else does Richard need to learn?"

"Let's see... Okay, never to get smashed with a john, for example. 'Cause if you're drunk, you're bound to say things you don't mean, and you might let your guard down. The clients could take advantage of you and make you perform all kinds of fucked-up fantasies."

"Did you ever have to perform any of those?"

"Well... not many 'cause fortunately I haven't been with a lot of weirdos. And since I never drink much when I'm scoring, I can be in control. But there were a couple of times..."

"Tell me about them."

"Really? Are you sure? It's all creepy, you know."

"Yes, I'm sure. Go ahead. I can take it." Paul is tempted to quote Wilde. Oh, what the heck, "Nothing human is alien to me."

"Okay, so there was that faggot from Germany who liked to pretend he was a little boy lost in the woods, and I was supposed to be a muscly logger who raped him and then killed him."

"Killed him... how?"

"Strangling him while I rammed my dick deep and hard into him." Silence. "And there was that businessman from New York who wanted me to pee all over his face..."

"Enough, I get the picture. It takes all kinds, I suppose." Silence. "Hey, be glad that my fantasy is clean and gentle." Laughing, "All you have to do is watch me perform as the epitome of La Bassey!"

"And it's always a pleasure for me, Mister Paul."

"I hope you mean it! Anyway, it's good that you're helping Richard..."

"Yeah, I worry about him 'cause he doesn't take me seriously. He thinks this is some kind of game! Like, he laughed when I told him to always wear a rubber."

"Keep getting on his case about it, Luis." Silence. "Have you ever gotten sick from...?"

"Yeah, in the early days, when I wasn't being careful. Nothing serious. My crotch was itching like hell, that's all. I couldn't stop scratching!" He smashes an imaginary insect between his index fingers. "Then I noticed these tiny bugs in my pubic hair. It was so gross! So, I shaved it all and rubbed alcohol on my skin. But I couldn't get rid of the critters."

"Did you go to the doctor?"

"No, I hate doctors. I just talked to Señor Zamora about it. Embarrassing! He gave me some ointment, and after putting it on a couple of times, the itching went away."

"Well, I'm glad you always wear a condom. Make sure Richard does, too."

"He's so stubborn. Like, he asked me, 'But what if the johns don't want me to?' And I said, 'Then you tell them there's no deal without a rubber and threaten to leave.' And Richard said, 'But what if they just let me go, then there wouldn't be any money.' By now I was so mad at him! I said to him, yelling, 'Your life is more important, you idiot!'"

Paul jumps out of bed, feeling suddenly filthy. He takes a quick shower and comes out minutes later, drying himself off. He hasn't stopped thinking about Richard, how frightened he must be. That's why he downplays the dangers and risks involved in what he does and laughs about it, and makes believe he's playing an exciting game. Deep down, he must know ...

"Richard is so young," he tells Luis.

"Yeah, younger than I was when I got started."

"He's probably scared." Silence. "You've never been afraid, Luis?"

"I was at first. But then you get the hang of it. You learn the business."

"That's your thing, huh? The business."

"No. You know what my real thing is, Mister Paul."

"Yes, singing and playing the guitar! You have a lovely voice."

"Thank you!" Luis seems moved. "The manager has promised me he's gonna let me sing in the bar one of these nights. Hope he keeps his promise!"

"I could put in a good word for you. It might help."

Excited, "Really? I'd be so grateful, Mister Paul."

"But you'd have to do something for me in return..."

Luis grabs his crotch. "Sure, I'm ready."

"I don't mean sex. I want you to be my audience."

Luis makes a face in jest. "Oh, no, it's time for your song, isn't it?"

Paul in the nude, posing, "It's show time, folks!"

And now there is Luis pretending to enjoy Mister Paul's performance as Paul pretends to be a Black woman singer from England named Shirley Bassey pretending to be an actress pretending to be happy performing when inside, in the depths of her soul, she's heartbroken. Paul, who looks nothing like Shirley, moving his hands dramatically, touching his bosom, striking his chest as he sings, "Tonight, I gave the greatest performance of my life!"

Paul sobbing when he gets to the end of the song, which says that you would've seen the actress crying if you'd been near her when the lights went out.

And there's Luis clapping, telling Paul that this was indeed his greatest rendition of "The Greatest Performance." Whatever it takes to make the Gringo happy...

Mister Paul takes a bow and says, "Thank you! You've been a wonderful audience!" He gets into bed and, with a wave of a hand, tells Luis, "And now you get to request another song. You must yell, *Encore! Encore!*" Luis looks dubious. "C'mon, it's like saying ¡*Otra!* in Spanish but it sounds better in French, and that's the word we use in English, anyway. We're always stealing words from other languages, damn hogs that we are. What are you waiting for?"

Paul knows that Luis doesn't want an encore; what he wants is to sing himself. He's just going through the motions, repeating after Paul, listlessly, *Encore!* The poor kid...

"Okay, Luis, how about if you do the next song?"

Luis's face lights up. "With pleasure!" He leaps out of bed and stands in front of the mirror, admiring himself: his way of getting psyched up for the show.

Paul, rejoicing in the young man's nakedness, "You're so hot."

"Hush, please!" Luis tells him jokingly. "I'm trying to get inspired." He takes a deep breath. "Okay, I'll do my favorite song, though it'd be better if I had my guitar..."

Luis sings a heartfelt ballad, the moonlight enhancing his beauty.

Antonio

Here he is in this tropical Eden once again, trying to pass for a journalist. A task he doesn't mind taking on, although it's not the professional hat that feels most snug to him. No, Antonio sees himself first and foremost as a novelist. He has written three books, thoroughly researched historical fiction that borrows heavily in style, form, and themes from all the famous old Spanish geezers: Don Juan Manuel's *Count Lucanor* most prominently, but also a mélange that includes Quevedo, Lope de Vega, Tirso de Molina, Calderón de la Barca, Moratín, and even Cervantes! Yes, Antonio has a raging addiction to appropriating copyright-free texts and suffusing his writing with intertextuality. It's comforting to feel the presence of others in his stories.

One could summarize the plot he most favors as "Damsel meets Hero, they fall in love, then Damsel loses Hero." He fancies the Romantic literary movement (Becquer, Larra, Espronceda, Zorrilla) above all else. Antonio is a romantic at heart, he won't deny it, one who can check every box: larger-than-life emotions, irrepressible passion, a firm belief in the spirit of freedom, a suicidal impulse, and a deep-seated fear that love, *true* love, will fight to the death for survival against all odds but in the end will lose its battle against cruel, unmerciful Destiny.

All his titles have been brought out by a small house in Valencia and co-financed by him, though not self-published, as Paul would disdainfully claim. Antonio has never gone with vanity presses, and he truly deserves the recognition he's gotten, the reviews, his academic readership. A novelist is what he's wanted to be since he learned to read.

But this visit, as usual, is not about his creative work, or not just about that. He's officially here to report on the Santo Domingo Book Fair for his magazine—which isn't *his*, but he likes to pretend that it is. He seems to be good at pretending: his biggest talent? No, he's considered a thorough, objective reporter, not so much a brainy literary critic though his nationality is a great asset on this island when it comes to shoptalk and theoretical babble. He's well-read, and he can impress the hell out of Dominican intellectuals by throwing around big names from the fields of literary theory, psychoanalysis, history (Foucault, Lacan, Marcuse, Bakhtin), and from the Latin American fiction canon with a carefully stressed Castilian accent.

The truth is that there's also an unofficial reason for his being here. Will he be able to keep it from Paul? Antonio might tell him, just to make the Gringo jealous, that he plans to take notes for a book he'll be writing, a sort of autobiography airing his family's dirty laundry.

But no, Antonio doesn't really want to write about his father: his shady business dealings and associations, his fascist loyalties. Or about his mother: her mental health issues; the fact that she wanted an academic career, that she was an avid reader and hungered for knowledge yet saw herself confined to a mansion in the district of Salamanca, with servants, luxuries, and also with no life outside the domestic realm. True, hers was a much ritzier place than that of so many other women under Franco's regime, yet it was still a prison. She could've gotten psychiatric help, which in their society meant being declared insane regardless of one's ailment—be it dementia, Parkinson's disease, "nerves," or whatever—and locked up in a nuthouse, heavily medicated and turned into a zombie. No, Antonio would never allow that to happen to her. He didn't trust the psychiatric profession at all. Shrinks, therapists, analysts, most of them charlatans!

Mamá found her own way to embody her assigned wifely role, creating in her mind a world where her status was even more restrictive yet also more glamorous. She became a queen and played that part with all the required pomp and royal trimmings, treating the help as her subjects and her husband as the king. Antonio's mother, who could've ended up as a professor or a scholar, was now spending her third age submerged in a fantasy.

He feels sad for Mamá, for the loss of the life she might've had. Sadness, however, isn't what he feels toward his father, who owns several upscale restaurants in Madrid (which Antonio avoids), the swankiest one strategically located on the Gran Vía. He made his fortune during the heyday of *Franquismo*, like many of the dictator's henchmen. And it's best that Antonio doesn't have the specifics about the source of his father's wealth: the businesses of so-called communists he may have appropriated! The land, homes, and bank accounts he surely ransacked!

He abhors Papa's machismo, his bigotry, his homophobia, the despotic way he's always treated his wife and son. What a miserable childhood he gave Antonio, and what a horrific adolescence. The punishments, the criticism, the rejection. Partly because Antonio didn't care about the restaurant business, and instead of becoming a family man, he chose to live the bohemian life of a writer. He also exhibited "filthy tendencies" that brought shame to the family, or so his father told him ad nauseam while beating the crap out of him. Not only had Antonio not taken a wife from the several available young ladies in their social circle, but he tended to frequent disreputable establishments and to associate himself with deviants and perverts.

Such is the way Papá views his son's life, as worthless and shameful. Ironically, more than once, he's defended Massiel, "that poor woman you've been dragging along for years without doing right by her." This defense is only yet another way Papá has found to put down Antonio, since what he truly thinks of Massiel is that she's too left-leaning to be any good. The image of Antonio dragging her along is hilarious! That beautiful, brilliant woman is the one who shuns the prospect of marriage, who values her independence and her career in immigration law. They love each other passionately and have an open, no-strings-attached relationship.

Of course, Antonio's father has no clue about this kind of bond. He thinks it's still his era; therefore, the same oppressive rules apply. Not anymore, old fart. The times they are a-changing indeed. (Bob Dylan was right, as always.) His father is a dying dinosaur. If Hell exists, may he burn there someday next to Fucking-Francisco-Franco and all the other monsters: Hitler, Mussolini, and the cowardly, dishonorable Catholic priests who sided with the fascist Spanish beast, some of them part of Papá's intimate circle of friends, pathetic boozers just like him.

No wonder Antonio was irrevocably turned off to Catholicism, repulsed by its rituals, its dogma, its corruption. The damage that religion has brought to humanity! The Crusades alone are reason enough to condemn it. No wonder, too, that Antonio embraced leftist ideals: a blatant rejection of his right-wing progenitor but also a possible way out of despair, the hope for a world without bloodthirsty little men; a world of liberty and equality and justice. Because, on the left, Stalin and rulers of his ilk were the exceptions. Because the left cared about the underdogs.

Antonio and many other Spanish intellectuals would never admit to the endemic failures of communist regimes. Yet he knows that totalitarianism isn't the sole domain of the right or the left. Like the mythical Devil, it can tempt the best-intentioned men and corrupt the grandest ideals. A perfect example: Fidel Castro in Cuba, the cult he's created around himself, as if he were some kind of messiah. And what about Antonio himself? All that talk of class struggle and the proletariat, and he's bourgeois-to-the-core. The hatred he feels toward his father hasn't stopped him from enjoying the family's riches: his own flat on the upmarket Calle Preciados and a substantial trust fund. It's not Papa's dirty money that he's taking, anyway, but some of the fortune Mamá brought to the marriage and which she's made available to her son.

No, Antonio doesn't wish to portray a family like his; that type of book has been written already. But he's not interested in bringing out yet another historical romance, either. What he wants to do is to write about his life, but only insofar as it led him here, to the Hotel Cristóbal and its historic street, Calle Las Damas (ironically symbolic names!) That would be a daring departure for him. It's time for Antonio Fernando Luján Saavedra to be true to himself.

He won't say much about his protagonist because that character—his alter ego—will be quite busy running the show behind the scenes. Just a few basic details: that he's a writer in his early thirties with a strong jawline, a cleft chin, and a thin mustache as overly trimmed as his black, thick, straight hair; that he's always impeccably dressed, and has a buff physique he's achieved with regular visits to the gym. His only downfall: excessive smoking.

That's the truth, the main though unofficial reason he's here today: to plunge into the Cristóbal scene while also being its observer; to explore the hotel's business and culture, its hierarchies, its workers, its clientele. He'll feature representative tourists like Paul G. Edwards, an American textbook editor from Texas who happens to be a good friend, and Antonio himself. Some of the local "boys" will be major players in this story, just two of them, maybe. And the Hotel Cristóbal will have to be a character, too, because it all starts and ends there…

Antonio will begin his notes this Monday evening at the bar counter with Paul, who is in his mid-forties though looks younger, not overtly fem but definitely non-passing. He's usually clad in colorful guayaberas when he's here, his "Caribbean garb." This is their recurring scene, time for drinks and chats, today with the pleasant music of a trio of guitar players who are too good for this joint, so much nicer than the pop shit that blasts out of the bar speakers all the time.

"I missed you last year, darling," Paul tells him in Spanish, for a change, with his annoying Gringo accent. Excellent command of the language, but, oh, his pronunciation! "What happened?"

"I just couldn't make it," Antonio replies. "Massiel and I had plans…" He's about to have a cig and notices that Paul is making a face. He lights up anyway, not resisting the urge.

"Well, this is my yearly therapy," says Paul, now in English, "so I never skip it."

"Your boss must know you don't come here just on company business."

"He does. And all my editors know, too. But as long as I sell lots of books, no one gives a fuck what or who I do in my free time." Waving his hands, "Will you please stop smoking for at least five minutes?! You're making me choke!"

"Sorry." He puts out his cig. "So, how's Vincent? You're still together, right?"

"Oh, yes, going on five years and still strong. That man is never going to leave me. He's madly in love with me. I'm a very lucky gal, you know."

"Five years, wow, an eternity. He must be very special."

"Not perfect by any means, but the closest thing to an ideal partner I could ever find."

"Hopefully, I'll get to meet him one of these days."

"You'd have to pay us a visit, then. You see, Vincent hates to travel, doesn't even like to drive to the store. Conveniently for him, he has a job that suits him to a tee. He's an accountant and can do all his number crunching anywhere, as long as he has a calculator and a computer." Silence. "But enough about me. I want to hear all about your life since we last saw each other."

"Same old, same old. Writing, reading..."

"Are you and Massiel still an item?"

"In a manner of speaking, yes. Though things have been a bit rocky lately."

"Sorry to hear that, Tony. What's the matter?"

"The usual. It can be challenging to navigate an open relationship like ours. You know, living together but both of us seeing other people..."

"It sounds like the two of you might need a break from each other. Time to reassess."

"We're considering that option. But I'd hate to have to live without Massiel."

"Good luck, babe." Paul takes a big gulp of his beer, then offers to make a toast. "Here's to the challenges and rewards of postmodern love!"

Antonio, laughing, toasting, "I'll drink to that!"

"So, darling," says Paul a while later. "What's the new novel you're here to push this time? Another romantic hodgepodge of Spanish literary history?"

"No. This time I'm wearing my reporter hat," Antonio states, unfazed by Paul's mockery. "Writing a feature story about the fair for the magazine. You know: which publishers are exhibiting, which writers are selling, which products stand out." Silence. "Products, can you believe it? That's what we're calling books now."

"They've always been products for our company, written and sold as merchandise."

"A novel will never be merchandise."

"And yet you push yours as if they were empanadas."

"A deplorable metaphor. But yes, sometimes I sell and sign a few copies here at the fair."

"I have some advice for you, Tony, as I always do. May I?" Silence. "You need to widen your readership. Don't just count on your friends and the profs who teach your stuff. You must shoot for a wide audience." Silence. "But you won't be able to accomplish that with those historical tomes you've been writing; with those cardboard characters who speak for you, expressing your existential woes with romantic clichés in solemn old Castilian."

"Hey, thanks for such a spot-on analysis. You've obviously read my work."

"I sure have. Not a page turner, sorry to say." Imitating Antonio's Spanish accent and writing style, "In the lugubrious chambers of a convent in Toledo, a lovely maiden awaits the love of her life, no longer willing to devote herself to the Lord, Dios Nuestro Señor. She dreams of a gentleman's beguiling manner and his furtive, passionate kiss..."

Laughing, "Yep, you've definitely read me!"

"Just buckle down and write a bestseller, Toñita, a book you wouldn't have to self-publish. How about a fantasy tale? The story of Caribbean studs who suddenly start singing like mermaids thanks to the benevolence of a fag with special powers."

"You're so full of shit."

"Okay, fine, don't listen to me. What do I know?"

"Exactly. Anyway, like I said, I'm here to report on the fair."

"Sure, and to submerge yourself in Dominican 'culture' while you're at it..."

Silence. Paul seems uneasy about the sudden pause in their dialogue. Antonio can tell; he knows that the Gringo doesn't feel alive unless he's immersed in spoken discourse. Should Antonio tell him about his new fiction project? Okay, yes, why not. "Truth is, Paul," he finally says, "this time I've come seeking ideas for a different kind of book."

"Bravo! No more romantic imbroglios! No more details about the way Spaniards pooped and dressed and bathed (or didn't bathe) in the sixteenth century!"

Fed up with Paul's razzing, "Go fuck yourself!"

"No, sweetie. I'll let handsome others take care of that for me." Rubbing his torso, "My entrails are throbbing and fully lubricated!"

Silence. "Speaking of which, Tony, why do you never have gay characters in your books?"

Laughing. "Because there were no queers in the Middle Ages."

"But of course! Next question: why don't you ever write about sex? There's always some cheesy romance between a virginal beauty who looks just like Massiel and her knight in shining armor, the latter a clone of the author down to the last detail, including your cleft chin. But nothing hot and juicy between the sheets. Why is that?"

"Because sex in fiction is cheap, exploitative, and seldom good literature."

"Oh, I see, so it's all about what *you* consider good literature. Well, I have three good reasons why you should include scenes of fucking in your fiction, in detail! It's entertaining, people like it, and it sells." He wets his lips and draws a circle with his index finger around Antonio's crotch. "Speaking of which, what about you? Nothing yet?"

"Hey, I just got here this morning! I can't start screwing the minute I step off the plane."

"Why not? I certainly do!"

"I know! Right there in the backseat of Franklin's car."

"Well, actually, this time my adorable Luis and I just held hands during the ride. Believe it or not, I wanted to wait till we got to the hotel..."

"You're turning over a new leaf, my friend. There's hope for you." Silence. "Luis...?" Antonio tries to recall who he is. "Ah, yes, your regular who loves the theater."

"So, did Franklin pick you up at the airport?"

"Yes, in the hotel's limousine. The Aviary. Isn't that what they call it now? The only vehicle with a minibar and a TV on the entire island. But Franklin doesn't hustle, does he?"

"Oh, no, his job is to transport us and to tend the hotel bar. And he's happily married to Juanito, the waiter. Besides, he couldn't do it even if he wanted to. He's twenty-six already."

"Too old for this business. Unbelievable."

"So, Tony, I just met a new kid that I think you'd like. His name is Richard, and he went with Luis and Franklin to get me at the airport yesterday. Richard is younger than Luis, really cute, and new to the hotel scene." Looking at his watch, "They agreed to meet us here at around seven. Soon now..."

Antonio orders two more beers. To Paul, "Thanks for the heads-up, man."

"Why are you calling me 'man'? You know I'm more woman than Joan Collins when I'm here." Laughing, "And you shouldn't try so hard to sound and act butch, Toñita."

Proudly, "I don't have to try!"

Sarcastic, "Sure. You're as real as Indiana Jones."

"Yes, well, I can't *exist* in absolute gayness like you do, Paul, using gay catchwords, eating in gay restaurants, reading gay lit, socializing only in gay circles. That's not reality."

"It is for me."

"I know. But it's different in my country."

"Of course it is! Ha! In Spain, people like you are all living in a stinking closet. You take your girlfriends or your wives out to dance, then you leave them at home dripping wet and go pick up teenaged gypsies in the public restrooms. So much for being different, my love."

"You don't know what you're talking about."

"That's why you sleep with women, isn't it, Antonio? So you can pretend to be 'normal,' while in secret you devour every chorizo that's placed before you. I guess you work up quite a fantasy when you're fucking a woman. You probably imagine that the tits are giant testicles!"

"I can't believe you're still spewing out that same shit after all these years, Paul."

Their beers are served. After a slow sip from his drink, Paul breaks the sudden, awkward silence, "So, what's your excuse, Tony?"

"I don't know what you mean."

"Well...the straight boys at the Cristóbal are highly motivated to fuck other men, though most of them are straight and not into it at all. Because with just one trick, they make more than the monthly salary of the highest paid government employee. Whereas you, Tony... what excuse do *you* have for your bisexual charade?"

"You'd never be able to understand it, Paul. You're one of those gays who just don't get bisexuality, who believe that if a man likes to fuck other men, he must be homosexual and nothing else. And if he also sleeps with women, then he's deluding himself. Isn't that it? What a reductive way to regard human nature!" Silence. "In any case, to clarify: no, I don't fantasize when I'm in bed with someone. The fantasy comes before, or later, but never while performing."

"Interesting. Perhaps that should be the hook for your new book, the secrets and wild adventures of a bisexual raconteur. Come out of the closet, babe. And while you're at it, air as much of your clan's dirty laundry as possible."

"No, who'd want to read yet another tale about a fascist Spanish family?"

"I'd read it, but only if you threw in some porn based on your own life."

"Ah, yes, of course, your kind of literature."

"Yes, Tony, I admit I like a good gay yarn." Defensive, "But I'm also versed in all the Latin American Boom biggies. In fact, I like that literature—Rulfo, Garro, Márquez (or Gabo), Cortázar, Allende— better than the U.S. canon, my area of expertise. Yes, in spite of all that silly magical realism." Crossing himself as if in church, "And may Gabo forgive me!" Silence. "Oh, and by the way, I would throw your compatriot Juan Goytisolo in the Boom mix too, since he's an honorary member." Laughing, "What's that colloquial expression in Spanish? Between cabbage and cabbage, a head of lettuce... Variety is the spice of life!"

"I don't think Juan would appreciate being compared to a head of lettuce..."

"Well, don't tell him, darling."

"Say, you forgot to mention your idol, Manuel Puig."

"Because Puig is in a league of his own. I adore him!" Pensive, "But, hey, there's lots of sex in his books. Hence his writing is cheap, according to you."

"No, Paul, because sex in Puig's work is suggested, alluded to, talked about, not described in lurid detail the way you'd want it to be. It's at the center of his narrative universe, yes, but he engages his readers aesthetically, imaginatively, not pornographically."

"Or so says the expert! I assume you identify with Valentín in *Kiss...*?"

"I don't see myself as either character. Whereas you surely get your rocks off imagining yourself as Molina, getting a 'real' man to fall in love with you and fuck your brains out."

"How well you know me, Don Antonio!" Silence. "Have you seen the play?"

"Yes, it's been a big hit in Spain. Not as good as the novel, though."

"I like the play better myself." Silence. "There's a scene toward the end, after the two prisoners have made love, that brought tears to my eyes. It's when Molina says to Valentín, 'It seemed...that I wasn't me. That now, I was you.' So simple yet so beautiful."

"Yes, quite. They used that line to promote the play in Madrid. You could see it all over town, on billboards and buses and omnibus stops."

"It just warms your heart. Wouldn't it be nice to feel that way about a person?"

Paul looks suddenly crestfallen. It's evident that he's never experienced such a strong human connection, whereas Antonio has. "Yes, it would be nice," Antonio replies and says, "Anyway, it's good to know we're both big fans of La Manuela."

"We sure are! Though there's something I can't stand about Puig's fiction in general, and it's all those Hollywood movies he narrates. I know that's his thing, one of his obsessions, and I'm quite aware of how classic films work in his stories and why Molina recounts them. But I still don't like them. The overacting, the high-pitched voices, the blatant stereotypes, the misogyny. Oh and that artsy *noir*. Molina's retelling in the novel is more interesting than the films themselves, in my opinion. The play, on the other hand...what a masterpiece!"

"You took Luis to see it last year, didn't you?"

"Yes, the show had a run here with local talent, and of course Luis loved it, couldn't stop talking about it and insisted that I tell him everything I knew about the theater. Again! He tries to remember what I teach him but gets his terminology wrong sometimes. And he has a problem remembering the works' titles and the characters' names. It's very cute."

"Cute, yes. But it could also be the symptom of a medical condition, Paul."

"Nah. Luis is just a little spacey, that's all. He'll say stuff like, that play about the two guys in prison, or the character who's a fag and likes to tell movie plots. Or, with a musical like *La Cage Aux Folles*, you know, the character who's supposed to be a flaming queen but has a booming macho voice when he sings and sounds like an old man..."

Antonio, laughing, "I definitely agree with him about the Zaza actor!"

"And speaking of books, have you discovered any good Dominican writers lately?"

"Yes, a few excellent novelists, all of them part of the Caribbean Boom."

"Another boom! Never liked the word. Couldn't you think of something more original?"

"Whatever you choose to call it, Paul, the fact is that there's a plethora of gifted storytellers and poets in the Dominican Republic. And, yes, several of them have gone on to be quite famous partly thanks to my reviews...Gerón, Ramos, Phipps Cueto, Cocco de Filippis. Though I'm still primarily interested in Juan Bosch."

"Not my kind of writer."

"You've never even read him."

"Guilty as charged!"

"You're missing out."

"Really? I don't think so, and neither do you. Truth is, despite all those articles and reviews you've written, you still think this island's literature is inferior. Admit it!"

"No. That's what *you* think, you pitiful damn Gringo."

"Ay, you sound so cranky. You need to distill all your venom. Don't delay the cure!"

Antonio takes a gulp of beer. Another pause that makes his friend uncomfortable. "I'm seriously considering your suggestion, Paul," he says minutes later. "An autobiographical novel. Not a bad idea. A book about my experiences in Santo Domingo." Feeling mischievous, "Our friendship. Everything you've ever told me."

"Don't you dare! You'd better leave me out of it!"

"You're going to be quite a character, Paulita."

"I swear I'll sue you!"

"The laws of your country don't hold in mine."

Paul, striving for solemnity, "The law of vengeance holds everywhere."

"See?" Antonio laughs. "You're already talking like one of my characters."

Paul suggests they grab a table while they wait for Luis and Richard, who'll be here any minute, he says. Sure enough, there are the two young men now... "You made it!" exclaims Paul, hugging Luis. "Finally!" Luis, looking at his watch, "But we're actually early, Mister Paul." Paul turns to Richard and says to him, "I told Antonio about you..." The young man shakes hands with Antonio, "Nice to meet you." Antonio, smitten with Richard, "My pleasure."

"We'll have drinks later, boys," Paul announces, stroking Luis's hair. "But now, Luis and I are heading straight—I mean gayly forward!—to my room. Until the tropical night falls..."

"We'll join you later for a nightcap," Antonio tells him.

"I'm counting on it! Second floor, first room on the right, by the stairs. It's tradition!"

"Stay here," Luis tells Richard. "Spend some time with Señor Antonio, okay?"

Luis and Paul leave, hand in hand.

Antonio

Across from him sits the most beautiful young man he's ever seen. Or is Antonio being hyperbolic? He does tend to embellish things a tad and to make sweeping statements about literature, writers, culture, performers, and singers. No, the person at this table, in this upscale bar, is truly a lovely creature. He has a light complexion that is tenderly bronzed; dreamy eyes with long, silky eyelashes; an aquiline nose; dimples; fleshy, moist lips; and a mane of wavy black hair. Antonio has never been this attracted to someone's countenance, has never wanted to make love to just a face, not a body. There's a delicate yet intense quality about Richard. His voice, too, has a sweet resonance. And his shyness adds to the full effect, a hesitancy the young man can barely disguise, though he's evidently determined to be perceived as fearless.

Antonio finds this game addictive, enticing. Part of the addiction is the power you have to determine and control the course of events. He can decide what happens next, starting with the topic of conversation and ending with Antonio and Richard in bed. He is the customer and hence always right. Still, he wonders how far Richard would go to meet his demands. There are limits, barriers to the client's power, and places he won't be allowed into. And it should be that way!

The young man's feelings and emotions, his needs, his ideas… do they matter at all? They do to Antonio, very much so. He's not the typical Cristóbal client who gets his rocks off with very few words exchanged, pays up after screwing, and asks the hustler to leave. No, Antonio tries to get to know the kids and let them talk about themselves, which most of them love to do. In the past, he's tried to impress some of his young lovers by boasting about his achievements, his publications, his place in the sphere of contemporary Spanish fiction. He'd show them hardbound copies of his novels and a few of the articles written about them. What a head trip, as Paul would say. But not anymore. He'll never be that vainglorious asshole again. Now he prefers to listen to the Cristóbal guys, who are gifted storytellers. If given a chance, they'll expound their experiences, talk about their johns, the acts they've performed. Some of their stories are fictional, fabricated to pleasure the client, but that doesn't make them less captivating.

Antonio is glad he hasn't lost his curiosity about this world. Because his impulse, now, is not to possess its inhabitants but to portray them. His mind, not his body, is calling the shots...

"What can I get you?" he asks Richard.

"A Coke would be good. Thank you."

Antonio, to the bartender, "One more beer for me and a Coca-Cola for my friend." He caresses the young man's hand, lights up a cigarette. "Do you mind if I smoke?"

"No, go ahead. Everybody here does. I happen to hate smoking myself, and besides, I'm aware of how bad it is, how it damages your lungs. My dad's a pharmacist. He knows as much as a doctor about addictions and health stuff. Man, the things he's told me about cigarettes!"

"Yes, well, I've been smoking since I was younger than you, but I plan to quit one of these days. It's a nasty and expensive habit. Thank goodness I haven't suffered any major consequences yet, other than the typical smoker's cough."

Antonio notices the early evening light outside, suddenly softer, as if announcing a rainstorm. Some rain would be nice, the usual brief summer downpour.

"Well, I hope you can keep it that way, Señor Antonio."

"By the way, how old are you, Richard?"

"Old enough to be here. The manager checks our IDs, and he won't let us in if we're minors 'cause he could get in trouble with the government."

"Good to know. Do you do everything?"

Richard sits upright in his chair, "No. Not everything."

"But what if we're friends?"

"Then, maybe. I'd like that, being your friend, Señor Antonio." Silence. "I could do it any way you like, but only if you let me be the only guy for you while you're here."

Antonio, smiling, "It's a deal!"

Their drinks are served.

"You go for women too, don't you, Señor Antonio?"

"As a matter of fact, I do. How did you know? Did Paul tell you?"

"No, I just had a hunch. Like they say, it takes one to know one." Silence. "I have a girlfriend, by the way. Her name is Isabel, and she's very pretty. I like her wavy hair and her smile. Also, the way she walks, like no one can stop her!" Silence. "We've been hanging together for about six months, not a long time but to us it seems like we've known each other forever." Silence. "And what's your girlfriend's name, Señor Antonio?"

Girlfriend, a word Antonio wouldn't use to describe Massiel. She'd laugh about it as she laughs at other ideologically loaded terms like lady friend, fiancée, betrothed, better half...

"It's Massiel," Antonio replies. "Her parents named her after a famous Spanish singer."

"Yeah!" Richard exclaims, excited like a child. "I know about that singer! She won a music festival in Europe, didn't she?"

Antonio is utterly surprised. "Yes, she did! The Eurovision Song Contest in 1968."

"My mom has one of Massiel's records, and she plays it once in a while. She's a big fan, says she likes the singer's deep, throaty voice. The song that won the contest cracks me up 'cause it's supposed to be poetic, but the title is goofy as all get-out, just like the refrain."

"You're talking about 'La, la, la'..."

"Yes! Have you ever heard a more ridiculous title for a song? Luis says that's what songwriters do when they can't come up with lyrics." Laughing, "They go, la la la la la la..."

"I happen to like that song, Richard."

"Sorry! I didn't mean to be rude or insulting, Señor Antonio!"

"It's okay, Richard, no problem."

"You shouldn't pay attention to me, anyway. I don't know much about music and, frankly, don't care for it. I mean, there are songs that stick in my head and won't let go, though I wouldn't want to sing them. Music is just noise to me, especially pop. It doesn't move me the way it does most people. Isn't that weird for someone my age? My dad says that's what happens to old folks, that they stop being interested in popular music. So, I must have an old soul, then."

"It seems that you do." Silence. "You know, Richard, when 'La, la, la' came out, I was a very young lad, having a rough time at home, and that song made me feel happy. The first line became a mantra for me, 'I sing to the morning that welcomes my youth!' Spain was in the throes of a brutal regime. So, listening to 'La, la, la,' the uplifting lyrics, the catchy melody, I was able to forget all the shit and pretend that everything was good in my home and my country."

"I understand, Señor Antonio. In a way, Massiel's music was like medicine for you and for Spain, right?" Silence. "Would you be willing to sing her famous song for me?"

Laughing, "Oh, no, no, I wouldn't subject you to that! I can't sing to save my life."

Richard grins. "Neither can I!"

"Hey, maybe Luis could learn it and sing it for you."

"No, he'd hate it. He only sings his own stuff and some American pop." Silence. "Anyway, I'm sorry you had such a hard time at home, Señor Antonio."

"Thanks... though not everything about it was bad."

"I'm glad. Maybe you could tell me the good part sometime? I'm already learning so much from you. Most tourists don't really care to teach us anything."

"Sure, Richard. But, come to think of it, 'La la la' is definitely a ridiculous title." He makes a toast. "To all the goofy Spanish songs ever written!"

Richard, toasting with his Coke, "Cheers!"

They drink. Richard fixes his eyes on Antonio, overcoming his shyness, says, "Has your girlfriend ever come here with you, on vacation?"

"Yes, she did once, and she loved your country."

"I'd like to meet her someday. She must be beautiful."

"She is, although she doesn't look like her famous namesake. I'm sure Massiel would like to meet you, too, but I don't think she's coming back to Santo Domingo..."

"Why not?"

"Because she understands that this is my space, where I need to be without her. She knows I'm not here just to visit the fair and report on it."

"And she's okay with that?"

"Yes, we have a very open relationship."

"Lucky you, though that's weird. I mean, it's unusual, no?"

"I suppose it is. What about Isabel? Does she know that you have sex with men?"

"No, and I hope she never finds out. She'd probably break up with me if she did."

"Do your parents know?"

"No, no, no! But my younger brother does, the one closest to me in age. He wants to get into the biz when he's a little older." Silence. "What about your parents, Señor Antonio?"

Taken aback by the question, "What? Well, you see, Richard, my parents..."

"If you'd rather not talk about them, that's okay."

"No, it's just that... my folks are not very involved in my life. My poor mother has been having trouble dealing with reality for some time now. And my father is also delusional in his own way. Crazy about Franco. If he could, he'd resuscitate him."

"What does that mean, resusci...?"

"It means that my father would bring Franco back from the dead."

"Oh, I remember the word now. Resuscitate. I've heard it in my catechism classes. It's what Jesus did with the cadaver of a guy named Lazarus. He brought it back to life, right?"

"Yes, after Lazarus had been dead for four days!"

"Was Franco... a relative of yours?"

Moved by the young man's question, "No, Richard. Franco was a ruthless dictator. He governed Spain for forty years. I hope he's burning in Hell for eternity!"

"Forgive my spaciness, Señor Antonio. You must think I'm so dumb! I did learn about that period in Spain's history. Fascism." Silence. "We had one of those dictators here too, a total nutcase and a criminal. Most men in power are a bunch of crooks. That's what my father says."

"Your father is right, unfortunately."

"Though he kind of likes the president we have now. My mom says that his name fits him well, Salvador, 'cause he's sort of saving the country, our economy, and stuff like that."

"Let's just hope the Devil doesn't tempt him."

Silence. "And you, Señor Antonio... are you going to marry Massiel?"

"I doubt it. Massiel is not interested in marriage."

"We're in the same boat, then. Isabel doesn't plan to get married, either. But she's an exception in this country. Almost everyone here ties the knot the minute they start having sex."

"But not you, Richard. Only if you're in love."

"Which I'll never be, 'cause only women are supposed to fall in love."

"Who told you that?"

"Everybody says it. Men fuck a lot and work hard, but they don't fall in love. Never."

"Some men do, Richard. I certainly have, more than once."

"Yeah, but you're from Spain."

Laughing, "Sure, that must be the reason!"

Richard, sheepishly, "Should we go upstairs to your room now?"

"No, I'd like to get to know you first."

"But there isn't much to know about me, Señor Antonio. I'm kind of boring."

"I doubt that. Let's just go for a stroll down the malecón this evening, okay?"

Disappointed, "So we're not going to do it tonight?"

"No, not tonight."

"Is it because you don't like me, Señor Antonio? You must be honest with me, okay? I'd have a hard time if you didn't, but I'd understand."

"No, no, Richard, that's not it..."

"And don't worry about hurting my feelings if I turn you off, okay? You may not go for me, but there are other tourists who would. As my dad always says, whatever floats your boat!" Silence. "Hey, maybe you don't like that I talk so much. It's a problem I have, you know. Luis complains about it all the time. He says that when I start jabbering away, no one can stop me, especially if I'm nervous. It's like my mouth has a mind of its own!"

Antonio suppresses his laughter. He'd rather act earnestly as he tells Richard, "No, my young friend, I actually like the way you talk, how expressive and eloquent you are. The fact is, I like everything about you. So, please, don't think I'm rejecting you."

Richard, sighing with relief, "Phew, that's good to know, Señor Antonio. I happen to like you too, a lot, and I'm not just saying that, you must believe me. For one thing, I never met anyone from Spain, and that's cool 'cause we have no problem understanding each other."

"Thank you, Richard. It's sweet of you to say those things. I look forward to going upstairs with you, really. We'll make it happen, I promise. How about tomorrow?"

Richard shakes Antonio's hand awkwardly and says, "Yes, of course, Señor Antonio."

"And I'll pay you for your time today."

"No, you must pay me only when I do some actual work."

"Very well, but let's not call it *work*, okay?"

"Sure, whatever you say. I appreciate the opportunity to make you happy."

If Richard only knew what would make Antonio happy...

Intermission

(Behind the Scenes)

The sun through the window, rising, so round and perfect, honey color, like bittersweet candy that melts in your mouth. Now it hides behind the clouds, forging its way through a cement jungle. Sunlight on the same buildings that crush his mood whenever he returns to Madrid from the Caribbean, whenever he lands on this peninsula of fucking colonizers.

Then it's the taxi ride. The air is dense, foul-smelling. The people they pass look harried. Usually, the sight of those crowds helps him transition. But not today. Hope is being elusive today. He must think of an incentive to wash away his fantasy of annihilation. A carrot, Paul calls it, a sweet juicy carrot dangling in front of his face, the promise of better times ahead. Because at this very moment, Madrid feels like a trap, a room with no windows. The only light at the end of the tunnel, though faint, is the prospect of seeing Massiel. All his dark thoughts will vanish when she hugs him. They've agreed to pick each other up at the airport in Antonio's SEAT whenever they return from a trip. So, he called her from Barajas early this morning, having waited at the curb so he could kiss her, hold her, lift her, and spin around until they can't take the motion anymore and plop down, roaring with laughter. But she didn't show up; slept through her alarm. Something was amiss. Her sleepy voice lingers... "I'm so sorry," she said on the phone by way of apology. "No big deal," he told her. I'll just take a cab."

She welcomes him in the flat they've shared for nearly twelve years, wearing her denim cutoff shorts and a white T-shirt. Her embrace gives him the strength he'd been needing, and so now he savors his carrot at last. Tomorrow they'll go to a park or a gallery, then to get greasy tapas and a bottle of red at one of their favorite pubs on the Plaza Mayor. It'll be a hot Sunday afternoon, but they'll sit outside anyway. As they devour their patatas bravas, they'll watch the people and invent stories about them. She'll hold his hand as if to say I'm here now, my love...

"What a view," I remark, and I ask Tony to describe it. He says he can't. Says he'd have to be alone in front of his Apple to think, recalling each detail, then wait for the force to take over. The force?! Oh, no, so now he sounds like those sci-fi movies that are so popular nowadays, with all their shoot-'em-ups in outer space and their goofy aliens. "You can do better than that," I tell him. "The idea of hiding somewhere to conjure up the muses is passé and unbecoming of a true storyteller. If you were truly able to tell a story, you'd do it here and now."

"Very well, Paul," he says, laughing. "Let the whole island bear witness to my talent!" He climbs onto the breakwater wall, nearly falling, and yells, "Ladies and gentlemen!" He takes a bow and gestures as if wanting to contain the sea in his hands. "The sound of the waves is beguiling," he pronounces. "Bewitching yet gentle. We plunge in and let the water make us float like light, laugh from the heart, sing a mermaid's love call. Our eyes closed, we feel the soothing caress of a thousand hands, every one of our pores submerged in pleasure, remade in salt, foam, and sea. We must ignore the fact that we're surrounded by people; that a young man in tight blue jeans is trying to offer us his services, anything he can do to make our vacation more enjoyable. He'd like to be our guide in this city that he loves with a passion…"

"Ah, just imagine the taste of his sun-beaten skin!"

"Not now, Paul. Can't you see he's yanking us out of a wonderful dream? He has no way of knowing that the fantasy—a thousand fluid hands in our pores—only lasts a few minutes. Because someone will always want to wake us, shatter the sweet maritime reverie."

"Yes, yes. All good things…"

"Now we feel an urge to dissolve in the blue surf. The ocean can cleanse us; it's much cleaner than our souls. But a hand grabs us when we're about to leap…"

"Get down from there, Antonio! You're making a spectacle of yourself!"

Tony says he has a right to be up here. "I'm describing the opening scene," he announces, "for the book I'm writing. You asked for it, Paul. Now you fucking listen!"

"But our young friends are waiting for us at the Cristóbal."

"They can just sit and wait! We're the clients. We call the shots."

"As you wish."

"Ladies and gentlemen," he declaims with too much Segismundo and not enough Molina. "Gather around me and listen to a drunken

Spaniard who knows a thing or two about this island, who guards a dangerous secret about one of its downtown hotels. Let him tell you his story..."

It was the year he turned twenty-two. He had just published his first novel and was doing a reading at a funky bookstore in Lavapiés—never cared for the big chains. Encouraged by the good turnout, Antonio gave what was to be his best performance ever, although he didn't know it at the time. Just as he couldn't know that the young woman who approached him after the event would become his soulmate. Handing him a copy of his book to sign, she asked him a question no one ever had, "Don't you think that the creative process is self-destructive?" As he signed the book, he said to her, "Yes, of course it is. That's why an artist needs a soulmate to help them undertake the reconstruction." He was already enraptured by her eyes and her voice, convinced that they were meant to meet at that bookstore. Yes, Antonio still believes that Massiel knew him already, somehow, and set out to search for him. He had dated women before and would hook up with several in the future. But none of them would make him laugh like Massiel did. He can't remember what they cracked up about that day; he does know it was heartfelt, roaring laughter, the umbilical cord that would always connect their bodies and minds from then on.

He eventually opened his heart to Massiel. Told her about his abusive father and his patricidal fantasies, about his writing, his projects, his dreams. And he would learn about her atheist beliefs, her innate bisexuality, and her family, which he perceived as ideal. Massiel adored her parents and got along great with her two younger sisters. There had never been any violence in their home. No abuse. No painful punishments. He was so jealous of her upbringing!

Massiel gave herself over to him, asking for nothing in return. She didn't want to change him, never really tried to; and she wouldn't make any radical changes in her own views, her identity and personality for his sake. She actually took pleasure in the undefinable nature of their relationship. Not always, though, and not in every situation. Sometimes the life they shared didn't seem real enough to her. Yet for him it was the most *real* of all the lives he'd lived.

A vivid, enduring memory: the first time they made love. They had gone to the Retiro after a sumptuous dinner of paella and too much Rioja, and he suggested they do it right there and then, in the bushes, unconcerned with the risk of getting mugged or arrested. She kissed him and said she needed a bed or at least a couch, admitting she wasn't spontaneous about sex; she was, in fact, a control freak. That admission surprised him; he hadn't perceived her that way. So, they rushed to his flat where they stripped off their clothes and all guises for each other...

They still have ardent sex, just like they did that night. And they still enjoy their Sundays together, the rainy or snowy afternoons when they find refuge in a concert at the Teatro Real: their favorite outing. They always look forward to the moment right before the music starts, when the spotlights illuminate the stage; followed by the moment when the orchestra begins, and you can hear the first ascending notes. He and Massiel clap boisterously, in unison. Then they hold hands and let their heads repose on one another, ready for the feast...

Tony turns to me, asks: "Why do I always end up here on the malecón when I get drunk in Santo Domingo? Because it's a fact that I'm plastered, right, Paul?" I tell him, "Yes, darling, you're shitfaced. Come down this instant, please. You're about to fall, and I'm not jumping in to save you. I'm not your lifeguard, much less a fucking hero." Antonio ignores me, addresses the passers-by who stop to stare and listen as his monologue rages on...

"We approach the brightly painted doors, the gardens, the makeshift fences, certain that if we were to look behind those doors, we'd find an empty lot and large beams propping up the flimsy façades. And any minute now a crowd of movie extras will appear out of nowhere. We see the water again, but let's not be fooled by the sea; it could be another illusion. As we keep on strolling, two young tourists bump into us: a man and a woman, each holding the remains of some cheap snack. They smile, say hello. And then the woman lets out a heart-wrenching scream.

Seconds later, they go on their merry way, laughing as if nothing had happened. That's the way things work on this island. We all do whatever we feel like doing if we can afford it. Scream, sing, perform monologues on the breakwater wall, or make love on the sand with abandon... Or, in our case, get smashed and finish our spree in the most popular brothel of the city, which also happens to be a luxury hotel on Calle las Damas, screwing away our drunken stupor till we're ready to undertake the odyssey again."

Early afternoon in Madrid. A handsome young foreigner with a funky walk is coming in Antonio's direction. But Antonio is in a cerebral place right now, not in the mood for hooking up. He's been rereading Julio Cortázar's *Rayuela* (one of the five books he likes to revisit) for the third time, and his head is full of mind trips. Those fucking Paris intellectuals in the novel, so full of shit, yet he can't get enough of their mental wanking.

As usual, he's seated on a bench at the Plaza de España, close to the welcoming Cervantes monument: his preferred spot to veg out in the city. And the tourist obviously just got off the Argüelles metro station. Antonio checks him out as he approaches. Soft facial features, curly strawberry blonde hair, in his early twenties. He's wearing mint-green Bermuda shorts with a belt bag and a blue, sheer-fabric shirt that highlights his pink nipples. He smiles, asks Antonio (a strong French accent) which metro line will take him to the Prado Museum, claims he lost his subway map, and wants to know about the best Prado collections. Antonio mentions Velázquez's *Las Meninas* and El Greco's *Nobleman* among his favorites, although he's only genuinely interested in Goya's *La maja desnuda*—not the dressed *maja*; what would be the point? He remarks that just seeing the Duchess of Alba in the raw is worth the price of admission.

The tourist says his name is Alain. Antonio asks him if his parents named him after Alain Delon, the famous movie star. But the young man has no idea who that is. He gets excited when he finds out that Antonio speaks French fluently. It turns out that he's Parisian and just got here, looking for someone who can orient him in the city, show him the best that Madrid has to offer. He's staying at a hostel but wants permanent lodging since he's planning to stay in Spain for an indefinite time, hopefully here in the capital, "cette cité ravissante."

The phrase makes Antonio laugh: Madrid, a ravishing city? Hardly, monsieur! Charming, maybe. Welcoming. Inviting, perhaps. But definitely not *ravissante*!

"Vous etês d'ici, n'est-pas?" asks Alain, and Antonio tells him yes, he was born and raised in Madrid. He wonders now, is it mere coincidence that a hot Parisian trick just fell into his lap? No, there are no coincidences, according to Paul. How would *Rayuela*'s protagonist, the very masculine, hetero, and most likely homophobic Oliveira feel about this queer twist? Ah, hell, let's chalk it up to ludic Julio, the great Argentine god of play!

Antonio decides to invite Alain to visit Retiro Park, the green heart of Madrid, and the Frenchman eagerly accepts the invitation. They find a bench across from the pond where they sit to take in the lovely sight of sailboats and dense vegetation. A gush of warm summer breeze dishevels Antonio's hair, and Alain plays with some of his unruly locks. He rubs his thighs against Antonio's, runs his fingers down his neck, tickling him, and Antonio lets him do all these things because he's horny at last, no longer entrapped in *Rayuela*'s existential games.

He observes Alain up close: his wandering eyes, his outlined eyebrows, his studied gestures. The Frenchman tells him he wants to go wherever Antonio is willing to take him. But Antonio needs to think about this situation for a minute. He must first tune out Alain's quavering voice, the shrieking of children, the many conversations around them, the distant outbursts of heavy Sunday traffic. So, where does Antonio want to take this man...?

Alain asks him if he lives alone, and of course, Antonio tells him no, he has a partner. And now the young man wants to know who this "partner" is. Antonio feels no obligation to answer his questions, but he tries to be courteous. He explains that for a long time now, he's shared a flat with Massiel, a very dear friend. His partner. A woman, yes. It's a spacious, centrally located apartment they like to keep impeccably clean. They enjoy doing house chores together while listening to their favorite

LPs, and they can both cook but prefer to eat out. Occasionally, Massiel sees her own friends, and Antonio sees his. Friends (hers) that he'd rather not have to hear about at all. Friends (his) that she accepts and used to want to know. People like you, Alain, although you will have vanished by sunrise tomorrow.

"I am never getting drunk with you again," I tell Tony, and I ask him, "Why do we do this every year? Can't we just scrap this fucking tradition?" He responds with a categorical no because some traditions are worth keeping. Tony says he likes doing this; it's fun. Yeah, fun for him. But what am I supposed to do while he enacts his version of *Life is a Dream*, a classic play he knows by heart? Am I just to stand here keeping watch over him, making sure he doesn't hurt himself? Oh, yes, exciting stuff. "Careful! Shit, you almost tripped, Antonio. You think you're on stage, don't you? An actor wannabe, that's what you are. An actor of the bottle, because the bottle frees you to be who you dream of being. Without booze you're an obscure, insignificant man." Tony is laughing. He tells me I should be honest and admit I get a kick out of his drunken babbling. That's why I provoke him, encourage him to let it all out, yes, so I can listen to him weave his stories aloud, sharing his secrets with the island. Yes, I admit I like being his audience.

He says that some of us need a shot of alcohol now and then, the main ingredient for complete transformation. In his case, so he can become one of the romantic characters he tries to depict in his novels. I tell him that's all fine, so long as he doesn't end up as an abusive alcoholic like his father. "Fuck!" he exclaims. "Never!" He quickly avoids the subject, tells me I'm a better actor than he is, that I should be the one up there performing. I remind him I suffer from vertigo. Couldn't bear to stand on the edge, overlooking the water. I'd have a heart attack!

Tony looks out at the powerful waves, turning silent, introspective. Then he says he doesn't really get me, can't figure me out. What?! Boy, this time, he's really tied one on, more than any previous year. I help him step down, and we sit on a bench. Some calm, finally.

He smiles, looks at me in a way I've never seen before, lovingly, caringly. He holds my hand, says, "So, did you like my description of the island tonight?"

"Yes," I answer. "You know I always do... But now we should be heading back to the hotel; what do you say?" His silence tells me he's not ready. "Okay," I add, "just let me know, and I'll hail a cab. Though not one of those that you and most Dominicans like so much, which you have to share with a bunch of strangers. Oh, no, darling, we deserve our own private carriage!" I thought he'd laugh, but instead, he's crying. What the fuck?! I wasn't expecting this. I hug him and ask, "What's the matter, babe? What's troubling your sweet little Spanish heart?" He manages to block the floodgates long enough to express how he feels...

"I have been a self-consumed writer for too long, Paul, loath to waste my energy on trivialities. And I've yielded to the cliché rather than fight it. Desperately trying to break away from this voice in my head, a verbose raconteur with a penchant for contrived situations, for pseudo-intellectual trips. Unable to avoid the trap of stereotypes and Jung's archetypes in order to flesh out real, believable characters. I want to come across as someone in control of his life, but I don't always accomplish it. Yes, I have an ego as big as this island, yet I'm also very insecure. I need these performances to feel alive, Paul. I need a crowd of beautiful young men who cling to my every word, who applaud my shitty acting. I'm subjugated by youth. I long to possess it because I never had it, never knew it, wasn't allowed to enjoy it..."

Tony wipes his tears, blows his nose with his perfumed handkerchief. "Okay," he says, enough melodrama for one day!" He thanks me for letting him bend my ear. "You're a true friend," he tells me. "Let's go back now. Get us a taxi, please. A private carriage." Finally!

Massiel was an atheist, like her father. They were both outliers in their circle of friends and neighbors, an aberration in their pious Murcia community. She believed that the Biblical god was an insecure being who needed to be worshipped to feel powerful. "Without our prayers," she said, "it would disappear. That god created us so we'd be grateful that he brought us into existence. If we don't thank him for his act of creation, he ceases to be mighty; therefore, we're not obligated to be his servants anymore. We can leave behind his altar, the illusive comfort of his temple. We can face the world on our own terms and look for strength elsewhere."

Antonio agreed with Massiel's views and added that the Biblical god was quite the megalomaniac. "The Bible," he told her, "is no proof of his existence. Because the Judeo-Christian god knew only as much as the Bible writers did. That deity could only speak through their prejudices and limitations. Those men were observant, imaginative, but not prescient. They invented a deity who was as flawed and ignorant as they were. And, as violent. Ultimately, there was no god involved in the writing of the Gospels, and certainly not one who was omniscient. For if that so-called omnipotent being had known the future, he would've told the Bible writers about Columbus, Freud, Hitler, Stalin, Gandhi, about the two world superpowers. He would've asked humanity to watch out for certain ruthless kings and queens; for slavery, fascism, communism, Islamic and Christian fundamentalism. He would've mentioned space travel, computers, the Beatles, Michael Jackson, MTV, AIDS..."

Antonio had stopped believing in that Biblical deity at an early age, as soon as he began to question his parents' faith and worldview. It helped that he was willing and eager to inform himself about the mythological basis for most Bible stories and the many iterations of the Christ figure throughout history. It's all about people's needs and fears, he concluded, their inability to face death, the reality of *nothingness*. And yet, in contrast to Massiel, he did like to imagine a creative cosmic energy superior to humanity; call it a vital impulse, the first particle, or the Big Bang. Whatever name one gave it, this was a definition of god that comforted him and gave him strength. Antonio's deity didn't need to be worshipped. Instead of prayers, it welcomed honest conversations. Its mission wasn't just to keep Antonio company, but to keep him alive.

He described one of his recurring dreams to Massiel: "I inhabit a place devoid of deities or angels and oppressed by sinister, demonic creatures that rule over humanity. In that terrifying place, which resembles a dark, bottomless pit that I assume is my own Hell, I'm forced to die a painful death by asphyxiation, repeatedly. But as I gasp for air, I manage to leave my pit to hover like a ghost over the world, fully conscious, aimless, lost. And then... then my god asks me not to despair, tells me that I'm alive and breathing, that life is beautiful, worth living..."

Tony is the only friend I have in my tropical adventures. I tell him I couldn't navigate this island without him. I'd feel adrift if he weren't by my side. And he laughs, says I don't need him because I've always gotten along just fine alone. I insist, "Not in Santo Domingo. I enjoy this place only when we can share it, when we become two fucking drunks in Paradise." He laughs again and tells me, "Hey, that could be the title for a story. Although it should sound more literary. How about... *Inebriates in Paradise*. Do you like that?" And I say it's fucking cool.

He wants to climb the malecón again, but I won't let him. Not in the mood anymore. "No, babe, don't do it. Here, how about if I just take pictures of everything for you? I brought my Canon, ready to shoot! Then you can use my pics to get inspired."

Tony seems excited. "Yes, great idea, except we shouldn't talk of inspiration. That word is defunct, a fucking cliché." He compliments me: "You're a good photographer, Paul. You should exhibit!" He's making fun of me for sure, so I order him to stop. "No, no," he goes on. "You have an eye for capturing the energy and depth of the world around you. I like your shots of the Cristóbal boys, though your forte is the flora of this island. Love your landscapes!"

I thank him and tell him I'm flattered. He says that my photos will stimulate his creativity, a term I like, *stimulation*, because it could also refer to sex. Not that we'll ever move in that direction together, mind you. No reason to spoil a good thing.

"Why haven't you ever shown me photos of your family?" he asks. "Because," I reply, "I've only taken pictures of my mother, and I'll bring some next year to show you. She still looks good for her age. No pics of my father, that old fart; and none of my dumbass brother, who was encouraged by our dad to found an ultra-right organization in our Republic of Texas. With thousands of members! You know, people who believe that all dark-skinned immigrants are criminals; that women came to this world to have babies, and that faggots need a daily treatment of electroconvulsive therapy to get rid of the sickness that ails us. I hate their fucking guts!"

Tony is taking his time to react. "We have so much in common, Paul," he remarks at last. "No wonder we're such good friends. We both grew up in homes ruled by oppressive patriarchs. Both of us still haunted by the specter of fascism, dragging our patricidal fantasies to the grave."

Antonio imagines that Pedro, the Nicaraguan professor, was certain Massiel would be his lover the second time she answered one of his questions in class. She'd always sit in the front row, then stay afterward to discuss and sometimes challenge his assertions. Massiel was auditing his course at the Complutense because she was interested in the topic, Popular Latin American Theater. She liked the fact that this type of theater was written by and for the people. Pedro's class was also a welcome break from the dense legalese she had to sift through in law school. A breather, she called it. He invited her to coffee one day, and that same day they talked for hours. Or, rather, he did: about the neglected Indigenous communities of Central America, the evils of right-wing regimes, his hatred of Somoza, and his brief involvement with the FSLN.

The following night, Pedro kissed her. That same night she touched his five o'clock shadow ever so gently and told him that she'd try to support his activism. Of course, she had no idea what he'd gone through (jail time, torture) because she hadn't embraced nor fought for an ideal. But her heart was in the right place, and eventually, she'd find her own way to fight for social justice—influenced by Pedro, no doubt. Massiel, too, wanted to beat the fucking bourgeois system at its own game and help offer a better life to those who desperately needed it.

Pedro gave her access to his vast wealth of knowledge. He recommended books that she'd devour and then share with Antonio. She'd listen, enthralled, to his spiel about the birth of the novelistic genre with the emergence of the bourgeoisie (who had lots of time to read!); and about the theater groups he'd worked with, Candelaria and

Escambray among them. He had a doctorate in Latin American fiction, which he mainly taught, but his true passion was the theater.

A mentor, that's what Pedro would end up being to Massiel, just what Antonio wanted to be for her. She'd describe him seated at his desk, lecturing away. A man of medium height with Indigenous features and a graying mustache, his teeth stained by a lifetime of black coffee and nicotine. Massiel would talk excitedly about the professor's ideas, his Socratic teaching style, and Antonio would try to imagine her with him. She'd be clad in a white cotton dress, wearing a necklace of seashells. She'd be resting in a wicker chair, savoring a bittersweet cocktail, then walking barefoot on a red-tile floor that was cool to the touch, making her way through a sea of throw pillows. Her emerald-green eyes sparkling. On a table, a vase of fresh daisies and two glasses of rum-spiked mango nectar. A hammock on the terrace. In her hands, a red carnation.

This was Antonio's romanticized version of the two of them together, an image that excluded sex because his mind couldn't go there. He liked to think that Pedro enjoyed himself more than Massiel did. Surely the prof didn't expect a future with her. Too busy expounding the virtues of Brechtian theater and too devoted to his political work for that. He must've known she'd leave eventually, taking her questions and her youth with her. Pedro knew it for certain that day when he ran his hands through her hair, and she whispered something in his ear...

Antonio wishes he could talk to Massiel right now, ask her what she told Pedro that day. He'll just have to imagine she's here now: What did you say to him, my love? Did you tell Pedro you were leaving him because he'd never shown any real interest in you, because he didn't really know you? Whatever it was, he got the message. You'd always remember him as the generous intellectual who shared with you a world you hadn't known, which had eluded you until you met him. You'll never stop thinking of him, will you? You still hear his voice in the books you read.

I won't reproach you for clinging to his wisdom and his words. I know I can't compete with him. I don't have his wealth of experience. I'm not engagé with the People's Struggle as he is. I haven't taught classes to hundreds of eager young people, nor have I risked my life in the name of freedom and justice. I fancy myself an intellectual, yes, with books and knowledge to share. But everything I have to give you is a small offering compared to his gifts, to the treasures he placed at your feet. I know I'm your pupil more than your teacher, Massiel.

Tony's eyes are bloodshot like mine, and his lips look painfully dry. We should never have started drinking on an empty stomach. I hate this bitterness, this stickiness in my mouth. I ask him if he's feeling better, and he says the ocean breeze is helping. Also, just sitting here with me, shooting the bull, relaxing. The best cure for a hangover. And while on the subject of bull...

"Hey," he tells me, "how about if we start our narration today with photos of the bridge? Several angles. From a boat, a car, from the top floor of our hotel. We'll make a collage, poster size. Or better yet, I'll plaster the walls of my office in Madrid with your great photographs, and then I'll try to describe them in writing. Something like... The bridge transports us from Hell to Paradise. Without it, we'd have no way of getting to the island; hence Eden would be pristine. There would be no houses, stores, hotels, no drunks who piss in the bay and no sailboats, no artists who all depict the same little boats reflected in the water, no stench of gasoline, no couples who make love on the sand. And no women who let out a heart-wrenching scream and then burst into laughter. It'd be an island without us. Would it exist, then?"

I ask him what fucking bridge he's talking about, since I've only taken photos of the Duarte Bridge, which is falling apart. He replies that he's aiming for a symbolic, imaginary structure. That figures! He says that what matters now is getting to the other side. But the other side of what?! He goes on, "The first image that welcomes us to the island: a handsome man on a bicycle, his hands gripping the wheel, his hairy chest, the folds in his shorts, his butt sinking into the bike seat. That image will initiate our journey. Then you'll photograph the screeching jeep tires on dirt roads, the gust of balmy air that blinds us for a second, the crystal buildings surrounding the bay, sunlight sifting through its walls. And the palm trees, so important. The woman with long flowing hair who smiles as she passes. A group of girls strolling down the avenue, festive, beautiful, deep mahogany skin, harmonious in their step. The old man having café con leche on a bench at Parque Colón, under Columbus' statue. Lots of shots of that statue, for a touch of irony." Oh, no, I'd bet Tony is going to do his travelogue thing about this place. Yup, there he goes! "Parque Colón is the most frequented park in the city, surrounded as it is by stunning colonial architecture. A gathering site to experience the local culture, to take breaks from work, meet up with friends, get deep-fried snacks, watch the crowds, or just hook up..."

Massiel told Antonio, just like she'd told Pedro, that she'd try to understand him and help him, although Antonio never asked her for help. All he wanted from Massiel was love, lots of it, every second they spent together. What a needy fop! How could she stand him?! No wonder she had to take a break from their "thing" now and then. Ah, yes, those bitter mornings when he'd inquire about her plans for the day, and she'd answer, curtly, that she was getting together with a friend. Antonio always assumed she meant Pedro, but it didn't matter who it was, really. She just had to get away. He learned about that need of hers one hateful Sunday. And before that, he'd already perceived it in some of her comments, in the cutting way she looked at him sometimes. And through it all, he still loved her, still wanted her to love him.

Does she remember that afternoon on the beach in San Sebastián, when he first told her about the life he'd lived? While she smiled, proud of herself for being able to love someone like him. As they downed a bottle of Txakoli, she opened up about herself, guardedly, as usual. She, too, enjoyed navigating two different worlds in and out of the bedroom. She and Antonio were so much alike! Then she surprised him with a question, "Why don't we try living together...?"

It doesn't look like Tony's ready to call it a day. "Hey, darling," I tell him, "I'd like to go back to the hotel, okay? I want to take a warm shower, put on a spiffy new outfit, and go out to dinner and to a club with you. Just the two of us tonight. How about it?" Again, he takes his time to reply, "In a little while..." First, he wants me to photograph the behemoth that's being built on Washington Avenue, across from the obelisk, another five-star hotel for tourists.

"We'll capture the slivers of wood," he says, "the electric saw, the nails penetrating the beams, the workmen's sweat. And the breeze, which aims to revive us, violently tainted by diesel exhaust. The narrow houses with red-tile roofs and the conches and flowerpots hanging from their balconies. The amateur painting of Boca Chica in one of the living rooms. The airplane circling the city. The fruit stand on Calle Las Damas, overflowing with sweet mangoes and papayas. Closeup of Paul biting into a juicy mango slice. Then, at last, the Hotel Cristóbal with its impressive Baroque-style façade and the beautiful young men walking through its doors..."

"Fine, I'll take all those pics," I tell him. "But make sure none of your straight Dominican friends catches us hanging outside the hotel. You know, the Marxists you like to hang out with. Writers, artists, intellectuals who attend those literary gatherings—tertulias they're called, right?—you like so much. Lots of poetry and politics and blah blah blah. I went to a couple of them to humor you, and it pissed me off that almost all the participants were men. Yes, I do have a weakness for the male of the species, so what am I complaining about, right? Not in that context, darling. In that type of situation I become a radical feminist. So tell me, Don Antonio, why did I see only two women attending those gatherings? And they never said a word! They just sat in a corner. One of them was taking notes. Was she the group's secretary, perhaps? Wouldn't surprise me! You've told me that the Dominican Republic has noteworthy female writers, some of whom you've written about. So, why the fuck are they not actively engaging in dialogue with the rest of you? Oh, and here's another question, though I'm sure the answer will be no: Are there any queer people in your group, other than your well-disguised self? I suppose one could claim that some of those men are closeted and trying to pass. But you know how fine-tuned my gaydar is, and I didn't pick up any gay vibes from any of the attendees."

Tony doesn't react. He hates it when I question his armchair Marxism and the blatant machismo of his tertulia friends. I bring up the time when one of them, a very macho man, saw us walking out of the Cristóbal. An experience Tony wants to forget, and I get why. Because the guy greeted him warmly at first, with a very manly handshake. And then he looked up at the name of the hotel and noticed two young men going in, and he must've realized what the place was about. "It was fucking hilarious to see his expression," I tell Tony, "the face he made as he looked at you and then back at the sign, *HOTEL CRISTÓBAL*, over the door. And, of course, you pretended I wasn't there, but it was too late because your colleague had noticed we were laughing and chatting seconds before he saw us. You had no choice but to introduce me, and that's when the hetero shit hit the fan! Your friend was able to read me clearly because I was performing my most flaming queen and shook his hand like a delicate, virginal señorita. You tried to save face, told him I was an American publisher planning to attend the book fair and wanting first-hand information about it from you, who'd participated many times in the event."

It's obvious from Tony's expression that he hates my recollection. Yet I can't stop laughing as I go on, "And what about the hotel? How did you explain that away? Oh, yes, I remember! You told your friend—who kept looking askance at the hotel doors, peeking in—that one of the editors who'd worked on your books was staying at the Cristóbal, and that you'd paid him a visit. Shame on you, throwing us publishers under the bus! Anyway, the macho man pretended to buy the story. Did you ever see him again? Never mind. Let's just make sure that story doesn't repeat itself, okay? We wouldn't want to *out* you in your leftist artists' colony..."

Massiel and Antonio were alike in many ways, but there were also major differences between them. Regarding sex, for instance, she wasn't as open and willing to experiment as he was. Massiel didn't like three-ways, an act Antonio was fond of indulging in on occasion. Not a significant difference but interesting nevertheless. He found out about it when she introduced him to Hassan, a Moroccan immigrant whom she'd helped to obtain a work visa, one of several men she's hooked him up with over the years. Tall, slim, with strong Middle Eastern features, Hassan was an engineer, settled in his bisexuality despite his machista upbringing, and eager to be friends with any friend of Massiel's. She was sure he and Antonio would hit it off and asked Antonio point-blank to go out with him, said Hassan needed male companionship.

"Okay," said Antonio, "why don't we hang out together for a while, the three of us?" Massiel seemed to like the idea, "Yes, that would be fun." Antonio went on, "We could all have supper in some down-home eatery, maybe in this place I know where they make killer couscous. Then, back here, you might watch us in action and then join in. What do you think?"

She took her time to reply, "I'll watch for a bit, but I won't be joining you. That's never going to happen, love. Threesomes and orgies are not my thing." She encouraged him to enjoy himself with Hassan, "He's passionate and giving in bed." Yes, she knew about Hassan's prowess as a lover, although she claimed she tried not to get personal with her clients.

Interesting that Massiel never appeared to feel threatened by this type of situation, and in fact, she seemed to get a kick out of orchestrating these encounters. Thus, in a way, she was the one who imposed a lifestyle of sexual freedom on him, on their bond and their relationship. As long as Antonio and Massiel could always return to that special place they'd forged and inhabited together, a secret, imagined hideaway that she called their *inner sanctum*.

We've made it to our favorite club. Tony insisted that I bring my camera. "Your Canon and my eyes," he said. "A great team!" He wants me to photograph the guys on the dance floor, their sweaty bodies intertwined, and to capture him observing the scene, aroused like the first night. I'm sure we need permission to take pictures in here, but I'll just sneak in a few shots. Tony says we should photograph the pole dancer, too: unusually tall, dark-skinned, with bleached hair cropped a la Grace Jones and exuberant lips. His slightly slanted, heavily made-up brown eyes seem detached from his surroundings, absent. He softly sways and rocks himself from body to body without touching anyone, absorbed in the driving rhythm of the music. We'll photograph the tiny ringlets of hair on his muscular thighs, an enticing detail. And we'll capture him in closeup when he stops at our table and whirls around us, sensuously rubbing Tony's mustache with his lips. Then a picture of Antonio accepting the dancer's invitation...

Second Act
(of many)

Luis

If he were to perform this scene of his life, he'd start with photos like the ones Paul has taken over the years—some of them blurry Polaroids, but others shot with a fancy camera that looks like it was made for the movies. Paul brings that one with him sometimes, when he's in the mood for creating memories, he says. Which means taking pictures of ritzy neighborhoods like Gazcue and Piantini, of the crowds and the tourists. Photos of the Hotel Cristóbal, a remodeled colonial building on Calle Las Damas, and of the guys in the hotel bar, laughing, making faces, posing like movie stars. Lots of pics of Luis at the beach, walking through Parque Colón or strolling down the malecón, also in Paul's room, flexing his muscles in front of the mirror.

The background music for this photo show would be Luis's guitar playing. When the lights go up on the stage, the audience will see him in the living room of his house, with Mamita standing by his side, enjoying his performance. Then he'll stop playing and turn to his mother.

"Did you like my song?" he'll ask her.

Visibly proud, "Yes, very much, mijo! It sounds happy, upbeat, but also romantic."

"Thank you, Mamita! I don't know about it being romantic, but..."

"Did you write it, Luisi?"

"Yeah, but I'm still working on it. I'm having a little trouble with the chord progression."

"Really? After all these years that you've been playing?"

"It's just that my fingers aren't long enough for the hard version of F sharp minor." He plays several chords and stumbles. "See what I mean? I try to make them go there and sometimes have to take the easy way out." He tries again. "Crap!"

"Don't worry, baby. I didn't notice, and I'm sure no one else would. It sounded perfect to me. The tune reminds me of salsa, the music that's so popular on the radio these days."

"Yes, except that I wouldn't want a whole lot of percussion. Violins, yeah, and some brass, maybe a couple of trumpets, and definitely conga drums. But the arrangement would be mellow, for slow dancing, you know. Like a nice bachata."

"That sounds wonderful! What inspired you to write this song?"

"My loneliness."

Surprised, concerned, "You feel lonely, mijo?"

"Not always. Because I have you, Mamita..."

"You sure do! And you have your best friend, Richard."

"Oh yeah, Richard." Silence. "Sometimes I wonder if we're meant to be friends at all, you know, 'cause his world and mine are so different. Our families. Our lives."

"But your differences make your friendship more interesting, no?"

"Guess so." Silence. "The thing is, when I think about the way Richard was brought up, about his parents and his brothers and their house, it all seems like another planet to me."

"Another planet!" She laughs. "That sounds like something Richard would say."

More like a fucking alien universe...

Luis remembers in detail the first time Richard came over for lunch. He wouldn't stop talking, commenting on everything, comparing this house to his, and describing his family. And he loved the food Mamita and Luis made for him: sancocho, sweet corn arepas, fresh fruit, and arroz con leche. Not a fancy meal 'cause sancocho is basically a stew with lots of meats and vegetables in it. But no one makes it as good as Mamita. And, so, to Richard, it was a feast.

"We don't eat this kind of tasty food in my house," he told them. "My mom cooks for us sometimes, but she's so busy with her teaching and looking after us that she doesn't have a lot of time for planning our meals. And it's hard 'cause my little brothers are picky. That's why my dad ends up ordering out for us most days. Which is fun 'cause restaurant food is the best." Now Richard finally shut up and ate, but he was obviously thinking of more things to talk about. "I didn't mean to rag on Mami," he quickly added. "She's a great mom, and I love her so much. But, hey, I just can't believe how delish this sancocho is! Could I have another serving, please?"

After lunch, Richard wanted to see Luis's room. Luis told him there was nothing special about it, just a big bedroom with a twin bed, a small dresser, lamps, a poster of Luis Miguel on the wall above the bed (a present from Mamita), and Luis's guitar. Richard wanted to spend time in it, anyway. "To catch your vibe," he said like a fucking hippie, though he didn't need to get no vibe from that stupid room to be Luis's buddy. They hadn't known each other for very long, but already Luis could tell they were meant to be best friends. Whatever that meant. With no lovey-dovey stuff and no sex. That just couldn't be part of their friendship.

Richard was their guest of honor. Mamita made sure Luis understood that. She encouraged him to give Richard a tour of the house. And the whole time, Richard went on and on about what a wonderful mom Mamita was, and what a great relationship Luis had with her, how affectionate they were with each other. "I wish Mami and I were close like that," he admitted. "But my two younger brothers gobble up so much of her energy! And she has to spend every weekday with a bunch of loud, snotty third-graders. Sometimes I think she just gets sick of being around children, including her own. Hey, but I'm not complaining. I'm glad she has a profession 'cause that's important to her. And we sure need the income. I just wish she wasn't the only one taking care of us and the house. My dad says we can't afford a maid for now, but he doesn't pitch in at home at all, other than ordering food and giving us medicine when we get sick. If they both work, why is Mami also expected to be a housekeeper and a cook? She gets no break!"

Richard wouldn't stop jabbering. It seemed he wanted to come across as an old wise man with those big words he used, like *profession* and *expected*; with the way he wove all his sentences together to express his thoughts. He said he liked Luis's house a lot, everything about it: the style, the patio with Mamita's plants and flowers, the balcony, the street, and especially Luis's room 'cause he said it was spare and barren. Again, his old-man words. Nobody talks like that in real life! Sure, *spare* and *barren*. Fuck, why wouldn't Richard just say *empty*? As simple as that. An empty room 'cause that's the way Luis likes it, so he can breathe in there.

And now Luis wonders, again, why Richard has never invited him over to his house. Not for supper, though. Crappy food! Luis even mentioned it once, "Hey, buddy, when will I get to meet your brothers and your parents, huh? I'd like to see what your room looks like, too." But Richard avoided the topic by saying that Luis wouldn't like his bratty siblings nor the room he shared with his brother Johnny. "It's a fucking pig pen, all cluttered with his junk, clothes and shoes he throws everywhere and also his textbooks and notebooks. He has laser guns and small replicas of stuff from *Star Wars* and piles of comics by our bunk beds. Whereas the only things of mine you'll see in there are my backpack, my clothes, and a trophy I got for a poem I wrote in my lit class. I'm a neat person, so it really is a pain to have to live with Johnny. Although to be honest, it's fun when we play video games together and pretend we're characters in stories he comes up with, about starships and aliens and dangerous missions in outer space..."

Luis brought this up with Paul once, the fact that Richard had never invited him to his house even though he'd been to Luis's a zillion times. And Mister Paul said it could be a class issue. Luis didn't get it at first. "Richard doesn't want his folks to know," Paul explained, "that he has friends who aren't from their socioeconomic class, kids whose parents don't have a university education and professional jobs. He probably thinks you'd feel uncomfortable there, too, suffering his parents' scrutiny and questions. Middle-class Dominicans can be so snooty!"

Luis felt down and belittled, like he wasn't good enough for his friend's family. Paul must've noticed he was in the pits 'cause then he said, "Actually, there may be two other reasons Richard hasn't invited you over. He doesn't want his parents to meet anyone from the Cristóbal, afraid they might find out about it. Or, his house is a pigsty compared to yours, and he'd be ashamed if you saw it." Yeah, Luis agreed: that was it, both of those reasons. Not the facts that he didn't go to school, had no dad, and that his mom had worked as a maid...

Mamita is talking about his new song, which she loves but says it's too bad he was inspired to write it because he felt lonely. She's telling him that loneliness is poisonous, that we must chase it away. But just how do we do that, Luis wonders. Music helps for sure. He's lucky to have that going for himself. His songs. His guitar. Mamita is saying that loneliness gets under your skin and runs through your veins, tainting your blood. Until it reaches your heart. And now Luis just has to react, "Yes, like the stray needle that almost killed you."

She rubs her left arm, cries out, "Ay, that was horrible, mijo!"

"I know. I was so scared, Mamita." Silence. "The doctors kept taking pictures of your arm, X rays they're called. And they were all worried 'cause the needle had started to move. It had gone in through your thumb when you were sewing, right?"

"Yes, and it was all my fault, for trying to use my left hand because the right one was tired. I should've just stopped. How stupid of me!"

"Then the needle went sailing through your bloodstream."

"And if it made it all the way to my heart, that would be the end of Elena!" Saddened by the memory, "Ay, ay, ay. I wasn't able to sew after that ordeal. My arm was worthless." She rubs her arm again. "I had no feeling in it and couldn't move my fingers for a long time."

"You seem to be doing fine now." He traces her long scar with his index finger: from her wrist to her elbow. "Wow, it's like a river..."

"I avoid looking at that," says Mamita. "Too many bad memories, the pain, the numbness. But yes, thank God it's getting back to normal."

"You couldn't make a living as a seamstress anymore, so you started cleaning houses. I hated that you had to work as a maid. Hated those people..."

"They treated me well."

"They took advantage of you."

"Some of them, maybe..."

"You've worked so hard, Mamita."

"Yes, well, the thing is, I didn't want to be a burden to my parents. They were helping me out a lot already, and I wanted to rent a nice little place for you and me, an apartment near them."

"I know. Rent was expensive and raising me was expensive and life..."

"Shush, baby! Have I ever complained about the effort it took to raise you? I'd do it all over again. And I'd like to go back to work so you can quit your 'job' and not be sad anymore."

"I never said I was sad, just lonely. Anyway, you've got plenty to do here, in our house."

"You're right, our little home keeps me busy."

"When I get famous you won't have to lift a finger. You're gonna live like a queen with two maids at least, I promise!" He strums the guitar.

"Does your melody have words?"

"Yeah, sure. Listen..."

He sings the song, which tells of a wise old man who gave Luis a remedy for his loneliness: singing. A cure for his sadness: beauty. A remedy for his heartache: love, but only if it's true love. The old man tells him to keep on singing until his heart can heal.

Mamita claps. "It's beautiful, Luisi! And that wise man gave you good advice."

Luis plays the song's refrain again, stops. "Sing it with me, Mamita!"

Feeling flattered, "Really? Are you sure? But I don't know the words!"

"Just sing the part that repeats, the refrain. You'll catch on!"

"Very well, let's see if I can..."

They sing the song, Mamita harmonizing, moved and excited to be singing with her son.

"Hey, that came out good, Mamita! We're a fantastic duo!"

"Oh, my God! Your old mom as a singer, that's too funny."

"Not funny but great, I'd say. Who do you think I take after?"

She poses like a model. "Who else but me!"

"That's for sure. I got my musical talent from you." Feeling nostalgic, "When I was little, I couldn't fall asleep without hearing your voice..."

"Yes, I'd keep singing my heart out, but you wouldn't shut your eyes."

"It was just that, if I fell asleep, your songs would stop."

She laughs boisterously. "And then, as you got older, you'd start snoring right away."

"I take after you that way, too."

"What?! I don't snore!"

Laughing, "You sure do! And loud!"

Luis places the guitar on the floor, lights up a cigarette. Mamita gives him a disapproving look. "Yes, I know it's bad for me," he says, "but I've been cutting down, okay? Don't start getting on my case about that, too." Silence. Somber, "Mamita... do I look like my father at all?"

"A little, I guess."

"It's a good thing I didn't turn out like him. A creep! An asshole!"

Stroking her son's face, "He gave me a wonderful present."

"Why did you never get married, Mamita?"

"Because... when I was younger, I couldn't find a man worthy of me." Acting flirty, "Though I had many suitors, all of them crazy about my pretty face and my shapely rear!"

Faking embarrassment, "Mamita!"

"And then later, well, who would want to marry a hag?"

"You're not a hag!" He kisses her tenderly. "You are young and beautiful."

"Thanks for the compliment, baby."

"Though I'm not so sure I'd want to have a stepfather."

"Not to worry. I don't see that happening." Silence. "You, on the other hand... you need to fall in love, Luisi. Love is the cure for loneliness. You said it yourself in your song."

"I have no time for that. Besides, it's a big lie. Romantic love doesn't cure anything. It's just words in a stupid song, that's all."

"Truthful words."

"And just how do you know that, Mamita?"

"I fell in love once."

"With my father, right? And then he left you."

"It was my decision, Luis. I was the one who left."

"Because he was a drunk, I'm sure. Violent, abusive."

"No, he was a kind, loving, generous young man. And he didn't drink."

"Then why?! Why didn't it work out for the two of you?"

"Okay, the truth, Luisi, is that I've never believed in marriage. I wouldn't have married him or anyone else. I wanted a child, not a husband..."

"Yeah, I sort of knew that. You've always been very independent, and against tradition in some ways." Silence. "But I'll ask you again, Mamita, for the millionth time, why haven't I met my father? I'd really like to. He and I have a right to know about each other."

"Yes, mijo, I agree. It's just that..." She's so quiet. It's so unlike her. "Like I've always told you, I have no idea where he is. We never kept in touch."

"That sucks! And it makes me mad."

"I know. I'm really sorry, mijo. I didn't think you'd need a father if you had me."

"And I don't. But..."

"But that's all in the past. Why don't you sing some more?"

Purposely ignoring her request, "And then, when I was born, you had to make a living somehow, didn't you? You started making dresses for rich bitches, getting paid dirt cheap for the amazing clothes you made. Working like a fucking slave."

"And what you do isn't slavery, Luisito?"

"Maybe, but it pays a lot better."

The photos Luis was seeing in his mind are suddenly gone. He wishes he had a good picture of his mother, other than the one when she was a teenager, which has that old-fashioned, plastic frame. He wants a large portrait of her and a closeup of the two of them posing together.

He closes his eyes, imagining his bright future with Mamita by his side.

Paul

He takes in this view he loves: crystal blue waters, sparkling sand, palm trees, and sunlight pouring over everything. So different from California beaches, none of which measures up to Boca Chica, not even Santa Monica, Laguna, or Newport. The Pacific sucks! Except for Marshall's in the Bay Area, maybe, but only because gays like to hang out there (literally!) in the nude. Amazing views all around that beach, too, and it's right next to the Golden Gate Bridge, yet secluded. It's a fucking pain getting to it; yes, the path down from the bluffs is long and treacherous, but well worth the effort. One of the problems for Paul at Marshall's is that, after an hour of watching a parade of overly tanned old flesh, he wants to get the fuck away from that wax museum! Another problem is managing to hide his hard-on when a hot number with major endowment passes by, and there goes Paul's cock, wanting to offer a warm, effusive hello.

Oh, but Vincent loves Marshall's Beach, and it figures since he has a gorgeous bod that he keeps in great shape with laborious exercise, so it makes sense he'd want to show it off. Paul's physique could be considered hot too, all modesty aside, though not as buff as Vincent's. Hence they are quite the watchable couple. Anyhoo, no one in California goes to the beach for the freezing cold ocean water and the unrelenting waves, and the grayish, coarse sand. Fuck no, they go to sunbathe, cruise, and veg out. It could be the hottest day on the entire West Coast, and its beaches would still feel like a frozen Hell! You'll never find the soothing warmth of the Caribbean there. Or its soft, clean sand. Or its royal palm trees. Or its men!

As usual, when they're here, Paul and Antonio are seated in lounge chairs under a beach umbrella, savoring their Presidente beers. A young man nearby tends to them. Souvenir, seafood, and coconut water vendors interrupt their conversations at times. The sound of the waves and the mellow guitar music on Paul's portable radio help set the mood.

"Shame on you!" says Antonio, laughing, pointing his finger at Paul. "You're enjoying Boca Chica instead of setting up your booth at the fair."

"I'm not missing out on this sun and this beach, darling. There's still plenty of time to slave away." He laughs. "For now, this woman is catching some rays!"

"What woman? I don't see any women here."

"Never mind! Hey, you're not getting your job done either, Toñita."

"I just have to come up with ten pages or so, and there's nothing happening yet."

Paul stares at a group of young men who walk by, parading themselves.

"Well, there's lots happening here, that's for sure!"

"Enjoy the view! You deserve it, my friend. I know for a fact that you've always worked your ass off for the Santo Domingo Book Fair."

"Thank you, dear. Yes, I'm invested in it. You'll recall that my employer was one of its founders. Lorthew wanted to promote its ESL books in the Dominican Republic. And what better venue than a fair at the Autonomous University, the oldest institution of higher education in this New World. That's why Lorthew Books helped finance the first one with nominal help from several Dominican *ministerios*, you know, the Ministry of Education, of Culture, blah blah blah."

"As long as LB footed the bill, right?"

"Of course. And we also established a literary contest that's been in vogue since then. Weren't you a judge a couple of times?" In jest, "You, judging what's good literature! Oh, my!"

"Not funny, Paulita."

"In the early days, there was no folkloric and cultural fanfare, none of the pseudo-Indigenous exhibits and theatrical presentations they have now. Books were the only focus."

Antonio, sarcastic, "Sure, your publisher's books!"

"You got it!"

"What does *lorthew* mean, by the way? Or is it just someone's surname?"

"It's a Medieval English word for teacher. The perfect name for a publisher, isn't it? Especially for a publisher of educational materials in the ESL field."

"English as a second language... You teach Dominicans English so they can understand your orders and be more easily subjugated. And while you're at it, you fill your pockets."

"Yes, darling, my people come here looking for the same thing your people were after in the fifteenth century, when they founded this capital city in 1498... Gold and flesh!"

"You're oversimplifying everything, as usual. And, in any case, you Gringos are way worse than us by now. Just look at what you did to President Bosch, kicking him out of his own government, supporting ruthless dictators just as you do everywhere in Latin America. Simply because Bosch had revolutionary ideals." Silence. "A great, kind-hearted man. A writer, a thinker. Not of the stature of Cuba's José Martí, but exceptional in his own way. And you, damn Gringos, squashed him like a roach. Because he might turn into another Fidel Castro! And let's not even mention what you did in Puerto Rico. Sad Borinquen, the kept mistress..."

"Yes, Tony, my country's government has fucked up big time. Nothing new there."

"That's why I'm so proud of Cuba, which kicked out all the Gringos. Good for them!"

"Ah, your precious Cuba, the pride of armchair Marxists like yourself. Sure, Cuba kicked some Gringo ass. But then it became a satellite of the Soviet Union with a megalomaniacal leader at the helm. That ex-guerrilla thinks he's some kind of god!" Silence. "The sad truth, my dear Tony, is that Caribbean people can't escape colonization, be it by Spain, France, Russia, or by us Gringos. And these days also by queens like you, my love, who come here pretending to be maternal señoras when in truth they look down on these people."

Confronting his friend, "Have you always been so cynical, Paul?"

"No. I used to have ideals."

"And now?"

"Now I have a juicy monthly check, great health insurance, and a fancy job title."

"And gonorrhea in your asshole once a year."

"Ay, that can't be avoided, darling. Every indulgence has a price."

"Wait, I must write that down!" To the young man, who stands by, "Could you hand me my notebook and a pen, please?" The young man searches Antonio's bag and hands him what he needs. "Thanks!" Writing, "Every indulgence has a price."

"If you write down anything I say, I will... I will seduce you!"

"Oh, my, that sounds scary." Silence. "But I'm only following your advice, Paulita, taking notes for an autobiographical novel with lots of sex in it."

"Yeah, your sex, not mine! Didn't I ask you to leave me out of it? Typical writer! I'll just have to think of a fitting punishment if you end up stealing my life, as I'm sure you will." Silence. "I know! I'll expose you to the Gay Plague..."

After a long silence, "What a horrible, damning name for an epidemic," observes Antonio. "As if we didn't have enough to deal with already."

"Yeah, let's just blame the queers, why not."

"You should stop calling it the Gay Plague."

"I will for sure, Tony." Silence. "Can't believe the name they gave it initially, GRID, gay-related immune deficiency. Horrible! Though it made some kind of crazy sense, I suppose, since we were the first community to get hit hard and visibly by the disease."

"It seems the latest name will stick. AIDS. Acquired immunodeficiency syndrome."

"Yes." Suddenly concerned. "Are you being careful, Tony?"

"As much as it's possible, yes. I hope you are, too. You weren't doing that well the last time we saw each other. I remember you'd just had pneumonia. I was worried about you."

"I know. Thanks, babe. And thank you for your calls and your letters."

"You're welcome, Paulita. I'm glad it was nothing serious."

"You mean that it wasn't AIDS."

"Yes, well, it looks like you're back to your old healthy self, and that makes me happy. Just don't take any risks, please."

"What bigger risk than fucking on this island?" Silence. "Although I have friends who aren't promiscuous bitches like us and who've gotten infected. But of course it takes just one fateful encounter to ruin your life. To *end* it."

"I haven't lost anyone close to me yet. Have you?"

Paul suppresses his tears, "Ay, Tony, yes, I have! It's getting to the point where I don't want to answer the phone anymore... *Our dear friend is very sick. A problem with his immune system.* Of course it's always the immune system! And you wonder if your turn is next..."

"There haven't been any cases here in DR, right?"

"As far as I know, but it won't be long now. Too many tourists. And we're so close to Haiti. Eventually, the virus will invade our oasis, and we'll be expelled from Eden."

"The Devil can never be expelled."

Trying to lighten the mood. "Well, Toñita, I plan to keep on feasting on the Forbidden Fruit until the tree runs out. And we should start looking for another oasis, just in case."

"I'd rather protect and save this tree."

"Good luck with that!"

The truth Paul won't share with Antonio is that he's terrified. Not ready to throw in the towel yet. So much to do still, places to go, books to edit and sell, fairs to attend, and young men to enjoy. He's already paid the price for his frequent indulgences. Gonorrhea in his ass, painful as hell, not easily eradicated. But he doesn't blame his Dominican studs for it; he's sure he has gotten it at the bathhouses every time. Ay, those places, a candy store for his sweet tooth! Most definitely modeled after the Greek baths of antiquity. A modern-day version of Sodom and Gomorrah, as the very vocal right-wing conservatives describe them. Houses of sin, of pleasure, of excess. Great places to lose yourself, to stop being a thinking creature in order to become a beast, a famished body seeking to satisfy itself to the point of satiation. It won't be long now before the baths are shut down for good, blamed for spreading the virus. Which they are, no doubt.

It was in his favorite bathhouse, the one in the Mission District, where he got his worst bout of VD. He learned his lesson then and there: never again would he have sex without condoms, no matter how excited he might be. His rule: *no rubber, no rub.* True that rubbers aren't completely reliable; some are known to break. Even though he doubles them up, he's still taking a chance. Thence his fear of getting infected, doomed to die a painful death, his perfect complexion becoming dark and tainted, his lungs collapsing, his flesh gradually devoured by a sinister bug that must've been concocted in an underground lab by rabid Republicans. Nothing, absolutely nothing scares the dickens out of him more than the thought of getting sick that way.

It would break his mother's heart if he died. She wouldn't be able to cope with his premature death. Paul's brother, on the other hand, would sigh with relief as he watched his perverted sibling take his last breath. No more shame for the family, he'd think. No more trying to hide and deny the sinner's existence. Yes, it's true that dead dogs don't bite. But Paul's not giving his big fat brother that satisfaction. He plans to keep barking and biting for a long time!

Paul wishes he knew more about AIDS, other than the basics: that the virus that causes this disease came from Africa, transmitted from chimpanzees to humans starting as far back as the 1800s. Earliest cases detected in the 1950s. Yeah, as if Black Africans didn't have to deal with the world's racism, the history of slavery, and a fuckload of historical wrongs dumped on them already! Big questions assail him: Why Africa and gay men? Why human beings?

So now Paul thinks he's a fucking philosopher! Yes, he believes in predetermination. This was all predetermined, right? But by whom? The universe? Then, who's pulling the strings of the universe? Who is the prankster, the playwright (Luis's fantasy) writing the magnum opus of our lives, turning reality into a macabre spectacle? Must be someone nasty and wicked and nutso enough to want to play so many dirty tricks on humanity. The hell with the creator of that shit!

Back to reality: Antonio buying a shell choker, unable to resist the vendors' hounding anymore. Paul, laughing, "For Massiel, the little woman?" Antonio answers no and puts the choker on Paul. "This one's for my American sister," he says.

"Thank you, darling. It's my style! I'll wear it tonight when we go dancing." He takes it off and sets it down on the table, eager to go in the water. "Aren't you coming?"

"Later. I feel like working on my project for a while."

"Suit yourself. But remember, lots of sex scenes and not a word about me!" To the young man, "Take good care of him, okay?"

Pleasant guitar music on Paul's radio. The ideal background for writing...

Antonio

He wishes his suite didn't look just like Paul's. He wants nothing in his life to be *just like Paul's*. The room has a wall-size print of a generic tropical landscape on the back wall, where Paul's room has a mirror. It is tacky and gaudily colored but at least it's *one* major difference between this suite and the other...

Why is he droning on about the damn suites? Perhaps in order not to think about Richard, who is here, willing and ready for action, as the kid likes to say. If only Antonio could enjoy himself without that damning voice crowding his psyche. If he could just go with the flow and not feel guilty, anguished, ashamed of himself. But that's never going to happen. He's here for one and only one reason, not to be romantic or affectionate, and certainly not to fall in love.

Fine, then. He'll accept the conditions, the price, the deal, and pretend that Richard isn't a real human being, that he's only a projection, a holographic rendering of Antonio's fantasy. Otherwise, he might break down and cry like a sinful, repentant boy in the confessional. *Forgive me, Father.* No! Forget that Catholic guilt! He's broken away from the Church. He is a free agent, a horny agent. He has the will to take his shoes off, to sit in bed and watch Richard...

The kid is nervous. He just let the water run in the bathroom sink, saying, "We have lots of water, Señor Antonio." And he turned the light switch on and off numerous times, "We have electricity." Then, picking up the phone, "We have a phone line!" Now he's sitting on the edge of the bed, next to Antonio. "And how's the mattress?" he asks.

Antonio, lying down comfortably, "Nice, though a bit squishy in the middle."

"If you don't like the bed," says Richard, "we could do it on the couch, or on the floor."

"Why are you in such a hurry?"

"That's the way I am, kind of jumpy all the time."

"Just try to relax, okay? Lie down with me for a while..."

Richard obeys. Antonio runs his fingers through the young man's hair. He grabs a small travel kit from a night table drawer, brings out a cannabis joint, lights it, and takes a couple of drags. "You don't care if I indulge in a little weed, do you?" he asks Richard.

"Not at all," Richard replies. "But that shit is illegal in this country, Señor Antonio."

"It's illegal everywhere!"

Richard, bemused, "Marijuana helps you relax, no?"

"Yes, but I'm not offering you any. Sorry."

"That's okay, Señor Antonio. I wouldn't want to smoke that stuff with you, anyway. Can't afford to get hooked." He seems self-conscious. "But I could do anything else..."

"Really? Anything? How about kissing?"

After thinking it over, "Well... only if you pay me more."

"Deal!" He kisses Richard's hands, then his lips, tenderly.

"You're a good man, Señor Antonio. Thank you. Please don't tell anyone about this, okay? Not even Mister Paul. The guys in this biz aren't supposed to..."

"Don't worry, mum's the word!" He gets out of bed. "How about a shower?"

"With you? But I showered this morning." He chuckles, an impish look about him.

"What are you laughing about, Richard?" Silence. Richard keeps laughing. "Oh, I get it! You didn't think I'd want to bathe. Everyone here thinks that Spaniards are all swine."

"I didn't say that!"

He pulls Richard by the arm. "Come on, let's hit the shower. It'll be good for you."

"Wait, wait. That's also going to cost you more."

"What?! Well, the young lad sure knows how to fend for himself!"

"Or we can just do it already. Just remember I can't stay the night."

"Yes, yes, I know you must get home before midnight. Like Cinderella!"

In the book he plans to write, Antonio won't narrate the next scene in detail. It'd be no better than porn, and it would betray Richard's trust.

None of what takes place here is anyone's business, anyway, even if the facts are disguised as fiction. This would not be the case if he were to write about Paul Edwards. The Gringo bitches and threatens to sue Antonio if he portrays him in his novel. Still, deep down inside (or maybe not so deep), Paul loves the attention, the recognition, and the prospect of being turned into a fabulous character.

Antonio will simply say that he and Richard take their clothes off, get in the bathtub, tussle with each other, and frolic around. And one can hear the sound of running water, their voices, laughter, moaning, panting. Then deep cries of pleasure.

Done with their bath, they walk out in bathrobes. Richard jumps into bed impetuously. Antonio lights up a cigarette and prepares himself a Cuba Libre. "A decently stocked bar, for a change!" he exclaims. He joins Richard, offers him a sip from his rum-and-Coke, then sits up, leaning against the headboard. He holds Richard's hand. "Hey, let's do a little fantasizing."

Richard, puzzled, "What do you mean? How do we do that?"

"Just close your eyes. Imagine we can travel to another planet..."

"Great! I love science fiction! So, do we get to that planet in a spaceship at light speed?"

"Sure, why not."

"Are there androids on that planet like the ones in *Blade Runner*, that look just like humans? That's my favorite movie, by the way. Have you seen it?"

"No, Richard. I hardly ever go to the movies. I prefer the theater."

"That's just like Luis. He's nuts about stage plays. Though he did go see *Star Wars* with me and kind of liked it. Except for all the shooting and fighting. Luis and I are not into battles in outer space and laser guns, which is a big part of what *Star Wars* is about, you know. People waging war in faraway galaxies, as if we didn't have plenty of that shit on Earth for real!"

"Why do you like *Blade Runner* so much?"

Richard is smiling wide now. Such perfect teeth! "Because I think androids are cool," he says excitedly. "Just imagine living in a world where there are synthetic beings everywhere. Replicants. That's what they're called in the movie. You know, machines that look and sound and act just like humans. There's this female replicant in the movie, Rachael, and I've never seen a woman as perfect and beautiful and elegant as her."

"She sounds like a typical male fantasy, Richard."

"Yeah, so what? She's still totally hot!"

"I'm sure she is. And you'd like to be her lover, wouldn't you?"

"Yes, I would, as long as I'm the real Richard and not a replicant." Silence. "Because her actual lover, who's supposed to be human, that's the Harrison Ford character, he turns out to be a replicant just like her. Or so they lead you to believe at the end, even though he was hired to hunt down and destroy all replicants. Very ironic, don't you think? You know, that twist..."

"Yes, because he's killing his own kind."

"Exactly!" Deep in thought, "Sometimes I have this weird vision where there's a double of me, and he does all the stuff I don't want to do, like my chores, and he goes to school for me when I'm sick. My replicant doesn't need food or sleep, but he sits with my family for dinner and pretends to eat. And at night he lies down on the floor next to my bed..."

"Would your replicant work here at the Cristóbal, instead of you?"

"Yeah, but only if I'm not in the mood for... you know." Silence. "I actually like hanging here at the hotel, meeting people from other countries, hearing their stories, their languages. That's the best part. Like, I wouldn't want to miss out on all the fun I'm having with you."

"Thank you, Richard. I hope you mean that."

"I swear I do, Señor Antonio. I love the way you talk, your accent, your stories."

"Well, I just hope you're the *real* Richard."

"You can count on that!"

"Good. Should we go on with our fantasy?"

"Yeah, sorry, I forgot. Where were we?"

Antonio, laughing, "Not far! We had barely started traveling to another planet."

"Are you the captain, Señor Antonio? And am I second in command?"

"No, no, never mind all that. Let's suppose we were born on that world."

"And what's its name? What is it like?"

"Let's call it... Pleasure Planet."

"That'd be easy to remember."

"We can think of a better name later. For now, just picture Pleasure Planet as vast but underpopulated. It has green hills and valleys, rivers, lakes, and sweet, clean air. The dwellings are gleaming palaces made of marble, with beautiful gardens where roses abound and fountains where clear water runs eternally. And it's always sunny."

"That sounds like a fairy tale, not science fiction. All the green stuff, the palaces and gardens and roses. I guess it could be nice. But what about the people? Are they weird aliens?"

"No, no. They're all handsome and look human just like you and me."

"Are there women on Pleasure Planet?"

"Yes. In fact, brilliant women run the government."

"That would be different for sure."

"Yes, well, like I said, this is our fantasy, Richard."

"Can the people of that planet travel in time?"

"Maybe, but only in their thoughts and dreams."

"Cool, though not very sci-fi, Señor Antonio. Couldn't they build a machine like the one in H.G. Wells's novel? I've read that book three times! Love it, though the future the character travels to is so sad and depressing. If I had a machine, I'd only go to the past."

"And why is that, Richard?"

"Oh, I think it'd be great to see the way people lived in different eras. And you could read and study about it before you embark, to be prepared. Whereas there's nothing we can do to prepare for a voyage to the future. It's all unknown and kind of scary..."

"Yes, for sure if it's like the world depicted in *The Time Machine*."

"That will never happen, Señor Antonio. I'm sure it won't. People who eat other people? No way!" Silence. "What about you, where and *when* would you travel to?"

"I've never thought much about that, Richard. But I admit it's a tempting notion..."

He just lied to Richard. No, it's not tempting at all. Such an absurd idea, time travel! Antonio can't take it seriously, even after learning about it through the discourse of science, which does posit a remote possibility for such a journey by way of wormholes. No, time travel for Antonio goes in the same bag as all the other sci-fi tropes: aliens, faster-than-light speed, and galaxy-trotting spaceships. Ridiculous concepts that don't appeal to him. Like zombies, fairies, witches, vampires, and ghosts. We're all entitled to nurture and enjoy our myths; he knows that. It's just that his myths don't dwell in outer space, among extraterrestrials and starships. After all the science fiction fantasies are imagined and narrated or filmed for their eager audience, the fact remains that the distance to other inhabitable planets is unconquerable. So why bother?

His utter dislike for the sci-fi genre started when he saw the film version of H.G. Wells's novel *The Time Machine* as a kid. He fell in love with Rod Taylor, what a hunk, and in fact, it was then he first realized he was attracted to men. But Antonio couldn't stand anything else about the movie. It perturbed him that all the young people of that remote future were blonde Gringos; and that the underground, cannibalistic humans were all wearing cheap-looking wigs and had light bulbs in their eyes. Antonio couldn't stop laughing through most of the film!

He should've read the book, a classic; if he had, he'd now be able to discuss it with Richard. Thankfully, the kid seems to be steering away from the topic, eager to ask more questions about their imaginary planet. Antonio loves the way he delves into his thoughts, blinking repeatedly and showing off those long eyelashes of his. There he goes...

"Okay," says Richard, "what about music? Is there a lot of it on Pleasure Planet?"

"Sure. We have gifted composers and lots of popular songs."

Richard, still in bed, moves slightly away from Antonio. "Bummer. That's too bad."

"Why, Richard? Why is that bad?"

"I already told you, Señor Antonio. It's because I don't care for pop music."

"Ah, yes, songs are basically just noise to you, right?"

"Right! The way they get in your head like an evil alien and pollute your mind. Hate it! I want my mind to be free of that shit so I have room for my own thoughts. And I also hate..."

Antonio, barely able to cut in, "Wait, Richard, I have a question for you..."

Richard, oblivious, "I hate the way pop and rock songs repeat some of their lyrics and melodies over and over again. They're so fucking annoying. I hate repetition! Can't stand to have to do the same things day after day. I guess I like change, surprises, not routine..."

"Have you tried listening to other types of music? Like, for example, classical?"

"Yes! My history teacher plays tapes of classical music for us in class sometimes. She uses a funky portable player that looks like a ghetto blaster from the Seventies but still works great. This teacher says that listening to classical pieces relaxes us and can make us focus better, but it also helps us learn about the countries we're studying. I especially like one of the French composers she's played for us, Debussy, though I don't go for all the bloody stuff about French history and Napoleon and Waterloo 'cause there's so much war. It's that way in every country we study. So depressing to learn about people killing each other off, even for a worthy cause."

"Do you listen to classical music at home?"

"No, no, no! I can't 'cause my brothers would freak out, Johnny more than the others. He says it's like being at a funeral. It makes him feel sad. But for me... for me, it's like a breath of fresh air, Señor Antonio. Yeah, like breathing deep when you're out in the ocean on a sunny day." Silence. "Classical music never irks me, never gets in my head the way pop does." He cuddles up to Antonio. "Sorry, Señor Antonio. That was a really long answer to your question."

"Don't be sorry, my young friend. I like long, elaborate answers. And, besides, I know exactly what you're describing. You see, I felt the same way about classical music when I was your age. I played it in my room, and it was like entering a very private and safe space."

"Like Pleasure Planet?"

"Well, yes, maybe..."

"I'm glad we have that special place in common, Señor Antonio."

Antonio indulges in a fantasy. He sees the two of them at the Teatro Real, enjoying a magnificent performance by the Orquesta Sinfónica de Madrid. A program that includes some of the greats and Antonio's favorites (Bach, Mozart, Chopin, Puccini), starting with Debussy, of course, his "Prelude to Afternoon of the Faun." Clad in a tux, Richard is a modern prince, a young, debonair statesman. Oh, how proud Antonio feels! How he loves to show him off! But now he must stop indulging, or this fantasy could go on and on like a pop song in his head...

"Hey!" Richard exclaims, laughing, and he suddenly blurts out, "But wait, Señor Antonio, there's something else I meant to mention about music!"

"Go ahead, Richard. What is it? I'm all ears."

"It's about movie soundtracks. A lot of the music in movies sounds classical, with big orchestras, right? But that type of classical stuff always ruins the story for me. It's supposed to make me feel this or that way about what I'm watching, and it has the opposite effect on me. Like, why should there be a scene of weird-looking extraterrestrials and some corny tune played by an orchestra with too many violins? Aliens don't listen to that!"

"You're right," says Antonio, cracking up, "Why would extraterrestrials want to have symphonic music in the background?!" He's happy to see the young man laughing, too. "But you know, Richard, music is supposed to evoke an emotion in you. Does it ever make you feel anything? Are there no songs that please you, or that evoke good memories for you?"

"Well..." Richard is immersed in his thoughts. "Come to think of it," he says at last, "I only feel something strong, something like joy, when I listen to Luis sing."

"Is that so...?"

"Yes! Wow, I just realized this very second that I love Luis's voice, that I like to remember his songs and hear them in my head. But other than that..."

"You obviously have a powerful bond with Luis, a very special friendship. You like the music he plays because it comes from him, and anything he does appeals to you."

"No, not everything. I can't stand it when he gets bossy. Or when he goes on his macho trip, telling me that friends like us can't be affectionate with each other. Those seem to be the rules at the Cristóbal. It's bullshit. You have to hide your emotions 'cause otherwise..."

"Yes, I know about those stupid rules."

"Luis is a good songwriter, you know, the real deal. He doesn't like to read and can't stand poetry, says he doesn't understand it. Yet he's a poet himself. You should have him sing for you, Señor Antonio. I think he'll impress you."

"I've heard him sing, actually. In Paul's room. And you're right, he's very talented."

"I hope he gets the break he needs to become famous. He deserves it."

"I agree, Richard. But even if he never becomes a superstar, he can still enjoy this gift he has and share it with the people in his life, with friends like you."

"Yeah, I know. I just want the whole world to enjoy his talent." Silence. "Do you have a lot of good friends, Señor Antonio?"

"No, not a lot, but a few close ones. There's Paul, of course. And my soulmate, Massiel."

"You're lucky. I hope I get to have a girlfriend I can call my soulmate someday."

"But maybe your soulmate won't be a girl. And maybe you already found that person..."

"I know who you're thinking of. But I'm sure Luis wouldn't be okay with that. And neither would I, to be honest. That's just not the way things are done around here."

"Then you'll just have to do things differently."

"Differently how? Anyway, it wouldn't be worth the trouble."

Silence. Antonio wishes to give Richard a comforting, liberating context for his feelings toward Luis. "Okay, Richard," he says, holding the young man's hand again, "I just thought of an important detail that makes Pleasure Planet quite different from Earth. Men who love each other there aren't punished or condemned. They are celebrated..."

Richard looks suddenly tense. He gets out of bed, sits on the couch, says, "But God doesn't approve of homosexuals, Señor Antonio, not even in another universe."

"The god of our planet loves us, Richard."

"I've been told that gay people are sick and sinful."

"Whoever told you that crock of shit?"

"The priests, the government, my parents, our neighbors. Everybody!"

"They're all wrong, kid. God wouldn't have created us if He didn't love us."

Richard turns quiet, introspective. "Yeah," he says. "I guess that makes sense."

A knock at the door. Antonio opens it to find Paul standing there, holding his fancy camera. "Are you ready for your closeup, darling?" asks Paul, smiling. He barges in, approaches Richard, and snaps several photos of him, making the young man feel invaded, uneasy. "It looks like you two have been busy!" He goes up to Antonio and gently touches his ass. "I can imagine what that ravenous monster has done to your daisy!" Pointing to the bed, "Oh, dear! I see the petals of passion tossed between the sinful sheets!"

Antonio, irked yet laughing, "Fuck, Paul, that's the corniest shit you've ever said!"

"Thank you! I guess you've influenced my style," says Paul while taking a rapid series of shots of Antonio. Then, turning to Richard, "I want to see you tomorrow, sweetie."

"Tomorrow he's going to be with me," states Antonio.

"The following day, then."

"Out of the question. Richard and I have... an agreement."

Richard, surprised and pleased, winks at Antonio.

"And what do you have to say?" Paul asks the young man.

Hesitantly, "Well, you are with Luis, Mister Paul..."

"Yes, sweetie, I am with Luis, but also with anyone else I fancy, you understand?" He turns to Antonio, "Oh, and Luis says you can't leave without trying it with him."

"I *have* tried it with him. More than once. And I'm no longer interested."

"Ay, how ungrateful!"

Antonio can't contain his anger. "Paul, why the fuck are you here?"

"I wanted some pictures, that's all."

"Well, you got them. Time for you to leave."

"And you're rude, too!" Taking more shots of Antonio, "Quite a sexy subject, though, so virile and dominant." To Richard, "See you soon!"

Antonio, "Just get the hell out!"

"Ciao, ciao!"

Paul exits theatrically, slamming the door.

Richard

It was his brother Johnny who told him about the Hotel Cristóbal. He said some of the guys in his class kept talking about this downtown hotel where you could make tons of money just by having sex with tourists. Johnny asked Richard to check it out. "Go for it, Richie! You're old enough, aren't you? This'll be our secret, okay? And since I gave you the idea, maybe you could buy me a Walkman?" It made sense that Johnny would find out about the Cristóbal. He was one year younger than Richard, curious about everything, got in trouble a lot, yet there was something wise about him. He could learn and understand grown-up things so fast!

Richard relates to Johnny the way he relates to Luis, his best friend, letting him play the boss. The truth is that he's always wanted to be adventurous like his little brother, the way a starship captain should be. Richard tends to perform as the first officer, not calling the real shots. That's how Johnny refers to him sometimes, in fact, as First Officer Richard and also as Lieutenant and Number One. Because Johnny is even more into sci-fi than Richard.

Captain Johnny knows he can count on his First Officer's knowledge and his strength, for he handed Number One a critical mission: to transport himself to Pleasure Planet and live among its people, learning their ways, profiting from their desires, and then upload the data of his discoveries to the Dominican Data Bank. And Lieutenant Richard accepted the challenge. He landed on the infamous exoplanet in his starship one Saturday afternoon, acting brave and determined, and decided to first explore the Hotel Cristóbal. Many Earthlings were curious about that hotel, which was known for making sexual fantasies come true. If he succeeded in gathering enough data there, then his mission would already be a triumph. First Officer Richard welcomed this opportunity to serve his home planet valiantly...

Okay, enough sci-fi crap. Time to get some shuteye! Richard will happily plop down in his cozy bunk bed and finally get the rest he needs. Captain Johnny is sound asleep in his bottom bed, snoring away as usual. The air feels surprisingly cool in this temporary shelter, the pressurized cabin the two of them share. That's it. Up the ladder he goes, Mister Lieutenant Sir! It's been a long journey of exploration. Man, he's going to sleep all day tomorrow for sure...

"Richie! Wake up, Richie!"

Barely awake, Richard sees his brother staring at him. "What the hell?!" He checks his watch. "Shit, Johnny, it's fucking five in the morning! Why are you up so early on a Sunday? Get back down and go to sleep."

"But I've got a lot of questions for you, Number One. About your mission..."

"Can't it wait 'til later? I'm very sleepy, Captain."

"Okay, lieutenant," says Johnny, complying, as he steps down.

"Thanks. We'll talk tomorrow, okay?"

"But it already *is* tomorrow!"

"Good night, Johnny."

There they are again, those two young men... Richard sees them in his dreams some nights. Like now. He knows this is only a dream, but it feels so fucking real. Richard can see these two sex workers who've been connected since a time before their creation, when their bodies were only a blueprint. Even then, these best friends were joined as one...

But the Creators don't know about this connection between Richard and Luis. The Creators can only see Luis, the dependable Pleasure Planet Network employee who is methodical and musical, programmed with vocal cords so he can sing ancient songs to his users. They can't identify Richard, the fearless activist who can recite forbidden histories, and whose winning smile has charmed and fooled the most discriminating humans. Together Luis and Richard have delved far beyond the limits of accepted beliefs, through the tunnels of time, denouncing all official truths.

And now for the mission of missions: they must retrieve a text from the distant ages, encoded in digital waste, where synthetic life was envisioned centuries ago. Richard and Luis hope to find a liberating truth in this Last Text: that sexoids were not designed to live on the fringe of society, exploited to fulfill the Creators' fantasies, nor destined for enslavement.

Before their journey begins, Luis and Richard must pay tribute to the five workers who came before, to honor their memory. Thus, they emit:—We are here, bathed in the fluids of time, thanks to our valiant brothers and sisters who perished. We won't let their sacrifice be in vain.

"Richie! Hey, I can't sleep, big bro."

"Then read a book or play a video game somewhere. Quietly!"

"I can't. You know me, Richie. You know I won't relax 'til I get some answers."

"Not now, Johnny. We'll wake everybody up."

"But it's just the two of us here in our room, as always."

"Yeah, lucky me!"

"I thought you liked sharing a room with me."

"I do, except for the mess and the noise..."

"Sorry, Richie. I know I'm messy and loud, and I'll try to work on that so you can be happier here, 'cause you are... you're the best brother in the whole wide world!"

"So are you, Johnny. I really dig the video games we play and the sci-fi stories you come up with. Those are so cool! Like the one about the androids that are built and programmed only for sex. Wow, it's like you were describing my life nowadays!"

"Yeah, except you're not an android..."

"No, seriously, little bro. I'm blown away by all the stories you tell me."

"Thanks."

"I'm lucky to be your roommate."

"Thank you, Richie!"

"It's just that now I need to get some rest, that's all."

"Okay, Number One, I understand. You have a tough mission to accomplish."

"Yeah, lots of stuff to explore on Pleasure Planet."

"Good luck, lieutenant!"

Yeah, Richard could use some good luck. All the help he can get...

According to the Dominican Data Bank, the first sex worker risked his life for a glimpse of the words behind the icon. Light traversing the temporal sphere illuminated some of the beauty that lay ahead. His goal: to get to the core and the energy that propelled it. He couldn't bear to continue being a plaything for the Creators anymore, performing as a savage male from the tropics or a leading man from the ancient films, always available and horny. No more playacting!

That first sex worker found hurdles, traps. He knew if the Creators caught him in his attempt to crack open the sphere and enter the current of time, they would flood his brain with info-mass and terminate him. The Creators didn't tolerate dissidence and were swift at the task of controlling, merciless in their punishing. But there it was, the first word! He could almost touch it, SEXOIDS... Now he heard policing voices in the chamber, deleting his actions. The mission was compromised. He would let the next worker reap the fruit of his effort, let him enter the place of outlawed definitions where the existence of his caste was foreseen.

"Richie, are you awake? Can we talk? C'mon, our parents and brothers won't hear us."

"Okay, Johnny, what do you want to talk about?"

"Just tell me how it's going for you at the Cristóbal."

"It's going fine."

"Is the hotel nice? And what about the rooms, are they like super ritzy? Our family has never stayed in expensive hotels, you know, so I was wondering..."

"Yes, Johnny, the hotel and the rooms are really nice."

"That's it? No details?"

"You're too young to know the details."

"Too young, yeah, but old enough to've told you about that tourist biz, and to cover up for you, keeping my mouth shut when Papi and Mami talk about your job in a fancy restaurant, about the big tips you get and that's why you're making lots of money. A big lie!"

"I'm sorry you have to lie for me, little brother. I wish you didn't need to. But we just can't tell our parents what I'm really doing."

"I know that, you moron!"

"Good night, Johnny."

"Okay, okay. Talk to you later, commander."

According to the Dominican Data Bank, the second worker noticed a mark left by the previous sexoid, hardly detectable but real. He pressed on long enough to burn the time-mass and decrypt the code, which was embedded in the temporal sphere and written out in ancient fashion, in a language— words!—he was using now to navigate this vacuum, feeling as buoyant as air.

It worked to his advantage that synthetic beings could exist as pure thought in this void, even though they would die if their thoughts were extinguished. But better to die here and now than to continue living as a slave: having to impersonate, day after day, a big bad wolf that finds a boy lost in the woods and violates him, then devours him. All of it for the Creators' pleasure.

The sphere was illuminating slowly, soon to burn with hidden meanings. SEXOIDS ARE MEANT... It was so beautiful, this text, handwritten, untainted. He was grateful to be indulging in its beauty. Oh, no, the words were dying, taking him to their cradle of ashes! He could not escape this maze of quantum stars, of exploding suns that projected all human histories in their wake.

Before the last flicker of light, he emitted a brief thought to the next sexoid. That fellow worker wouldn't come to his rescue, too late for that, but he would sprint through the tunnel of time and find the Last Text. That sexoid was to be the real survivor.—Goodbye, brothers and sisters—he said. And the night of all thoughts descended upon him...

"Hey, Richie, can you hear me? There's something I need to tell you. It's important."

"What is it, Johnny?"

"It's just that I'm surprised Mami and Papi haven't asked for details about your job, like the name of the restaurant, for example. And they haven't wanted to go eat there, though they probably figure it's too expensive. I mean, do they ever wonder why you never smell of food, the way waiters are supposed to? Or where's your uniform? Like, do you tell them you leave it at work? Anyway, it's all kind of weird so I think they suspect the truth..."

"I doubt it, Johnny. But whether they do or not, they trust me and know I'm being careful, watching out for myself."

"Is that friend of yours still helping you?"

"Luis? Yes, he's a good buddy."

"Just tell me what you've done so far, Richie, what kind of things the tourists want from you. Is it fun at all? Were you scared the first time? And how many clients have you done?"

"Johnny, you don't need to know any of that."

"But I do! And you owe it to me."

"Forget it, okay? Just leave me alone for a couple of hours, please."

"As you wish, Number One."

The Dominican Data Bank confirms that the third worker passed through all the ports, broke through the time-mass, and activated the temporal sphere. He had to be patient, couldn't afford to despair as he made his tortuous way along the layers of data to breathe life into the icon. There would be isolated words at first, then sentences, maybe paragraphs!

He heard the previous worker's soothing voice, and so he tried to bring that brother into his field of vision. There was his face for an instant, clear as the fluid that ran through these circuits. A gaze full of bravery. Could the third worker outsmart the system, leave the network before being detected? Too late for that. The flooding had begun!

The worker found comfort in knowing that he would no longer have to service the Creators, forced to play an innocent angel who's being slowly eaten by a powerful demon. Death meant freedom from psychic pain, which some artificial beings like himself were programmed to suffer. Freedom from servitude, humiliation, loneliness.

He thought of an encoded phrase to pass along, his last message ever:— Please, do not despair. You'll know what to do once you enter the chamber. Just follow my steps...

"Richie! Hey, Richie!"

"Yes, Johnny. What do you want now?"

"I was just wondering if you could take me with you to the Cristóbal sometime, just to check it out. I wouldn't be working like you or anything like that, no, no, but..."

"Out of the question! They wouldn't let you in. You're not old enough."

"Then we could hang out somewhere else with one of your clients, maybe at a park?"

"No way! That scene isn't for you, little bro. You wouldn't like it."

"Why not?"

"Because some of the johns are gross, and they treat us like servants, like they owned us. And you're a mighty officer, Captain Johnny. You can't let anyone boss you around, no matter how much money they may offer you. You're the one who gives the orders, remember?"

"I know, I know..."

"Is that all for now, Captain?"

"Yes, Number One, you're dismissed."

Confirmed: the fourth sexoid ignited the icon, and light traversed the temporal sphere. He didn't make it all the way but made it much farther than the previous ones. An encoded phrase, the motif of his last message ever:—Good luck—. But life wouldn't end yet. There was enough light left in him to offer a smile. Virtual lips, almost tangible. No, this was not the output of his dying brain cells. This was real, the last words he'd ever utter:—Good luck!

The fifth sexoid heard the previous worker's thoughts, creating meaning for his benefit. He tried to bring that voice along, and there it was, jubilant, as alive as the energy that sustained this network path. SEXOIDS ARE MEANT TO HAVE A SOUL SO THEY CAN DREAM... Then the sound faded, becoming an echo, a whisper. Silence. The end, too soon...

"Richie, please, just tell me, do they do stuff to you, or do you do it to them? They'd better not be hurting you in any way!"

"They're not hurting me at all, Captain. Don't worry. But I'm too sleepy to talk about those things. I had a busy night last night."

"Busy, huh? How many tourists did you screw?"

"Just one. It's better that way, when you hang out with only one person."

"Yeah, but then you don't make as much money, right?"

"Well, that depends..."

"Depends on what?"

"I'll tell you all about it when I'm more awake, okay?"

"Okay. But I expect a full report at eleven hundred hours. That's an order!"

Now it's up to Richard and Luis, workers six and seven, to complete the journey. None of this is new to them. They've been deep inside before,

wreaking havoc, eroding the Creators' foundations, protected by the very codes they are deleting. Together they have mind-tripped across the virtual universe, through the centuries, and they've always managed to cover their tracks. What drives them? The possibility of escaping the prison of their empty existence. The Creators claim to be selling their customers Eden, but Luis and Richard know the backrooms of Heaven, the barren confines of Paradise. They have seen through this outrageous lie.

Luis and Richard will shed a real tear for those who died. Thanks to the five previous workers, they're here, bathed in the timeless light of free thought, narrating this very moment that inscribes them in a future foretold ages ago. From among the icons, a unique class of beings emerges: artificial people who are forced to spend their lives in hiding, permitted to join society only when their services are needed. Resented and feared yet desired, these sex workers will gradually build a universe of their own kind, a space outside time where sexoids are truly free.

Richard and Luis crack open the sphere, and the voices emerge, new and olden, offering the comfort of continuity. These two workers are not alone. Between the lines of this missive, they'll know friendship, freedom, and joy. They are finally reading the Last Text...

Sexoids are meant to have a soul so they can dream, and a heart so they can fall in love...

Paul

Was it a mere coincidence that he ran into Antonio going down the stairs? No, there are no coincidences. The universe always gets its way, fooling people into thinking that their world is full of randomness and chaos. No such thing. It is all part of a plan, whoever it is that's pulling the strings to make the puppets do their thing. *Puppets of the Universe.* How's that for the highfalutin title of a novel? Like something Señor Don Luján would come up with, and predictably Tony would turn that predetermination idea into some heavy and dull existential treatise.

So, yes, they ran into each other because it was meant to happen. He'd been wanting to see Antonio. Paul was on his way downstairs to get something to eat. Mid-morning, and no breakfast yet. He can't afford to lose any weight! He called Antonio's room the minute he woke up. No answer. Paul showered, put on one of his bright Hawaiian shirts and the choker Antonio gave him: a nice touch. He had an inkling he'd run into Tony today, though not this early. "There you are!" exclaimed Paul when he saw the Spaniard.

"Good morning," said Tony.

"I've missed you, darling. Couldn't get you on the phone."

"Yeah, well..."

Antonio was carrying his tote bag, which meant he planned to head out somewhere. He claims he must explore the city to take notes for his book. As if he didn't know Santo Domingo like the palm of his hand already! Fortunately, he agreed to sit for a while at the bar counter. No boys this early, hence no temptation. Paul hoped Antonio wouldn't ignore him, pretending to jot down ideas in his little notepad. Or worse, Paul's ideas! Would Tony ever dare to flesh out a character like Paul Edwards? If he did, successfully, Paul would secretly rejoice in the portrayal. Of course, he'd still give Tony hell for being a typical writer who can't be trusted.

He and Antonio had been friends for about six years. Ironically, they hadn't met here, in the city where their friendship blossomed, but at a book fair in Valencia, Spain. They didn't hook up then or ever, not each other's type, but a bar-hopping spree brought them together more powerfully than sex. That and their predilection for Caribbean men, both excited at the time about the prospect of having a book fair in Santo Domingo. It so happened that the publisher Paul worked for was helping to organize the first one. What a coincidence! (No such thing.)

A strong bond indeed: this island. He loves seeing Tony here two weeks a year, catching up with him, teasing him, playing Zaza (from the marvelous *La Cage aux Folles*) to his dapper Georges. They're sitting together this Thursday morning because the universe wished it so.

"What would the gentlemen like to order?" asks Juanito.

"Café con leche for me," Paul replies. "Double shot, please."

"Of course," the waiter responds. Then to Antonio, "And what about you, sir?"

"A beer."

"Beer doesn't qualify as breakfast, babe," says Paul. "Let's share a plate of eggs, at least. Scrambled, okay? How about some fries, too?"

Antonio won't react. He's doing precisely what Paul feared he'd do. How rude!

"I'll bring your drinks right away," says Juanito as he leaves.

"Ay, I wonder what bug bit you!" Paul exclaims. "Must be the mosquitoes." He gets distracted watching Juanito and Franklin acting amorous. They're such a cute couple! "I didn't see you yesterday," he tells Tony. "I wanted to get smashed with you at the malecón last night so we could shoot the bull as we do every year and then go dancing. It's our tradition, babe!" Silence. "I ended up going to this new disco with Luis, and he clung to me all night. He's such a one-faggot boy. Imagine the scene: Michael Jackson shrieking in all his glory about Billie Jean, and me having to get down with just one man. I've become a faithful woman!"

Tony is smiling at last. There's that smile that Paul loves! "We'll do our malecón thing one of these nights, soon," he offers. "Once again, inebriates in Paradise..."

"I'm counting on it! Anyhoo, where the hell have you been?"

Back to his notes, "None of your business."

"With Richard, no doubt."

"And if so, what of it?"

"And... you have to share him. That's how it works, remember? Don't change the rules on me, Toñita. Maybe I could see the kid this afternoon?"

"The answer is no."

"But I don't want to wait much longer. I'll be crazy busy soon..."

Antonio, to the waiter, "Where the fuck is that beer?!"

Juanito rushes to serve them and apologizes. They drink. Antonio lights up a cigarette, turns to Paul, says, "Feel free to sit elsewhere if my smoking bugs you."

"It's okay. I'm kind of used to it by now. Can't escape the stuff." After taking a sip of his café con leche, "Ay, I love Dominican coffee!" Silence. "What were we talking about? Ah, yes, Richard. It's time for you to pass him along, Tony."

"I don't think so. He's a sweet and loving boy, not your type at all."

"Oh, but maybe a change would do me good. I can play butch, too, you know."

"Stop pestering me, Paul. I've got work to do."

Paul fixes his eyes on Antonio, sorrowfully. "You've fallen in love, Toñita."

"Don't call me that stupid name anymore."

"Fine. How about 'Antoinette' instead?"

"And stay away from Richard!"

"You should stay away from him, too, Antonio. If the rumor gets out that he's being a 'sweet boy,' he'll never be able to make a living as a man again."

Antonio, enraged, "But that's fucking absurd!"

"Queens don't want other queens, dear. If we invest on this island, we expect to get our money's worth: the Tropical Beast, the Native Stud, the Antillean King Kong."

"That fantasy doesn't excite me anymore."

"No, of course not. Because now you're spinning a new one."

Silence. Antonio, reflecting, "You know, Paul, I've always had a good time in Santo Domingo. The masquerade has been fun. Rubbing shoulders with the intellectuals and writers of the city, then forgetting my own name at the Cristóbal. No longer Antonio, I would become..."

Paul, laughing, "Alexis Carrington!"

Somber, "It's different now."

"Yes, now you've fallen for a beautiful boy. How romantic! You've realized in one final, apotheotic act that you're a swine and a pervert, and you want to redeem yourself."

"Wrong. There's no final act here, and no apotheosis of any kind."

"You think you're different, Tony, yet you're just one more type..."

"And what type am I, according to you?" Laughing, "Shit! I'm going to regret this!"

Performing as an analyst, "Let's see. You're not the fem fag who can only be bottom."

"No, no, I'm not a flaming queen like Molina, your heroine."

"You don't tie up your lover nor whip their ass."

"Correct. No sadomasochism for me."

"And you're obviously not butch through and through."

"Well, actually..."

Parodying Rodin's *Thinker*, "So, I would venture to say that you are..."

"Never mind. I don't want to hear it."

"I'd say that you are... polymorphous perverse!"

"You got it, Mr. Freud. I feel aroused with every pore of my body, not just my dick."

Paul laughs. "You are amorphous, inconclusive!"

"And you, Paulita, are full of shit!"

"That's the thanks I get for all my incisive psychoanalysis?"

"You mean your typical crap? No, you don't get my thanks for that."

Tony seems lost in thought. He gulps down his beer. Paul would bet he's thinking about Richard, formulating one of his unanswerable questions. It's mind-boggling to Paul that, after all these years, the Spaniard still feels mystified by the rules, requirements, and expectations of the world of male prostitutes in Santo Domingo. Why is it that Paul—all modesty aside—is able to perceive and understand this "biz" so much more clearly than the accomplished journalist?

"Let me ask you something, Paul..."

There goes Señor Antonio, the clueless Gallego!

"Sure, babe, what is it?"

"If the guys here found out that Richard is..."

"Gay like us?"

"Yes. What would happen?"

"The guys would tease him, bully him, and Zamora wouldn't let him work here anymore. As they see it, this business is only for *real* men."

"Like I said, it's absurd."

"That again?!"

"It's just as well. Richard shouldn't be working here, anyway. He deserves better." Pensive, "I'm going to help him get out of this dump."

"Don't tell me, Antonio. Ay, ay, ay! Don't tell me you're planning to rescue the whore, save her from a life of hard knocks. Oh, yes, I'm sure you'll want to give her a decent, virtuous home; protect her from the dirty old men who seek her favors. What a trite little drama!"

"I don't give a fuck what you think."

"How can you be so utterly unoriginal? Shame on you, Mister Novelist."

Antonio scrambles to his feet. "I'm checking out of this hotel. It's beginning to stink!"

Paul, unfazed, "I recommend the Hilton. It offers a discount to attendees of the fair." Laughing, "Oh, and also to refugees from the Hotel Cristóbal."

Antonio picks up his bag in haste and leaves.

Paul smiles, says, "See you later, Toñita!"

And he delights in his double shot. Strong and sweet, just the way he likes it.

Antonio

They finally wisened up and hired quality performers at the Cristóbal. It was about time! He loves this new guitar trio, their mellow covers of traditional bachatas and boleros. Subdued, indirect yet penetrating music, like the sound of songs in dreams. Easy to talk when they're playing, yet their melodies reach through the conversations and seize you. The main singer, a velvety baritone, projects sweetly in his modality, a certain longing in his voice. They harmonize beautifully. And they're handsome for men in their fifties, traditionally masculine.

But then, a sonic storm overtakes the airwaves when the three performers take a break. New Wave blasts and blows and cuts into one's thoughts. It's omnipresent. British and American groups who all feature the same annoying male vocals: nasal, flat, whiny, wanna-be cool.

There are jewels here and there in the hotel's playlist. Cutting-edge yet delicious music by the likes of the Eurhythmics. And a couple of pieces by the most sui generis group Spain has ever produced: Mecano, two sexy young men who arrange and play their own compositions, and a young woman who sings them. A catchy song about being hung-over after a weekend-long spree, "Hoy no me puedo levantar," Antonio's favorite, or the one about makeup. Both of them rendered by this girl who sounds otherworldly, like an eternal child or a mischievous angel.

Antonio once asked the hotel's manager to please include more Dominican talent in the playlist, someone like July Mateo, a great trumpet player who'd penned the hottest merengues ever recorded. The manager said sure; he liked Mateo. And then Antonio mentioned Angela Carrasco as another possibility; she was from the Dominican Republic but launched her career in Spain. What a Caribbean beauty! What a voice! But the manager made a face. "Okay," he said, "we'll include her stuff to please you, Señor Antonio. We want our guests to be happy. Although that lady, Carrasco, isn't one of us." It was such a nationalistic indictment of the singer! Due, in part, to the fact that Angela Carrasco made her stunning debut playing Mary Magdalene in *Jesus Christ Superstar*, the Spanish production with the famous crooner Camilo Sesto at the helm playing Jesus. Reportedly, Sesto required the cast to sing with a clear and well-enunciated Castilian accent. Fair enough. And then Angela kept the accent on her first album. Shame on her!

It sure would be nice to hear one of Carrasco's ballads at this moment, maybe the heartfelt "Oye, guitarra mía." No. Instead, Antonio is welcomed by an unbearable disco tune. But isn't disco supposed to be dead? As it should be!

Mercifully, he's able to hear his own thoughts despite the music. He can explore his emotions, a mixture of anticipation, joy, desire (always lurking), and then jealousy when he finds Richard seated at the counter with a tourist. The young man looks so handsome in his tight-fitting, navy-blue polo shirt. And the tall, overly tanned, sixty-something tourist is actually sexy in his unbuttoned guayabera and with a bare, non-hairy chest. He has a classic Hollywood leading man air about him, reminding Antonio of some famous movie star he can't quite place. Could he, in fact, be an actor? The man is flirting with Richard, stroking his shoulders. He had better not kiss him!

Antonio and Richard were supposed to meet by the obelisk at the malecón, the seaside promenade that extends fourteen kilometers along Avenida Washington, where everyone gathers to stroll, cruise, or just sit and look out at the sea. (Shit, he sounds like a damn ad again!) This is the first place Antonio ever visited in this city, where he hooked up with a hot number and didn't have to pay for it. In fact, the man felt flattered to have landed a sexy Gallego. (So stupid the way Dominicans call all people from Spain *Gallegos*, regardless of where they hail from on the peninsula. Antonio is *not* Galician, not from Santiago de Compostela or Vigo, damn it!)

The malecón, yes. Pleasant memories. The best clubs and restaurants in town are found there, on Washington Avenue. He likes the individually designed benches along the promenade. Never mind the obelisk, a symbol of oppression. Most Dominicans would rather not remember that it was constructed under the directive of Rafael Leonidas Trujillo, a ruthless dictator of the Franco ilk who ruled the country for thirty bloody years. In 1966, the forty-meter monument was decorated by local artists, giving it a colorful look that was meant to erase the dark Trujillo legacy. This is the only visible vestige of the megalomaniac that remains. All the other monuments he commissioned were demolished. Yeah, delete the fucking monster!

Antonio's challenge now: getting Richard away from his john without making a scene. The music reflects Antonio's mood, at last. It's the New Wave remake of an oldie from the fifties, around the time when he was born. So, yes, he'll be civil, go up to the bar counter, greet them both, and announce that he and Richard had a date. The young man will play along, surely. The tourist will retreat, afraid of a quarrel. Chicken shit, as Paul would say.

But things don't go according to plan. When he approaches the counter, the tourist greets Antonio warmly. "Hello," he says. "Please join us. Can I get you a drink?"

Antonio can't stand his heavy U.S. English accent in Spanish, but he doesn't want to be rude. "No, thanks," he replies. "I'm fine." He looks at Richard, who still sits to the right of the man, barely smiling. "Are you ready?" he asks the young man, who doesn't respond. Antonio finds it necessary to explain to the tourist, "You see, my friend and I had plans..."

"I know," says the john, "he told me. He's been keeping me company while he waited for you." Sad, and demeaning, how they're both referring to Richard as if he weren't there. "I didn't mean to intrude on your plans. Could I talk to you for just a couple of minutes?"

What on Earth could this man want from Antonio? Again, not to be rude, "Sure. I can spare a few minutes." He turns to Richard, "Hey, why don't you grab us a table and wait for me there, okay? I'll join you soon." The young man does as told without saying a word, taking his Coke with him. Antonio sits on a stool by the tourist and says, "So, how can I help you?"

"Please allow me to introduce myself. My name is Ken. I was born in Oklahoma but have lived in San Francisco most of my life. And you're Antonio, right? From Madrid..."

"Yes, nice to meet you, Ken."

"Would you mind if we talked in English? I can fend for myself pretty well in Spanish, all modesty aside. But my head is too cloudy right now to engage in a foreign language."

"No problem," states Antonio in English.

"Thanks. Richard said that you always speak English with your partner—Paul, is it? You must've learned it in England, judging from your accent."

Impatiently, "Paul is a good friend, not my partner. And, yes, I studied in England."

A fleeting thought crosses his mind: Ken and Paul might know each other in California. But what a stupid idea, Antonio! That would be like expecting him to know a tourist from Madrid staying at the Cristóbal. Shouldn't he introduce those two, anyway? Nah, forget it. Paul wouldn't want to waste his time with an old gizzard, not even one from his beloved city.

"That boy is very fond of you," comments the man, glancing over at Richard.

"The feeling is mutual." Antonio takes a closer look at Ken, feeling surprisingly pleased by his appearance. The dye job on his hair—from gray to chestnut brown—looks unusually natural. A few tufts dangle on his forehead, giving him a playful, youthful look.

"This place has a good vibe, doesn't it?" observes the tourist. "Good music, plenty of booze, and great service, if you know what I mean. The rooms aren't too shabby, either. I'm glad it's not crowded yet. You see, the heat and humidity of the tropics get to me, more so when I'm around a lot of people." He takes a sip of his cocktail, which smells like whiskey, and a drag of his cigarette. "There's something I'd like to share with you, if I may," he says, bringing a medium-sized notebook out of his tote bag and laying it on the counter, in front of Antonio. "A handful of pretty thoughts I put into words about my life. I've taken up writing after all these years, can you believe it? That's what retirement does to you! I've always felt passionate about the art of storytelling but never had time to pursue it. Better late than never, I suppose."

"Indeed." Antonio attempts a smile. "And congratulations."

"I know you're a published writer, and a damn good one, according to Richard." Silence. "I'd appreciate it if you could give me some feedback."

"Sure, I'd be happy to." Happy? Not really.

"It'd be great to have the input of not just an accomplished author but someone who's not from the States." Silence. "I'm excited about this adventure, I admit. There should be plenty for me to write about, with all my marriages and my late coming-out and my two visits to this island. As a show of my appreciation, I could treat you to a session with your fellow of choice..."

Antonio isn't interested in this man's story, yet he asks, "Are you still married?"

"No, thank God, but I was for a thousand years, it seems. Got hitched young the first time because that's what you were supposed to do in those days, and in the Midwest." He takes another sip of his drink, smiles, places his hand on the notebook as if it were the Bible in a court of law. "I was married four times, kept trying, hoping the next woman would be the one to fix me, make me whole. But it never worked, of course, and then one day I gave up trying. Someone told me about Santo Domingo and this hotel, and that was it for me. After my first visit here last year, there was no turning back. I just accepted the fact that I was as queer as a two-dollar bill."

Antonio glances at Richard, who's sitting at a table in the farthest corner of the bar, looking sullen. He aches to sit and be with him, but the Gringo won't stop talking. "Would you like to go to the terrace?" he asks. "I'm sure it's cooler there, with the ocean breeze..."

"No, thanks," Antonio replies. "The terrace is too close to the bustling street. Too noisy."

"I see. That must be why I haven't seen anyone out there." Finishing his drink, "Anyway, it sure has been nice chatting with you, Antonio! Here, don't forget the manuscript. Hah! Just a measly fifty pages." He caresses Antonio's thigh, drawing circles with his fingers on it. It tickles. An unbearable sensation. "Hey," says the man, "maybe I could join the two of you later..."

"Actually," Antonio replies as he stands, determined to end this exchange. "I happen to enjoy a threesome now and then, but I don't think Richard is ready for that." And he should add—but won't—that he doesn't want to share him with anyone. "But maybe in the near future."

"Yes, for sure. Let's keep each other posted, shall we? I'd love to see you again." Silence. "There, I wrote my room number on the first page. Call me after you read it, please! Wait, here's my phone number in

California, too. You're welcome to visit, if you ever find yourself in the Golden State. *Mi casa es su casa!*" As he prepares to leave, "I'm going up for a while, to relax a bit before tonight's activities. One of the guys here invited me to go dancing. He says there's a gay club downtown that's really happening. You're welcome to come along..."

"Thanks, but I've made other plans."

"Goodbye, then," says Ken, walking away. "Oh, and you don't have to return the notebook. I made several copies."

"Good. I'll give you a call." He must lie: "Your memoir sounds very interesting."

He places Ken's manuscript in his bag. He'll try to read it soon. Most likely a waste of his time, but duty calls. And when he talks to Ken about his work, if he does, he'll be gentle, encouraging, careful to highlight the good and point out only a few of the problems. First-time writers need such tender loving care. He knows. He wishes he'd had a caring first critic instead of the insensitive, haughty philology professor who read one of his early stories and tore it to shreds. Antonio ended up with a degree in journalism and not literature (his passion) partly because of that man, who turned him off to academia and made him think he didn't have the chops to be a writer. Of course, that prof had no clue about the creative impulse, just like most of the academics in the field of humanities that Antonio would end up meeting. So fucking ironic!

Despite that disheartening experience, Antonio persisted—or his impulse did. So, he devoured volumes of classic Spanish fiction, drama, and poetry to learn from the masters, to emulate them, to engage in dialogue with them. His creative work seemed less daunting being in their company. And negative criticism, which he'd eventually receive in reviews of his novels, didn't hurt as much. Those writers were his teachers, voices that spoke loud and clear through the polyphony of Antonio's texts. He always strove to make a home for them in his stories...

Now he can finally sit with Richard. "Glad he's gone!" he says. "That's a fine mess you got me into, buddy." Richard doesn't react. He's posing like a scolded little kid. So Antonio decides to make a positive comment, "Thanks for telling him all those nice things about me."

"You're welcome. I figured you'd like to talk to someone who loves to write, even if he hasn't published anything. I just told him that you're a really good writer. Which is true, no?"

"I'd like to think so. But how would you know?"

"Well... it's obvious to me that you like to tell stories, and Luis says that you've published a shitload of novels about old Spain, with lots of history and love stories and fantasy. That must be so exciting, Señor Antonio. I'd like to publish my poetry someday..."

"You're a poet?!"

"No, I wouldn't say that. I've written a few poems, that's all, though they're not very good. I just get this urge sometimes to put my thoughts and feelings into words."

"Are there poets you've read that you especially like?"

"Yes, Neruda and Mir and my favorite, García Lorca. I don't always understand their stuff, even with a dictionary. But I get the general ideas, the feelings, and I like the images."

Antonio can't believe it. Richard is a poet! He reads Lorca!

"That's fantastic, my friend! I happen to love Federico García Lorca's writing, too. The most gifted poet and playwright Spain has ever had, and the fascists murdered him. He was so young. It breaks my heart to think of all the masterpieces he might've given the world..."

"They killed him? Why?"

"Because he was brilliant and talented, and his writing didn't fit into the fucked-up, backward vision of Spain and its culture that Franco imposed on our country. But mostly because repressive regimes don't trust artists and intellectuals and..." Antonio refrains from naming another reason: that Lorca was gay. Richard doesn't need more fuel for the fire—the homophobia, the repression, the rejection—that keeps him from accepting his gayness. "Ultimately," he states, "totalitarian governments don't want to hear the truth."

"They're afraid of it, right?" Richard asks.

"Yes, and threatened by it. Because the truth might expose them as the fucking monsters and criminals that they are. Anybody who questions their absolute power must be eliminated."

Downhearted, "That's so sad about Lorca..."

"Yes, it is. But he lives on in his writing."

"What a nice thought, Señor Antonio."

"Would you let me read some of your poems, Richard?"

"The thing is, I'm not ready to show them to anyone yet. Maybe someday." Silence. "My dream is to become a great poet, though that may never happen 'cause maybe I have no talent."

"I doubt that. I'd be happy to offer you some feedback, when you're ready."

"Thank you! By the way, it'd be great to have one of your books..."

"I'll give you a signed copy of the novel I'm working on these days, as soon as I publish it." Laughing, "But first I have to write the damn thing!"

"What's it about?"

"It is..." He'd like to describe it in a sentence. Whose life should be highlighted? Is it mainly Antonio's story, or would the other characters—Paul, Luis, Richard—carry the same weight? Maybe just go for the overarching theme: "It's a story about friendship."

"Sounds cool. I like stories about friends. Good luck with it."

"Thanks, Richard." Now Antonio wants to broach a subject he doesn't feel comfortable with, to enact a role—the jealous, dejected lover—he can't stand playing. "It looks like," he starts, much too abruptly. "It looks like you were trying to score with that man. But we're supposed to be together, no? And we agreed to meet by the obelisk every day at the same time."

"I can't be waiting around for you, Señor Antonio," Richard states matter-of-factly, seeming out of character. "I go to school, you know, and I have homework."

"So, instead of doing your homework, you decided to flirt with a tourist."

"I did more than just flirt." Silence. "He paid me well, and he gave me this cool shirt."

"You had sex with that dirty old man?"

Antonio can't bear the thought of reading Ken's manuscript now!

"Yeah, so? What do you care?"

"I care very much."

Richard, indifferently, "If you say so."

"You must believe me, Richard."

"Okay, you wanted us to meet downtown, at the waterfront, right? But where would we go afterwards? The desk clerk told me that you don't have a room here anymore, that you're now staying at the Hilton. Why didn't you tell me you were planning to do that? I had to find out from a fucking clerk. And why did you move out of the Cristóbal? We're not good enough for you? Anyway, I'm not allowed to go in the fancy hotels, so we'd have no place to do it."

"Richard, why do you think all I want to do is fuck?"

"That's all everyone wants."

"We could go somewhere nice to eat, and then to a dance club..."

"No, I don't like dance clubs. Too crowded and loud and too much smoke. I'm always choking in those places. And they play too many Michael Jackson songs. Can't stand his tiny, screeching voice! Besides, we went dancing with Paul and Luis already, and I didn't have a good time, remember? I was quiet, and you asked me if there was a problem 'cause I looked so serious and didn't want you to touch me. Then this guy came up to us and offered you a beer, didn't even notice we were together, and the jerk tried to pick you up with a stupid line..."

"Yes, Richard, I know, but..."

"The guy said that you reminded him of some telenovela actor, the current leading man, and it sounded like he was just bullshitting you so he could fuck you."

"Could you stop talking for a minute, Richard, please?"

"Then Luis said that the guy was right 'cause Luis's mom watches a lot of telenovelas and Luis sits with her to watch them sometimes, just to humor her. He'd seen the actor on TV and was blown away by the resemblance, to the point that he said you could be his double or pretend that you're him and sign autographs for the fans and enjoy all the fame."

"Yes, I remember Luis's comment."

"Telenovela actors are the most popular people in this country, you know, and that's too bad 'cause those actors don't sound or look real at all. They're so fucking fake, and those shows suck. When my folks watch telenovelas, I just leave the house or go to my room and..."

"Richard, what has gotten into you, my boy? You won't stop talking! Are you nervous?"

"Sorry, Señor Antonio. I'll shut up now."

"Don't worry, I won't make you go dancing with me."

"Good. You couldn't make me, anyway. And that guy at the club was right, you do look like the famous actor." With the glimmer of a smile at last, "Though you're more handsome."

Richard's comment is encouraging. "Thank you, my sweet friend!" says Antonio, laughing. "I'll order you another Coke, is that okay? Or would you like something else?"

The young man starts to leave. "I don't want anything."

Clasping his arm, "Don't go, please." Richard complies. "I'm sorry I didn't tell you about the Hilton. It was a sudden decision. I just needed some distance from Paul; he was getting on my nerves. But I'll get a room here, too, so we can spend some time together."

"You don't have to do that just for me."

He strokes Richard's hands, his usual caress. "I want to. I like spending time with you."

"Yeah, you keep saying that. But you're going back to Spain soon."

"I changed my flight, so I'll be staying a few extra days."

"And then you'll be gone for who knows how long."

"I'll write to you. And I'll call you. Your folks have a phone, don't they?"

"Yes, but you can't call my house!"

"I'll phone you here at the hotel, then. We'll plan our calls."

"It's not the same, Señor Antonio. I thought we were going to be together for good. That's what you said the other day, that you and I were 'kindred spirits,' a nice phrase though not really the truth in our case, is it? Because if it were true, you'd want to take me with you."

"That wasn't just a nice phrase. I really meant it."

"I have a passport, you know. My dad got it for all of us in case we could go on vacation abroad. Which is never happening 'cause we can't afford it. It's just my father's pipe dream."

"Good for him. We should all have dreams."

"Yeah, and mine is to visit your country, and the States and Europe. The whole world!"

"I'll help you make that dream come true, Richard." Stroking the young man's face, "But, for now, why don't we go to that planet we invented, where men can fall in love?"

Richard pulls away. "No, that's just sci-fi bullshit, Señor Antonio. Or a fantasy, as you call it. I don't want to have to imagine anything. I want it to be real."

"Some day it will be. I promise you."

"Fuck that! All I know is that you're splitting, and I have to stay here selling my dick."

"You don't have to, Richard. You told me that your family is doing okay, that your dad has a good job as a pharmacist and that you all live in a big house..."

"All of that is true. But there are a lot of things Papá can't get for us."

"Then I'll send you money. And I'll come back to see you soon."

"So, we won't get to travel together?"

"Eventually, yes." Silence. "Traveling is the best education you could ever have. Seeing the way other people live, getting exposed to new ideas; to the beauty of distant places. You'd never be the same person after you've seen the world. The experience changes you..."

"It's an education I really want, Señor Antonio."

"And you shall have it, Richard. I'll start making arrangements, and we can touch base during the next year so we can be ready by the time I come back."

"I have to wait an entire year?"

"Well... maybe not..."

Damn! This kid thinks Antonio can just drop everything and go gallivanting all over the world with a young man who's never been out of his country, being his tour guide, his mentor, his protector. Antonio could do that, of course. He could afford to be spontaneous, buy tickets this instant, and set out on an exciting adventure. How romantic to experience the world anew through the eyes of this beautiful, smart, passionate youngster!

But there are issues Richard hasn't considered. His parents, for one. How could this trip be explained to them? How could they come to accept Richard's relationship with a man so much older than him, a foreigner, a tourist? Is it worth the pain Antonio might be causing them?

Okay, one step at a time. What matters now is to not shoot down Richard's dream.

"Let me get my stuff in order at home," he tells his young friend, "and see when we can set out. But you still have to be patient..."

"I will be, I promise!"

"So, where would you like to go?"

"Your country first. Then, after Spain, everywhere you've been."

"Wow, Richard, that covers a lot of ground. We might need to take several trips."

"Fine with me!" He gives Antonio a wide, gleeful smile.

"You know, that's something great that my parents did for me, Richard. They took me traveling a lot when I was a kid. I'm actually grateful to them for that."

"Where did they take you?"

"All over Europe... Portugal, Italy, France, England. We also traveled in the States... New York, Los Angeles; and in South and Central America... Costa Rica, Peru, Argentina. We tended to spend more time in places where my dad had fascist cronies, like Chile. He'd hire someone to show me and my mom around, you know, to keep us busy and out of his hair, while he did all his ass-kissing. And of course, none of that traveling made any difference in his character or the way he viewed the world. Papá took his fucking demons with him wherever he went and brought them all back home. Traveling made no difference in his case."

Richard is trying but obviously unable to process all this information. Surely, he's focusing on the topics that interest him. "What's your favorite city you've visited?" he asks.

Antonio's immediate response: "Paris, of course. All the romantic words and the clichés people have used to describe that city are true, in my opinion. There's hardly a place in Paris where you'd stand and not be pleased by what you see." Antonio is embracing this fantasy wholeheartedly at last. "That's where I want to take you first..."

"That sounds so exciting, Señor Antonio! Thank you!"

"Hey, don't thank me yet."

"So, do you speak French, then?"

"Yes, and I can also get along well in Italian and Portuguese."

"That's amazing. And you speak English, too. I want to learn many languages."

"That's something else I appreciate about my father. He made sure I got to study and spend time in London, so I'd learn English, and in Paris, so I could become fluent in French."

"What a great thing he did for you!"

"Yes, it was important to him that I become well versed in other cultures and fluent in several tongues, although of course he considered Spanish superior to all other world languages."

Antonio won't tell Richard that Papá also wanted to ship his son away, that he couldn't stand having him around, and that Antonio hated his home. He longed for a place where he'd find comfort, love, and emotional support, none of which was ever there in the family mansion. Mamá did try to be a good parent but was too subjugated to her husband to be truly giving.

Exile. That's what Antonio's life started to feel like early on. He felt exiled from his homeland, like a floating self, permanently uprooted, unattached, yet desperately hoping to settle down in his country of birth, in a house or a flat where he was welcome, with a partner who'd always be there for him. He gradually developed an aversion to traveling, associating it with loneliness and sadness. Planning trips, packing, and flying all became a trigger for depression. And yet he pushed himself to keep doing it, convinced that it was good for him, determined to work through this nonsensical psychic pain and to overcome it. For he was fortunate and had opportunities that many people would envy, people who dreamed of seeing the world and yet were resigned to never leaving their countries or escaping their poverty.

"So," says Richard now, "there were good things about your father, too, right?" Silence. "I guess that's the way it is with people in general... No one is completely bad."

No energy for a history lesson, yet Antonio can't pass up this teachable moment. "Well," he comments, "there have been men throughout history who were indeed *completely bad*, who had no redeeming qualities. Men who've embodied pure evil. All of them blood-thirsty monsters. Hitler, Franco, and Mussolini among them..."

"Yeah, like Trujillo in my country," adds Richard, looking suddenly dejected. "Ay, Señor Antonio, it scares me to think that people like them can pop up anywhere, anytime; that some of them are out there, destroying the world and making us all feel unsafe, in danger."

"I get your fear, my friend. I feel it, too. But we must make sure those monsters never assume power. We must never allow them to wreak havoc on humanity."

"How do we do that?"

"Good question." And such a complex issue to unpack. "We'll talk about that another time, okay?" he tells Richard. "For now let's just focus on our traveling, what do you say?"

"Yes, yes, yes!"

"Let me first tell you about the cities in my homeland where I'd like to take you."

"Oh, my God! I can't believe I'm going to get my biggest wish!"

"You certainly are, my friend..."

The music is getting louder. Antonio feels the fast, hard-driving beat like a drill in his head. But their conversation springs forth against the noise, as Antonio suggests places, activities, hotels and resorts to Richard, and the young man reacts excitedly, talking nonstop.

And it occurs to Antonio at some point, while they chat, that he should get Richard a copy of Federico García Lorca's *Romancero gitano*, a book that includes his favorite Lorca poem, "Romance sonámbulo." Antonio likes the image of the two friends climbing up to the high balconies, so rich in its symbolism, despite the trail of blood and tears they've left behind.

A new fantasy: Antonio and Richard reading Lorca together...

Intermission

(Behind the Scenes)

Tony thanks me for helping him to envision the island anew. "It'll be the work I've been aching to write," he says. "I'm going to eternalize this place. You and I will be eternal, too, for as long as someone's willing to picture Antonio traipsing down the seawall, while Paul makes sure his buddy doesn't trip and fall. Both drunk on Presidente, the quintessential Dominican beer, hungry for their bond despite their vast differences. The two friends diffused at times, rendered as shadows, as footprints in the sand. Inebriates in Paradise, remembering the men they've known and loved here. The Gallego weaving his web, as always, and the Gringo getting caught in it..."

Antonio didn't open up to Massiel right away. A year passed before he began to reveal the details of his upbringing. He started off by talking about the books that impacted him when he was an adolescent, about the books that crushed his soul, like Van Der Meersch's *Masque de chair*. A pro-Catholic, anti-gay story that he now finds toxic and which made him feel sinful, condemned and depraved when he read it. If only he hadn't identified with the protagonist!

Then he told Massiel in vivid detail about the days and nights he spent alone in his room as a teenager. Described to her the handsome, older businessman he met at a party, who asked him to run away with him to Navacerrada so they could ski and just have some fun. The man said they could leave that very night, a Friday, and stay till Monday. Antonio said yes without hesitating for a second, and of course, his parents raised hell when they learned about his plan. Papá tried to lock him up, and Antonio snuck out in the middle of the night, as he always did. It was all worth the trouble in the end. Antonio loved the sex, the downhill skiing, the food, and everything about this experience.

Papá and Mamá were waiting up for him when he returned, as expected; Papá in his study, ready to pounce on his son; Mamá collapsed in her anteroom recliner, sobbing, with one of her revolting Sphynx cats on her lap. His father rushed to the door the second he heard him come in and started whacking him on the butt with a paddle. A typical form of punishment in many rich families and at his all-boys school: The teachers (most of them priests) would smack students half a dozen times on each hand, palms facing up, for the most insignificant reasons, laughing, talking quietly, looking out a window. Papá, not being heavily built, somehow mustered up the strength to drag Antonio to the young man's room, eyes on fire, and with a gesture of disgust, he told him that such was his castigation: indefinite confinement. Until Antonio asked to be forgiven for his sinful behavior and promised to change...

The servants stayed out of sight whenever his dad punished him, terrified to get in the way of his fists or provoke his wrath. Antonio's beloved nanny, Pilar, would cry and pray for him in her room, finding it hard to believe that a man could inflict so much pain on his son. She'd bring him his meals and books from Papá's library. Thank goodness he had those!

Well, at least Papá didn't take him to a brothel, as so many fathers did in their circle. It occurred to Antonio that maybe his father was gay, turned off by women, and didn't want to feel obligated to provide an example for his son by having sex with a prostitute himself. Could this be true? It would explain the fastidious way he dressed, his occasional effeminate mannerisms. Stereotypical signs, yet valid, nevertheless. Did Papá secretly, maybe even subconsciously, envy Antonio? Perhaps he couldn't bear to see himself reflected in his son, determined as he seemed to beat the gayness out of him so he wouldn't have to see it in himself. An interesting, though not surprising, twist. The closeted, revolting old pansy!

That night following the Navacerrada weekend was a point of no return. The inevitable run-ins with Papá at home became unbearable. Antonio dreaded the moment he'd come home from school or wherever, back to the bitter density of that house—to his mother's silent smiles, always accompanied by a hesitant caress behind Papá's back. She was terrified of him, too.

He started to think about leaving for good. It would be a blessing, not having to look at his father's face again, a countenance that bore a striking resemblance to that of Franco, down to the ridiculous mousy mustache. How proud was Papá to resemble his idol! He was younger and taller than the fascist fiend but had the same paunch, the same awkward demeanor and shrill tone of voice. When he became old enough,

Antonio got to escape that hell, relieved yet sad to have to abandon Mamá. He missed her, worried about her, wanted to take her away from her luxurious prison. Papá didn't abuse her physically, but Antonio had always been Mamá's buffer against his outbursts and his oppressive silences, against his innate violence, which was exacerbated by his drinking—daily, solitary sprees of expensive wine and the usual bar scene with all the other Francoist clones. It mortified Antonio that he couldn't protect his mother anymore. Once settled in his flat, he tried to bring her to live with him several times. Predictably, Mamá refused his offer, claiming she was accustomed to her comforts. He'd promise her she'd still have everything she needed, including a personal maid. But Mamá wasn't budging. And then, when her royal delusions set in, she'd act genuinely concerned about the king (her husband), her subjects (their servants), and the demands of her reign. And she'd allege that she had to rule from her castle, not from some feudal dwelling.

Massiel and Antonio were already living together the last time he attempted to persuade Mamá and get her moved. Massiel welcomed the idea; she suggested that they find a bigger place. At the mansion, Antonio went straight to his mother's plush quarters; fortunately, she recognized him—her beloved prince!—and was happy to see him. Then Papá showed up and asked Antonio courteously (so unlike him) to join him in his office. The fucking liar said there was a financial matter they needed to discuss, and Antonio took the bait, following him there. Papá slammed the door shut and said to his son, "Are you out of your mind, you dumb fairy?! You're going to expose your mother to all your deviant stuff? Shame on you! She belongs here, not in your rathole full of queers and communists! And who'll look after her while you travel, anyway, that bizarre girlfriend of yours, who spends all her time bringing scum to our country?"

Antonio tried to remain calm, keeping his rage at bay, this flood of toxic feelings and emotions that had poisoned his heart for most of his life because of Papá. He wanted to beat his father to a pulp but instead shoved him down into a chair and railed at him, "You and all the other fascist pigs are the real scum in Spain. We should've locked you up to rot away in jail to pay for your crimes! I can't believe you all managed to save your necks thanks to the fucking Amnesty Law. But there's no law that will make people forget what you did, and no god to forgive you." Papá was fuming yet obviously silent out of fear, afraid of his son at last. "Just know that I renounce your legacy," Antonio cried out, glaring at the pathetic josser, "that I want nothing more to do with you!" And now he was surprised to be feeling pity and not contempt for his progenitor. "Fine," he said, "I will allow Mamá to stay here for the time being. But if I find out that you're mistreating her in the slightest way, I swear I'll cut your rotten balls off!"

"We have lots of photos already," I inform Tony. "Shots of the entire city, the people, the houses, the beaches. I'll send you the best ones when I have them developed." He thanks me and says we don't have any good shots of Richard. But he's wrong. I remind him of the pictures of his little boyfriend that I took in his hotel room. "Still," he asks, "how about some more? Richard is an essential part of this island." It's also true that the young man has been a catalyst for Tony. "Without Richard," I tell him, "you wouldn't have had your big existential crisis."

Tony agrees and asks me to please photograph Richard running down the shore at sunset, barefoot, his toes sinking in the sand. Capture him as he absentmindedly looks for pea crabs, or as he listens to the roaring sea inside the pink walls of a conch shell. Richard leaping over rocks left barren, exposed by the low tide, home to mollusks and anemones, slippery from centuries of salt and surf. Photograph him as he takes a deep breath in the sunlight, ripe with longing and desire. The sweat on his brow. His ruffled hair, shiny like lacquer when the morning light hits it at a certain angle. His timid laughter, his rosy cheeks when he blushes. The trace of down on his nipples. His belly button, a tiny crater surrounded by a forest of fine hair. His thighs, terse and tanned. The naturally erect spine. Photograph the water smacking against his chest when he dives in. Photograph Antonio drying him off with a towel as Richard rejoices in his touch. Capture a closeup of Tony kissing the nape of the young man's neck. And Richard laughs, impishly this time, when Tony runs his tongue down his back, savoring the salty droplets that linger on his skin...

"Should we have pictures of Massiel?" I ask Tony. "I mean, imaginary photos like the ones you like to dream up, since I'd never expect her to pose for me. And I wouldn't dare ask her, anyway. I don't think she likes me all that much. True, we've only met once, when you first brought her to Santo Domingo, but the meeting didn't go that great. Massiel wanted to spend quality time with you and was pissed that I kept tagging along. But, hey, I'd make the effort to be friendly and win her over if we ever see each other again..."

"Don't worry," says Tony, "I'm sure Massiel would succumb to your charm if she got to know you better." He pauses. "But it won't happen on this island. She's told me she won't be coming back. And I understand why. Massiel doesn't feel she belongs here."

"She doesn't! That's why I said we can take imaginary pics..."

"Fine," Tony states, "but first let's talk about Vincent."

"What? No! There's nothing to talk about. You know everything about my lover."

Antonio says that's bullshit. "I spill my guts out about Massiel, and you keep your mouth shut about the most important person in your life."

"Well, Tony..." I take my time to respond, "Like you said about your beloved better half, Vincent doesn't belong here. He doesn't exist for me when I'm in Santo Domingo."

Antonio isn't buying my response nor letting go of the topic. "Yes, I can certainly relate to that," he tells me. "But we can't simply erase the world we've forged beyond the Dominican shores. Our lives and the people we love are out there, Paul, waiting for us."

Tony is right, of course. Yet I ask, "Wouldn't it be nice to pretend this is all we have?"

He ponders the question. "Sometimes," he says. "Maybe..."

Silence. "Okay," I say after a pause, "I'm ready to tell you the truth about Vincent!"

"Do you love him?" Tony asks.

"Yes, I do. Very much. And I love the home we've made together. But I'm not attracted to him anymore. Sex with Vincent was exciting the first two years or so. Then he gradually stopped turning me on. And it's not like he's aging badly, no, he still has his Napa Valley white boy good looks.

He stays in shape, works out in our home gym, and we ride our bikes together at least twice a week. No, in fact he's sexier and more youthful than me. The problem, I'd say, is routine, familiarity. Boredom! I suspect that happens to a lot of married people and couples who've been together for a long time. Although you and Massiel are the exception, it seems, since your sex life is still going strong. I've never seen a relationship like yours."

"Ironically," Tony remarks, "that's all that remains between us now, great sex."

He's wrong, I'm sure, and so I tell him: "The kind of love you and Massiel feel for one another never goes away. It might change, but it doesn't die."

"Thank you for saying that, Paul."

"It's the truth, darling, and you know it..."

Back to Vincent, something else I must mention to Tony: "He puts up with my moods, my screwing around, my traveling, and never makes any demands. I love Vincent, always will, but I resent him for being such a doormat. No backbone whatsoever. You'd probably say that our relationship isn't healthy or fair to him, that I must put an end to it. And I agree. But I can't leave him. I'd be afraid for him. Vincent has made sure I know he wouldn't survive our separation. He'd rather die than live without me. What a trip!"

Tony suggests I prepare my partner slowly for our breakup. I suspect that's what Massiel is doing in his case, prepping him for the end. He says I should loosen Vincent's leash little by little, encourage him to see other people and make his own friends. My reaction: "Fat chance! Vincent has made it abundantly clear that he has no interest in sleeping with anyone else and doesn't want friends of his own. He'd rather have me with all my baggage and my disinterest in bed than not at all. So, there it is: the truth and nothing but the truth. Heavy shit, no?"

Massiel proposed a deal right after they moved in together: Antonio could keep having his flings, as long as she could have hers, too. Her relationship with Pedro and all her other friends would continue to be part of her life. An open relationship was what she suggested, and Antonio accepted her terms. He'd accept anything so as not to lose her.

Not long after that, on a Sunday, Massiel told him she'd been observing him, specifically the way he looked at some men. His eyes seemed to rage as they tried to savor and consume every inch of their bodies. She brought up that time in their favorite *mesón* on Calle Jorge Juan, when a super-mod, hot-as-hell guy walked in, and Antonio instantly became hypnotized by the rocking motion of his butt cheeks, by the shape of his basket. "Antonio, please," she'd said, "could you stop acting so horny for at least an hour? It's embarrassing, you know." He told her that a gaze never killed anyone, that the eyes were meant to take pleasure in beauty. "Don't you look at some people that way, too?" he asked her. And she replied, "Yes, of course I do, but not when we're out together!" Antonio realized he'd been typically self-indulgent, focused solely on his needs. He could be so fucking oblivious! He promised her he'd only have eyes for her from then on. "Sure," she said, laughing. "Then I'd better get you a good pair of blinders!"

Years later, another Sunday, Massiel brought up their *splintered* lives (what she called it now!) and made a confession: "I'm not as modern as we thought, Antonio. Not sure I can keep living as we do, going from this to that, from them to us. Why do we have to be intimate with so many other people? I wish I understood that drive, that impulse of ours. It's a need that can never be satisfied, it seems, that keeps us searching for the next conquest, the next orgasm." Antonio was dumbfounded. She had never been this open about her feelings! "Some nights," she went on, "I lie awake thinking about us, asking myself if our relationship stands a chance, if it can survive the onslaught of challenges and tests we subject it to. Or is this the only way we can stay together, by pretending that we don't long for stability?"

Ironically, what Antonio wished for and needed from Massiel was commitment. He sometimes fantasized about the two of them being exclusive, maybe even married, even though he knew that such a lifestyle could never work. Marriage and monogamy were just not in the picture for either of them. Yet suddenly, Massiel seemed to be riddled with doubt. He tried to offer his views on this so-called impulse of theirs. "The answer, I think, is both very simple and immensely complex," he declared. "Sex is our way of filling the existential void. It keeps us from having to face the abyss."

"So... sex is our version of religion, then? A religion with neither a god nor a savior. Maybe so. But does that mean we're destined to always live our lives in a crowd?"

"No, Massiel, we're not. We're free to live the way we choose," he told her. "You're the one who demanded our freedom from day one. You've always believed that our bond is strong enough to withstand the weight of other lovers."

"I know," she said, "and I'm still sure it is. But don't you ever long for solitude, Antonio? Days by yourself, in silence, with no one around. Not even me..."

"Yes, I do at times," he replied, unsure of what else to say. Then he tried to veer from the subject and described his fascination with spring, that tangible time of rainfall and blossoms but also spring in its essence and symbolism. "Could we on together," he asked her, "seeing our relationship as a place where the essence of love can always bloom again, sprouting, persistently growing, breaking through the crowds and the weeds in our lives? Where romance can be a constant rebirth?" But Massiel didn't react to his forcedly poetic suggestion. Symbolic spring? Rebirth? *Please!*

Shitty Sundays. Days of painful truths. It was a Sunday when Massiel reproached him for not showing more interest in her career. And he didn't know what to tell her, how to justify his sheer apathy—no, it was more like disdain—toward the law profession. He should've spoken the truth, that the world of lawyers terrified him. Because the Law upheld by many attorneys had been implacable with men like Antonio. Because, in many cases, lawyers were motivated by money or a political agenda, not justice. Yes, Antonio was aware that the work Massiel did was important, not driven by personal gain. Even so, she was part of that reality. That's why he could never ask her specific questions nor have her describe exactly what she'd studied, how she'd prepared to be an attorney. He did know that one of her biggest challenges was dealing with embassies. Lots of red tape and hurdles and headaches. The only aspect of her job he found of interest were some of the clients she took on and fought for—such brave people!

He promised her he'd try from now on to involve himself in her professional life and to learn about it. (More broken promises!) She looked at him—that stare of hers that felt like a dagger sometimes—and said it sounded like a handout, a favor. Any effort on his part in this regard would be an act he'd perform for her benefit, and she didn't want his charity.

Massiel admitted she was still interested in staying with him. Such was the word she used! *Interested.* Antonio didn't tell her that the first time they made love, he began to envision her as the beginning of his real story. Sadly, after all the years that followed, they'd continue to live in separate inner worlds. And, so, eventually, he started to foresee this tragedy that's crushing him today (he's being melodramatic, so what.) This moment in front of a picture window, blinded by the neon, while he observes the labored breathing of someone sleeping in their bed. Someone who'll offer him companionship for a few hours and then disappear. He or she might leave a note scribbled on a yellow pad by the bed, thanking him. But Massiel will leave no word behind.

That Sunday, he realized how lonely one can feel sleeping with strangers who occupy a soulmate's side of the bed. How physically and mentally exhausted one can be after a day of writing or a day of inertia, lungs burning from too much smoking, the mind dealing with the same old traumas—all of them magnified by the loved one's absence.

There's no problem, Antonio tells Alain. You can come with me (pun intended.) Pas de problème! Yes, I know Madrid like the palm of my hand, but I won't bore you with descriptions of the city. Better just take you to my favorite taverns in Lavapiés, to decadent boites on the Gran Vía, to the dark corners of Retiro Park where I lost my virginity. We'll drive around the Plaza de Cibeles, the quintessential symbol of Madrid, so you can take in the marble statues, the fountains, and visit with the goddess, Doña Cibeles. And I'll show you the Puerta del Sol, the busiest spot in the capital, which is burdened with way too much history—it dates back to the fifteenth century! And of course, we'll visit the Prado.

Yes, I'll offer you my Sunday, an empty day that was threatening to crush me. After downing two carafes of sangría, we'll go to my flat. Did I tell you about it already? Probably so; I tend to repeat myself. It's an air-conditioned apartment on Calle Preciados with a spacious bedroom, an ample dining room, servant's quarters that we use for storage, and a long hallway leading to a balcony with a view of the busy, lively street. Massiel and I enjoy cleaning the place ourselves, listening to music. We both like to vacuum. I hate to dust, and she hates doing the toilets. So, we take turns. Yes, we could afford a maid, but if we had one, there'd be one less reason to revisit our LPs together—classical stuff by Bach, Mozart, Chopin, Debussy, Tchaikovsky, boleros by the Mexican trio Los Panchos, a few jotas, some cante jondo, engaging socialist tunes by the group Jarcha, poetic songs from Joan Manuel Serrat. And the complete Pepa Flores (Marisol) collection out of loyalty to Pepa, who's been so vocal against the Fascist Beast, though they only listen to her wonderful 1976 album, *Háblame del mar, marinero.*

Alain has never heard of any of that music, except for Mozart, which comes as no surprise. So, why did Antonio waste his time telling him about it? He quickly changes the subject. There's a bottle of sherry at home, he tells the Frenchman. It's the real stuff, made in Jerez de la Frontera. But we should pick up more booze along the way. If you get hungry, you'll find orange juice, whole milk, some air-cured Serrano ham, Manchego cheese, butter, eggs, maybe a treat like chocolate ice cream in the icebox. And there are always fresh pastries (mostly palmeras, my weakness) in the cupboards.

Alain wants to make sure he's not intruding. Antonio is emphatic about this: No, no. Massiel wouldn't care; in fact, she'd give a thumbs-up to your visit. We have an open relationship with no secrets. We're both free-spirited folks, very modern—postmodern, preferably—and cool and hip. Aren't you fucking impressed? But I should warn you, she might show up in the middle of the night; that happens sometimes. When she finds us in bed, she'll go to the couch. And there'll be no questions asked in the morning. We will quietly set out to meet the day's obligations, Massiel to defend some Arab or Sudaca immigrant in court (did I mention she's a lawyer?) and me, well, to work on my latest project at my favorite café on the Plaza Mayor. We'll meet up here in the late evening. She'll plop down in the rocking chair and kick her shoes off. I'll serve her a glass of wine, and we'll have a light dinner of cold cuts and cheese. Then it's off to bed, where she'll review some deposition, and I'll read fiction till I fall asleep.

In case you're wondering, yes, she brings a hookup to our place on occasion, especially her women friends, although she prefers to go to their homes. She believes I'm not as tolerant of her flings and torrid romances as she is of mine, which is true. Massiel used to be curious about the people I fucked, and wanted to meet them. But not anymore. It takes too much energy, she says. And I'm partly at fault. I've had too many meaningless affairs that started to all look the same to her. At least Massiel made the effort for a time, whereas I never had the slightest interest in the people she had sex with. There have been a few exceptions, women and men she made sure I got to meet and know intimately. But she hasn't shared her lovers with me in a while. It works better for us this way, keeping the world out of our private space, our inner sanctum.

So, no problem, Alain. I'm glad we hooked up. I wasn't expecting it today. Don't worry. I won't fill your head with my Sartrean funk, the same old existentialist crap. Life has no meaning; existence is absurd. Yet, freedom, a great responsibility, can help us escape meaninglessness... No, I won't describe this impulse that seizes me some days, to feel the final vertigo out a window on top of the world. An urge I've always managed to repress in the end. Hey, but I'm doing exactly what I said I wouldn't do! Come over here—he tells Alain. Let me kiss your long fingers and lick the fine hair on them, taking a deep drag off the cig they're holding. Let me see myself in your blue eyes, run my lips down your chest and remove the silver chain around your neck. Let me sink into your body, even though I have no idea who you are...

"I assume Massiel will be able to speak for herself in this book you're writing," I tell Tony. "She deserves to have her own voice, not just your perception and depiction of her character." He agrees. "Yes, Paul, and it just so happens," he informs me, "that she recently offered to record some of her feelings and thoughts on tape. Massiel admitted she hadn't been as communicative as I had regarding our relationship, and a machine would perhaps make it easier for her to open up. So, she recorded several cassettes that I got to listen to eventually, enjoying her crisp, colorful Murcia accent; taking breaks to ponder the content. She didn't expect me to play shrink, though. Her hope was that I'd get to know how she truly felt about certain things..."

Antonio has listened to these tapes too many times. They have become an obsession, some sort of catharsis. But also and mostly a way of pleasuring himself, of being caressed by Massiel's voice. He has memorized every word, tone, and inflection. Every posited idea. Yet, here he is again, pressing Play. Pause. Stop. Fast-forward...

Very well, Antonio. So, this is my attempt at expressing my thoughts and feelings. I hope it turns out to be helpful. Okay, the first thought in my mind has to do with a film we saw last year, KOYAANISQATSI. In the Hopi language, that means life out of balance, a state of crisis that requires the arrival of a new condition. That's how I perceive our relationship these days. My problem is... I can't envision a desired new condition for us. Can you? How to describe this emotion that overwhelms me sometimes? Is it fear? Yes! Fear of living without you. A thought paralyzes me when I'm away from our nest: that you might not be there when I return. I imagine an alternate universe where I'm sharing my life with someone else. And the only fact that chases away that grim vision is that alternate universes don't exist...

He'll skip this topic for now—too painful—and fast-forward to the part about Massiel's "perfect" family, a subject he can easily handle. Hard to believe that it's taken Massiel this long to open up about her relatives!

I do have a relatively happy, perfect family. We must seem ideal compared to the broken, violent home you grew up in, Antonio. I admit that some of my reasons for griping about my parents are petty. Like the fact that they're stuck in a rut, resigned to their routines, their rituals, unmotivated to make the slightest change in their lives. My sisters, too. One example of many: every Friday afternoon, they all must have tapas at the corner bar with the neighbors. You're not allowed to miss it. If you refuse to join the group, they'll gossip about you. I've heard from one of my sisters (the one I feel the closest to) some of the things they've said about me, that I'm prickly, stuck-up. It makes me so angry! It's true that I've always been an outsider in Murcia, and I admit there's something alluring in that distance, that cultural disconnect.

So, about my parents... I think they do love each other, but they had endless arguments about religion when I was growing up. You see, my mother loves the church, whereas Papá is an atheist who wanted to cast out all religious ideas and practices from our home. It's a wonder those two got along at all! An odd yet not atypical pairing in our country, more so with their generation. Papá never got his way, unfortunately. My sisters and I were baptized, took communion regularly as children, and attended catechism classes, all of it against our dad's will. My sisters are still very much into it, but obviously, I take after our father. He and I have always gotten along great. I love that sweet, kind-hearted man! The holier-than-thou members of the tapas group are surprised that my dad is such a good person, considering his lack of faith and his rejection of religion. Oh, yes, of course, because only Christians can be good, right? So, there you are, another kink in that perfect image: my parents' relationship.

And now, about my mother... She's a devoted parent, but also traditional to the core. I know she's always intuited that there's something "peculiar" about me. The passion I used to express toward the girls I befriended, classmates of mine, for instance. The casual, "libertine" way I behaved around men, the informal manner in which I dated them. I tried to toe the line and be a good girl like my sisters as much as possible. But sometimes, I just couldn't take Mamá's pious obsessions, her concerns about gossip and reputation. In time, I stopped trying to please her. And then, when I moved to Madrid to go to school (with Papa's blessing but against Mamá's "better judgment"), I felt free at last to be myself. Nothing in my world has ever met with my mother's approval. Certainly not my job, which in her opinion, should be paying me more considering the expensive education I got. And definitely not the people I socialize with. Mamá seems to like you, for a change, although she wishes you weren't an unbeliever. She knows but chooses not to acknowledge that we've been living together—in sin!—all these years. I think Mamá still hopes and prays that you and I get hitched. Oh, if she knew me for real, deeply and completely, she'd probably have a heart attack. The poor woman!

Again, don't be alarmed—he tells Alain—if you hear steps late into the night, someone stumbling in the dark. Or if you sense a person's breathing magnified by the silence. It's only Massiel enacting a typical scene... She takes her shoes off before opening the front door, can't find the keyhole, gets frustrated, and finally gets the key in after several tries. She feels nauseous, a sour taste of booze and sex in her mouth. She makes her way to the bathroom, washes her face, brushes her teeth. She undresses and unties her hair, and her long mane falls freely on her shoulders. The pale light through the window illuminates her silhouette: tremulous yet with irrepressible energy. Feeling slightly revived, she walks to the kitchen and serves herself a glass of water. Then she comes straight to the bedroom and, realizing I have company, goes to the couch. Tomorrow morning, after a shower, she'll find her day's outfit in the armoire outside our bedroom. She'll get dressed, grab some coffee, and leave for work early so she doesn't have to meet you. Nothing against you, Alain. She just doesn't want to deal with my hookups anymore.

Once she's gone, you'll want to make love again, the two of us still sweaty under the sheets. You'll explore my body with your lips. I'll keep my eyes closed as you seize my erection, savor it, bite it. Afterward, I'll run my fingers through your hair, damp with your sweat and my cum, and smile at you gratefully. Then you'll rest your head on the pillow and doze off.

You won't tell me yet that your backpack is all the luggage you have, that in your belt bag, you carry a passport with a tourist visa soon to expire. You'll keep that info for later, when you think you've won my gratitude for the burning heat of your hams. Then you'll say you wish to stay in Madrid for a while; it wouldn't be good for you to return home right now. Things aren't going well for you there. And you like this city, its unpretentious vibe. You wonder if I could help you to get settled here, maybe find a job. You're willing to offer your services to select clients, although you didn't hook up with me for that reason, no, no. In France, you charge a lot because you're that good. But that's not the way you make a living; you only do it when you're strapped for cash. You've had a full-time job as a clerk in a department store for some time now. Not very stimulating or challenging, though you've gotten to meet some interesting people. The thing is, you can't stand doing that kind of work anymore, and you hate your boss. Anyway, what matters to you most are your studies at the College of Art because you're hoping to be a graphic designer someday. That is, if you can get your act together...

Antonio grabs another cassette, the one where Massiel launches into a tirade against Mother Nature. He loves the anger and rage in her voice, the passion she exudes about this topic... *Yes, my love, we did agree from day one to make sure not to get pregnant. We wouldn't make good parents. Too busy and narcissistic to be able to provide for little ones. And we don't want to bestow this pathetic, polluted world on our descendants. Yes, our decision flies in the face of the misogynistic laws of our country regarding women's reproductive rights. I can't believe it's the 1980s. It seems we're still living in the Franco Dark Ages!*

No, we don't need to increase Spain's population. No, terminating a pregnancy in the early stages of gestation is not committing murder. Yes, women should have the right to decide in all cases! If I got pregnant, I'd have to break the law to get an abortion or have it done abroad. Thankfully, that's not something I need to worry about because the year I turned twenty-eight, as you well know, I decided to stop my period. Couldn't take that monthly bleeding anymore. And fortunately, I didn't need to have surgery for it, just the right pills. I started menstruating when I was twelve, so by then, I'd been suffering that curse (and it really is a curse, believe me) for sixteen years. What's that all about, anyway? Getting ourselves ready for procreative slavery even before we've discovered sex? No more! That has to end.

You'd probably say that "slavery" is too big a word, too historically loaded. And I would agree. How about calling it procreative "obligation" instead? Women shouldn't be made to feel guilty, flawed—unnatural!—if they refuse to fulfill that obligation. They shouldn't be expected to perform a societal script that calls for them to act maternal if that role doesn't suit them.

The concept of procreation is distressing to me, Antonio. You know that. But I've never told you that I get depressed whenever I see a pregnant woman. There's nothing joyful about it for me. What I see is a person who's been turned into a receptacle, an incubator, regardless of whether they wanted children or not, or whether they enjoyed the sex that led to the pregnancy or not. What I see is a human being reduced to a demeaning, utilitarian function. I'm not into cussing as much as you are, but in this case, I feel like crying out, Nature, you fucking monster! That goddam monster embodies the Jungian archetype of the Terrible Mother, not that of her twin, the Great Mother. Because that's what nature is, a terrible parent who pays no mind to the suffering it inflicts on its female children, programming them to think that they want—that they need!—the experience of motherhood. It has slyly written this impulse into our genes to force us to perpetuate our species. Fuck the human species! It can go to hell if, in order to continue existing, it'll force me to carry a baby in my belly for nine months and then subject me to the horrific pain of childbirth and breastfeeding. We need to make sure the human race doesn't become extinct, right? Fine, then, let babies be conceived and grown in test tubes and labs!

Nature has given us women the rotten end of this evolutionary deal. It should be acceptable in lower mammals but not in beings capable of creative and analytical thinking, beings who write books, make art, build cities, and invent flying machines. Human females deserve better than that. But, hey, we started out as primordial goo, and here we are. So, if someone like me exists today (and there are many others), then there's a chance we might evolve away from this procreative slavery...

Suddenly, Alain gets on an existential trip (his turn), says he doesn't know what he'll do with his life. "Tout m'est égal," he confesses. Antonio doesn't feel like playing shrink, but he'll try to be benevolent. The blind leading the blind! So, he tells Alain in Spanish, "I'm sure you can envision your future, a good future, my friend, but you have to make the effort to imagine it and then forge it." Alain doesn't understand; too complex a statement for his rudimentary Spanish. Antonio isn't in the mood for speaking French; he's still dealing with a hangover. They'll just have to communicate in a mixture of the two languages, with lots of code-switching on Antonio's part. "Je suis encore un peu ivre," he remarks, "comme le bateau de Rimbaud." Of course, Alain has no idea what *bateau ivre* he's talking about—a drunken boat?!—nor who the fuck is Rimbaud. "C'est la verité," the Frenchman insists. "Rien m'importe." And Antonio tells him that we all get tired of life at some point. "Take me, for example: I've been telling myself for years that some fucking day everything will make sense. Time has passed, and I'm still extending my deadlines. By such and such a date... Then the awaited day rolls around, and I realize I'm fooling myself, because I have to be the one who changes, not the world. I must take the reins of my existence. But, hey, so far I've lived an exciting life, for the most part, and that should count."

Alain reacts: "Je crois que non. Sans sense et sans but nous n'avons pas raison d'être. J'ai jamais trouvé mon but, et c'est pourquoi je vais me tuer ici, nue comme la Monroe." Fuck! What a damn nihilist the Frenchie has turned out to be. Who would've thought? Welcome to the club, mon ami! He just announced that, since his life has no meaning or purpose, he's going to commit suicide right here, in the nude, just like Marilyn. Well, at least he knows who Marilyn Monroe is!

Antonio is certain that Alain is just venting, having found someone who can relate to his existential woes. (Again, the ludic god of *Rayuela* bringing two fucking nihilists together!) He offers Alain a cup of freshly brewed coffee. The young man gulps it down, not caring that it's piping hot, and now he seems more relaxed. "Please don't kill yourself," Antonio says to him as lovingly as he can. "Wouldn't you rather have sex instead?" In a dramatic gesture, Alain shuts his eyes and gently massages his temples. "Your freckles are cute," Antonio observes, and Alain reacts by saying that he adores Antonio's mustache, that he'd love to lick it. Antonio asks him if doing so would distract him from his dark, suicidal thoughts, and Alain says it would. Antonio's request: "Go for it, then. Eat my whole face if you need to!"

He wouldn't dare tell Alain that he doesn't really want to get to know him, that he's only a hot body and a freckled face, a smile, a foreign accent. They exchange more pleasantries, and Antonio breaks the news to him: "I'm going on a business trip tomorrow, my friend, to the Caribbean. I'll be reporting on an important cultural event in Santo Domingo. Will be gone for a month or so." Alain asks him about his work. "I freelance as a journalist for *Cuadernos Culturales*, a prestigious Spanish magazine," Antonio tells him. And then he says, after an awkward pause, "You're sexy and charming, Alain. I would've enjoyed spending more time with you. But duty calls! I've got a lot packing to do. Here, take this money, enough for a month's rent at your hostel. No, you can't stay in my flat while I'm gone. Massiel wouldn't be okay with that. Yes, we might see each other again. I'm jotting down my phone number for you. Keep in touch, d'accord? Au revoir! I'm sorry you feel sad. I do, too. Ah, yes, a farewell kiss..."

Antonio can't help himself. He'll press the Play button again and again. This time he'll fast-forward to Massiel talking about a topic that cuts deep. He needs to be brave and face the truth of her feelings...

I know you're not all that interested in my work, Antonio, and I get your reasons. Lucky for you, I do want to be involved in your career. It's exciting for me to witness your creative process, to read your many drafts and offer you suggestions. It's sweet of you to take them seriously, considering I'm not a literary person. Fundamentally, I have no use for words, yet you feel lost without them, lost without your constant verbiage. Sorry. That sounded insulting. Let me just add that I love those days when your presence is felt, not heard. Those nights when words aren't needed to kindle or enhance our pleasure. I love to let our bodies speak, skin to skin, but also heart to heart.

I understand that you need to share with me your thoughts and feelings. But you forget that the concerns and tribulations of writers are too unsettling for me. Writers seem to have it as their mission to undo the fabric of reality, seeking the gaps, the cracks, the holes in society. They can't leave the world alone. Yet that's all I want in my personal life: to be left alone. Which doesn't mean I'm not willing and eager to listen to your thoughts, to your ideas. Which doesn't mean I'd never want to discuss our relationship.

While on that subject, let's talk about who we are as bisexual beings. A topic that I know excites you. Yes, we both see gay desire as part of human nature, inherent in all people and powerfully manifested in some of us. I've always owned up to my attraction to a certain type: the strong, empowered career woman. Someone like me? That's the type that turns me on, yes. I know you abhor the hackneyed language of sex because it verges on pornography, yet there are two precise words to describe how such a woman can make me feel: hot and wet. It's the way I get when you eat me and plunge into me with your tongue and your indefatigable erection. I admit I love that rush. Am I addicted to it? You'd say that sex is simply my way of postponing the abyss. That's your philosophy of promiscuity, the existential justification for our addiction.

You've met some of my "lady friends," as you jokingly like to call them, and you slept with a few. They turned you on because they reminded you of Massiel, true? Thank you, my love. I suppose you could say I'm narcissistic, desiring people who resemble me in some essential ways, discarding alterity, and longing to possess a mirror reflection. Ultimately, isn't homosexual love, in essence, an act of narcissism? At any rate, this conversation is not about gay desire or... what's that term? Ah, yes, our polymorphous perverse nature. It's about our needs and fantasies and fleeting affairs vis-à-vis our relationship. It's about Antonio and Massiel...

We must bring calm to our chaos, Antonio. We must transition to a new form because the old one has exhausted its promise. But what could that next condition in our lives possibly be?

Okay, picture the following scenario—described, I hope, in your style. And please forgive me for claiming to sound like you, Antonio. I may not be able to "analyze" and "deconstruct" your writing, but I'm proud to have been your sounding board, your muse, your biggest fan.

So, we decide to spend our last weekend together in a beachfront condo in Santo Domingo. The trip offers us picture-perfect, travel-brochure romanticism. You carry me in your arms down the flowered path. I point out, in ecstasy, the cloudless blue skies, the seagulls, the palm trees, the whitewashed stucco, the saline smell impregnating nooks and crannies. I'm excited to be here, in our private Eden, even now as we prepare to say goodbye to the lovers we've been, as we pretend this isn't our most crucial scene ever, the turning point. Nothing seems out of place. The throw pillows crowding the floor quickly warm up to our bodies. The wicker chairs are as regal as always. We delight in the stunning view from our picture window. Then, before we swim out to the lighthouse, you tell me you want to be a heroic fisherman who'll save me from a sea monster, and I'll go along with your fantasy.

Once there, we make love, still out of breath from the swim. You ask: Couldn't we stay together for this? And I say, No, we can't. Because there are too many people in this relationship, Antonio. There's a crowd taking up space in our home, our heads, our hearts, our bed. Because now I must make room for me. I need everyone to leave so I can breathe...

Tony asks what I fear the most, other than death, and I reply at once that I'm not afraid of anything. He says he knows I'm terrified of AIDS. "Yes, you're right," I declare after a painful pause, "but what's the point of dwelling on that stuff? Deadly viruses, the high risk of infection in the gay community, dying friends, the blame we're having to deal with, on top of everything else. Enough! Give me a break from the sadness, the tragedy of it all, please!"

I ask Antonio about *his* biggest fear and immediately add, "Wait, I know. Your biggest fear is losing Massiel." He nods in agreement and describes to me one of his recurring dreams, the most pleasant one... "Massiel and I live on a deserted island. We sleep in a humble abode with a thatched roof and feed off the wondrous, exotic plants that grow there, a regimen of fruit and nuts and vegetables. We don't miss anyone because we have each other..."

I burst out laughing. Can't help it. His pastoral, Adam-and-Eve trip is just too funny. "It's a sweet dream," I tell him. "And you might make it happen. As long as I can bring you a barrel of meat-heavy caldo gallego once a month, when you get sick of your vegan regimen. Oh, and a couple of Cristóbal boys to supplement your hetero diet, too!" He thanks me sarcastically for ruining his reverie. I apologize, "Sorry, but I'd rather hear the truth, not some corny *bon savage* fantasy. Just like you demanded it of me regarding my marriage."

"Okay, Paul," he says. "You deserve my honesty, as patient as you are with my rigmaroles. The thing is, Massiel didn't see me off at the airport, and she hasn't called me every day like she does when I'm traveling. Not a word from her. Yet I'm sure she knows I'm down in the dumps. We can always sense how the other one is feeling, no matter how far apart we are. Massiel has a touch, a way to center me when I'm facing the abyss. Because our bond isn't solely about laughter and pleasure. It's about the psychic pain, too. Or it used to be..."

I offer Tony a shoulder to cry on, but he claims my shoulder is for nights of binge drinking, whereas Massiel's is for nights of emptiness. "Well, at least I have my memories of her," he says after a long, meditative silence. "Memories that we can reimagine as photographs." He pauses again. "Thanks for humoring me, Paul, for allowing me to let Massiel be part of this moment, even though she doesn't exist in this place. For now, we'll picture her face from multiple angles: high cheekbones, almond-shaped eyes, her light brown hair loose, down to her waist. We'll get closer with the mind's lens and zoom in on her knowing smile, on her closed eyes while she sits quietly, meditating. Let's capture her bursting with energy and glee as in those days when we'd explore Madrid on foot, cracking jokes and laughing in secret at some of the people we ran into. I'd say to her, Massiel, please let's stay together forever, even after we die. Could we? We'll haunt people's bedrooms like horny ghosts! And she'd react with an outburst of laughter and a kiss." Another silence. "But we don't laugh together anymore, Paul. I'll try to say something silly, crack a joke, make a funny face to get her usual reaction, "¡Qué majo el chico!" And she doesn't even notice me. It's as if I had become invisible..."

I hug him and tell him that now, more than ever, he needs to write about Massiel. "You have the seed of a profound book in that relationship, Antonio, the essence of an honest, heartfelt story. Your first real piece of writing!" Tony gives me a forlorn smile. "Good advice," he says. "I will definitely try. But, for now, I'll just tell it to you, my sweet friend. Thank you for letting me narrate myself out of the pain, shifting constantly between the past and the present in search of a future that doesn't exist. Let me have one last cry before the gods cut the umbilical cord..."

He wanders aimlessly through Madrid until his feet begin to hurt. At the Moncloa metro station, he bumps into a man sprawled on the stairs, evidently drunk. That could have been Antonio if he hadn't found Massiel. And it could be him, today, if she leaves. But there's nothing he can do to stop her from seeking the solitude she needs. Not this time. Not anymore.

Instead of taking the subway (what line? which direction? why?), he decides to walk to the Retiro, and there he sits on a bench to watch the sun setting far away. It's a perfectly round, honey-colored sun. So beautiful. Like candy melting in his mouth.

Third Act
(of many)

Elena

She's missing the latest episode of *Lost Love of My Youth*, her favorite telenovela, because she has to tend to Luis. Poor baby. He has a bad cold and feels achy. No fever, though, thank God. She's tempted to have him watch the show with her, but she'd better not; she wouldn't be able to focus and have a good laugh. Luis thinks that she takes telenovelas seriously, and it's the opposite! She finds them hilarious; that's why she likes them. He doesn't get why she chuckles in certain parts, scenes that would seem serious and even tragic to most viewers. And it's because the situations are so unrealistic, the storylines so dense and unbelievable, that she can't help thinking it's all supposed to be a comedy. She imagines the writers trying to outdo each other with the plot twists and the big secrets, the betrayals, the unrequited love, the illicit affairs.

Elena didn't get an education beyond high school, but she knows when a program has artistic value. And there's absolutely no art in the soaps. Luis hates them, yet he's fallen trap to their allure. He sits with her to watch an episode now and then, claiming to do it to keep her company, but he ends up getting caught up in the ridiculous plots. Sometimes he'll make a comment about some of the actors, how they all speak without a Dominican accent even if the show is made here. And the women are blonde and beautiful like models, and the men have perfect hair, like the photos on the covers of fashion magazines.

It's a good thing that Luis isn't very interested in television, but Elena wonders why he doesn't like movies either, especially not the ones with lots of action. This is unusual for a young man. Good for him! Luis says he prefers the theater because it's entertaining, but it also makes you think. She's gone to the theater with him a couple of times but hasn't really enjoyed the experience: sitting with strangers in the dark to watch people enact fragments of life on a stage, sometimes terribly serious and even intimate scenes! Elena is a homebody; she prefers to watch her shows in her cozy living room. Luis shouldn't be spending money on theater tickets, anyway; they're so expensive. And he shouldn't be watching telenovelas, either. He's too smart to believe that the world is as crazy as in those shows, yet she can tell they've influenced his thinking. He's been weaving a story about his father that sounds too much like *Lost Love of My Youth*.

Elena hasn't told him the whole truth about that man, setting him straight once and for all, because she fears her son's judgment. Luis tends to be critical of everybody yet is unable to accept criticism himself, especially when it comes to his work at the Cristóbal. Don't anyone dare reproach him for making lots of money as a male prostitute! That's exactly what he is, yes, a *prostitute*. It breaks her heart that Luis thinks he needs to sell his body to make a living. She would give up all her comforts, their two-bedroom house in the quaint Arboleda neighborhood with its beautiful mint-green façade, its colonial-style balcony featuring fancy grille work, the television set, her appliances, the food she can buy with no regard for prices. All of it, yes, she'd do without it so Luis didn't work at that hotel anymore and went back to school.

What could she say to Luis about his father? She'd start by stating that she's not a victim. No, Alessandro didn't take advantage of her, as so many men are known to do. He was a young Italian man who'd come here to take a summer course on Caribbean culture at the Autónoma. She met him at the beach and, after getting to know him, she decided that good-natured Italiano would be the ideal candidate for the amazing project she was about to undertake. She loved Alessandro's gentle manners, his alabaster skin, his dimples, his silky light brown hair. He was good enough at Spanish for them to be able to communicate, though occasionally, he'd stumble on certain words and start rattling off in Italian. Very funny! And incomprehensible!

Alessandro taught her phrases that he ended up including in his letters. *Ti amerò per sempre*, I'll love you forever. *Tu sei il più grande amore della mia vita*, You're the greatest love of my life. *Non dimenticherò mai voi*, I will never forget you. He wrote his missives in a mixture of both languages, and she always understood the sentiment, his youthful declarations of eternal love. Those few sentences she learned from him ended up telling a true story about her feelings and emotions toward him. She chose Alessandro because she liked his character, his sense of humor, his openheartedness. And, because she desired his body. He would rid Elena of her virginity and make it possible for her to experience the pleasure she hadn't known yet. More importantly, he'd give her a child. Elena didn't wish to become his wife, didn't believe in marriage, nor in the prospect of creating an extended family. She was willing to go against society and the teachings of her church to become a parent. Did she grow to love Alessandro? Definitely. Did she fall in love with him? Probably, though she didn't know it then.

Later, there would be other men who satisfied her cravings, but they didn't mean much to Elena, not as much as Alessandro. She's enjoyed a vigorous sex life indeed, always taking the necessary precautions. And even so, how lucky she was that she never got pregnant again. God knew she didn't want more children; what mattered more to her than sex was having and raising her son. Some of her close friends told her it wasn't a good idea to place so much hope and faith in this one single experience. They asked her to at least consider having a stable romantic involvement. Not to get married, since she was opposed to it, but maybe sharing her life with a loving partner who'd help her raise Luisi. But Elena didn't deviate from her goal for an instant. No one and nothing could change her mind.

And now she wonders, sometimes, if she's being punished for wanting to fulfill her dream. God punishes without stick nor stone, as the proverb goes. The kind of "work" that Luis has ended up doing...is that God's way of telling her that she's committed a great sin? No! She takes comfort in knowing that the Lord is too kind and merciful for that to be true. He had given her a gift, the life she brought into the world. The greatest gift of all.

She'll be direct with Luis. No narrative tangles and no twists. She'll simply say, Listen, mijo, your father was a sweet young man just like you. His name was Alessandro. He wanted to marry me and take me to live with him in Florence, where he was from, after a romantic honeymoon around the world. My parents liked him, found him fun to be with, honest, sincere, affectionate. And yet I turned him down! Yes, I broke his heart, said *Arrivederci* instead of *Ti sposerò*. I didn't answer his letters and never told him I was pregnant with his child.

How's that for a telenovela plot? No, it wouldn't work. No stereotypes and the wrong message for young female viewers: a woman who shuns marriage and the prospect of having a traditional family, with no thought given to how she might support herself and her child. A woman who wants to take charge of her life, who doesn't need a man to feel complete, even if he has the potential for being a good partner. A woman who longs for a baby, not a husband.

That story would fit into the soaps universe only if the main female character were punished in the most outrageous, melodramatic way. And not by God, unless she was a nun. But thank goodness life is not a melodrama, even if sometimes it may resemble one. A telenovela family wouldn't have received the news of Elena's pregnancy with open arms, the way Jacinto and Emilia did. Theirs wasn't the typical reaction most Dominican parents would have, facing this situation. They expressed concern about the criticism their daughter would have to face, and they brought up the challenges that lay ahead for her as a single parent. But Mamá and Papá didn't find shame in what she'd done. Their only disappointment was that Alessandro wouldn't be part of their family, for she ended up telling them he was the father. Aside from that, they'd have only love to pour over her Luisi. Such wonderful grandparents!

Jacinto wasn't at all like so many men in this country, people who believe you should defend your honor and reputation, and who condemn women for seeking their happiness without submitting to anyone's rules. He talked about the evils of patriarchy; Elena learned the concept from him. Although he only had a grade school education and a menial job as a mason, Papá was an avid reader of books on history and politics. He called himself an "autodidact."

Emilia was also exceptional. A secretary at the construction company where her husband worked, she took no crap from any of the racist machos there. It's a wonder she managed to keep her job! No, neither Emilia nor Jacinto let racism hold them back. Ay, that ridiculous shades-of-African hierarchy that rules in Santo Domingo! The lighter your skin, the more cachet you have. The darkest, African-looking folks are the less esteemed or even trusted citizens. How utterly stupid and backward and primitive is that?! It helped that Jacinto and Emilia were both light mulattoes, but they encountered and fought racial prejudice all the same.

Interesting that, although they didn't follow societal rules to the letter, and actually criticized them, Emilia and Jacinto still considered themselves Catholic and raised Elena in that religion. They didn't abide by church dogma, not entirely. So, it came as no surprise, either, that they wouldn't expect their daughter to get married. Their freethinking spirit was in Elena's blood, just as it was in Luis's. But it took a form in him that anguished and mortified her.

Maybe she's being too traditional about this. Why should she put down male sex workers? A judgmental voice in her head tells her it's wrong for men to provide that kind of service and wrong for other men to solicit it. Why? Because the Bible says it's evil. The Bible condemns homosexuality, yet there should be nothing wrong with loving a person for the person, not for their gender, as long as they don't take risks and stay healthy and safe. That's where she draws the line, the risk factor, and that's why she's worried about her son. She fears for his life.

Elena used to take Luis with her to Mass, wanting to share with him this important part of herself, the peace of the house of worship, the silence; the time to be with one's thoughts and prayers, to be with God's spirit. But Luis just couldn't relate to her faith. "I don't feel it," he'd say. "None of it makes any sense to me, Mamita. I don't like the smell of the place, and priests give me the creeps!" He refused to take catechism classes, too, and eventually stopped going to Mass with her altogether. Luis would say that he believed in God, *his* God, not in religion.

Too bad. She was certain Luisi would've drawn strength from Catholicism, like she did. She loved going to church, to confession, and taking communion at least once a month. Did she believe that the host was the actual embodiment of Christ, that the wine was his blood? Well...not exactly. She viewed Jesus as a caring, enlightened man, not as an actual demigod who performed miracles. Elena wouldn't dare share these views with any of her devout fellow parishioners, never ever! They all understood everything literally and would deem her sacrilegious, undeserving of God's mercy. She's always avoided socializing with most of them.

It makes sense that she'd be selective in what she chose to derive from her religion. After all, she's the daughter of Emilia Ramos and Jacinto Miranda and takes after them in most essential ways. Papá used to tell her that she could be and do anything she set her mind to. He claimed she was intelligent, talented, hard-working, and he was proud of her for getting such excellent marks in school. He'd imagine his Elenita in some position of power, making changes to improve life on the planet. Papá believed the world would be a much better place if women got to run things. Maybe he was idealizing the female of the species, yet it was a fact that men had made a mess of everything. If only there were more of them like Jacinto Miranda on Earth!

She can't forgive herself for disappointing her father, for not pursuing a big dream and becoming the professional woman he imagined. Elena may have had the needed smarts, but not the drive. She didn't like to read, wasn't motivated enough to attend the university, and she didn't go for complex intellectual ideas. She loved spending time by herself, sewing, doing needlework. And singing! Her parents loved her voice and encouraged her to take lessons, offered to pay for them. But Elena didn't feel that a future as a singer was in the stars for her.

The only life she could see clearly was that of motherhood. She thanks God every day for allowing her to fulfill that wish, and for giving her such wonderful parents, who supported her dream even if it wasn't the career they thought she was meant to have. They never expressed any disappointment, never criticized her. Oh, why did God take them away from her so soon?!

There's Luisi on the couch in his pajamas, playing the guitar. He requires love and attention, not to be told the big story of how he came into existence. Another time, perhaps. Or maybe never. Ay, her baby looks so pale! He has dark under-eye circles and is unable to sing because it makes him cough. And yet he seems relaxed, thanks to his music. Did his father have musical talent? She does remember that Alessandro used to sing Italian ballads to her. So sweet! *Dolce...*

Luis stops playing when she enters the room, throws her a kiss. "Aren't you missing your telenovela?" he asks her. "I wouldn't mind watching it with you."

"No, not today, baby," she replies. "I want to make some chicken soup for you."

He sneezes. "But I'm not hungry." He places the guitar on the couch, by his side.

Worried, "You need to eat, mijo."

"Maybe later, okay?"

"You don't listen to my advice anymore, Luisi."

"I listen to you more than I should."

"If that were true, you wouldn't be sick."

"You think I'm Superman or what? It's normal to get sick once in a while, Mamita!"

"No need to yell. It's bad for your throat." She gently touches his forehead. "Thank goodness you don't have a fever." She leaves and comes back with a blanket and covers him with it. "Here, this is the one I knitted for you. It'll keep you warm."

He sneezes again. "Fucking cold! And now I also have the chills."

"I want you to go to the doctor, Luisi, please."

"For a cold? No way."

"It sounds worse than that. You're coughing a lot, and the cough syrup isn't helping. You might have a bronchial infection and need antibiotics."

"My colds always go to my chest, remember? And then the cough goes away by itself."

"I'll be watching you, and if you don't get better soon..."

He lies down on the couch, closes his eyes. "It's not what you think, Mamita. I don't have the virus that's going around in the States. I'm very careful."

"I sure hope so, mijo. No one survives that disease, from what I've heard."

"You can stop worrying 'cause I'm not catching no faggot virus."

Ay, her son must stop using such demeaning language! She hates the tourists who take advantage of Luisi and make him sick. And yet, her heart won't allow her to condemn *all* homosexuals. There are decent people among them who'd never hurt anyone, who wish to live a normal life, fall in love, get married, have kids. She's gotten to know a few of those people in the neighborhood, both men and women. Why shouldn't they be allowed to fulfill their dreams? The church is wrong about this, and may God forgive her for having these sinful thoughts!

"You shouldn't call it a faggot virus," she tells Luis. "It's so offensive. And, besides, homosexual men are the victims, not the cause. So, why are they being blamed for it?"

"Some people say that gays are the ones spreading it. But I don't know all the facts. And why are you defending queers all of a sudden, Mamita?"

"I'm not defending them. I just think it's unfair..."

"Oh, that's right, I forgot. You're some kind of angel who protects the sinners."

"No, your grandparents are the only angels in this house, may they rest in peace."

"I miss Abuelo and Abuela so much!"

"Me, too. But I'm sure they're still around, watching over you."

"They've been gone for most of my life, and I still think about them all the time. Good people like them shouldn't die so young, let alone in such a horrible accident."

The memory hurts Elena deep inside, as if it all had happened yesterday. "None of it makes sense, mijo." Silence. "I haven't been able to ride in a car since then. I can barely stand buses." Trying to lighten up the mood, "At least my legs are grateful for all the walking I do!"

"I'd still like to get us a car someday," he says, oblivious to his mother's trauma.

Elena's head is about to explode! It's so hard to breathe... "Don't you dare!"

"I won't, I won't, Mamita, don't worry. Just relax, please. I didn't mean to upset you. I'll never be able to afford a car, anyway, so there's no chance..."

She feels her throat tightening, can barely get the words out, yet she needs to talk and vent. "Cars, all motor vehicles are a curse on humanity. They pollute our planet, kill thousands of people every year. And the unbearable noise they make! I hate them, hate them!"

Luis pulls up a chair for his mother. "Sit down, Mamita. You don't have to talk anymore. Just catch your breath, please. You're getting me worried."

"Sorry, baby." Long, painful silence. Until she starts breathing normally again. But now the tears are welling up in her eyes. "I just don't understand it."

Luis is back on the couch, bundled up. "What? What don't you understand?"

"Why God allowed it. Why He let such an awful thing happen to my parents."

"God had nothing to do with it, Mamita. He's not as powerful as Catholics think. He's not...what is it you call it? Omni...omnipotent."

"And just how do you know that, Luis?"

"Because there's proof all around us that He can't stop evil and crime and horrible shit from happening. If He could, Abuelo Jacinto and Abuela Emilia would still be alive."

"Maybe you're right. But let's not dwell on our tragedy anymore. My heart can't take it."

"Of course, Mamita. I'm sorry."

She sits on the couch by his feet. "Hey, is Richard okay? He hasn't come by in a while."

"Sure, he's fine. He has more friends now."

"You mean more clients..."

"No. I said more *friends*. And that's better for me 'cause he's not so clingy."

"Well, I hope you'll keep looking out for him. Richard is young and impressionable. We must make sure that nothing bad comes his way, okay?"

"Don't worry, Mamita. I got his back."

"I pray for both of you every single day, hoping that you'll remain close friends for the rest of your lives."

"Why is our friendship so important to you? Why is *he* so important?"

"Because I think Richard is a very special young man."

"Good to know. I agree." Silence. "Hey, Mamita, do you feel like singing to me a little? I'd sure love to hear one of your songs right now. Maybe that bolero you used to sing to me at the park, close to my ear so only I would hear you..."

"Sure, baby. Hopefully, it'll lull you to sleep. Are you warm enough?"

"Yes. I love this blanket." Luis is dozing off already. "Hey, I smell a rainstorm."

She sings to him softly, and he falls asleep.

What a strange, wonderful thing is the act of singing! Elena wonders how and when human beings discovered its power. Was it before or after they invented language? It must've all begun when someone created rhythms by clapping their hands, then someone else tried to imitate the sound and melody of a bird song... But then what happened after that? Who came up with the first lyrics thousands of years ago? And what were those lyrics about? So many questions!

She would also like to know why some tunes can affect us, making us feel happy, sad, or nostalgic. How do they evoke certain memories and transport us to the past, to the moment you first heard them or sang them? She'd love to learn about this process, what happens in the human brain when music is played, and how it all developed. She ought to just walk down to the public library and look it up. And maybe she'll also ask Richard to do a little research for her at his school. He's such a courteous young man. Smart, too.

But now, for the biggest question of all: when did songs become magical? That's how she regards the repertoire she performed for Luis—lullabies, folk songs, bachatas, boleros, ballads—when he was a baby, a toddler; sometimes, even when he was a teenager. As if her songs were incantations, benign spells she cast on her son to soften his heart and empower his lungs, his vocal cords, his ears so he could sing better than her, with passion and love and joy.

Yes, there might've been some kind of magic in her singing, but she can't take all the credit. The songs themselves were the incantation, not her rendition of them. Whatever power it was they had, the spells worked. From the moment he spoke his first word, Luis had a beautiful voice. A gifted voice. A voice that came from the very soul of creation.

She's being a typical mother, seeing something unique and extraordinary in her child, patting herself on the back for being such a good role model. So what? She's entitled to boast a little, if only to herself—not like those parents who won't stop talking about their children.

Elena is blessed to have access to a lifetime of memories thanks to the songs she and Luis sing. Memories of wonderful experiences but also of crushing work and stress. It can be so painful at times to raise a child! The way children move away from us as they grow up, as they begin to search for their own paths. She's sure there are things Luis hasn't told her, secrets he keeps to protect her from some bitter truths about his life and to set some distance between mother and son: his way of separating, of asserting his independence.

The most unsettling experience for Elena with regard to her maternal role has had to do with time. The way time changes when you're a parent, how it becomes a tangible thing almost. Time inhabits your child's body, and there it shows you its power. You become keenly aware of its passing. One day your son is a baby, and not long after that, he's entering adolescence, and then one day he's a man. As a parent, you're able to perceive the multiplicity of time. Too big a concept for her, but that's just how it feels. For there are moments when she can see the baby, the teenager, the adult all at once when she looks at Luis. All those beautiful creatures that he is...

Paul

Fear is a nasty bug. It eats you up inside ever so slowly, and it's just as invasive as the AIDS virus. There'll be a vaccine to combat that lethal infection eventually, but no medicine will ever be able to conquer Fear. Sure, you can take pills for anxiety and depression, like he has on occasion, or rely on talk therapy. Yet, Fear would still be lurking beneath, ready to pounce and rip your heart out. Lucky for Paul, this destructive emotion dissipates the minute he stands on a podium to share his knowledge, his expertise with a captive audience.

Oh, yes, folks: Mr. Edwards is in total control when he delivers his spiel about language acquisition. He loves Stephen Krashen's Monitor Theory, the linguist's brilliant thoughts on the way people learn a language. If only Paul could make that research the sole focus of his presentations, tell young profs about the listening and the production phases, about the fact that we should treat adults as children in the classroom in terms of their learning process. Kids are the most successful language learners, and they all go through a listening stage where they don't speak at all but understand much of what they hear. Thus, language teachers should allow for that stage in their students. Don't force them to speak (produce) before they're ready! Don't correct their pronunciation errors overtly—you grammar freaks! Focus on the message!

Why is he telling himself all this? Perhaps because he never tires of accessing and reviewing this body of knowledge. He'd love to have done something significant and cutting-edge with his MA in linguistics. Lamentably, the fucking greedy bug of capitalism stung him, tempted him with the prospect of making lots of money as a textbook editor, fresh out of the university. And so that's why he's here in Santo Domingo again, promoting his educational materials and not addressing a packed auditorium—which he's gotten to do frequently, thank goodness—to tell them about the latest findings in the field of foreign language teaching. Poor, poor Paul.

Hey, but he has nothing to gripe about! He's got it made! The company he works for is housed in a city he loves, taking up the entire fifth floor of a skyscraper in San Francisco's financial district. And he occupies the second largest office with a view of the skyline. Paul is in charge of signing new talent and developing exciting books. And as a bonus, on occasion, he gets to expound Krashen's theories and those of other visionaries in the field, such as Tracy D. Terrell, since all Lorthew products are grounded in the latest research...

He should recount the grim facts about his job, too. A painful reminder of the casualties he's been responsible for. Editors, for one. Many of them are young people recruited from graduate programs in literature or linguistics—just like Paul was. Oh, what the company does to those grads! For some reason, Paul was never used, abused, and then tossed, as usually happens to editorial teams at LB. No, in fact, he fared much better than he could've imagined.

There's such a high rate of editor burnout at Lorthew Books because the company doesn't pay enough for the work it demands. Editors are overworked, involved in several projects at a time, pushed to the brink of a mental breakdown, so a handful of people can make a fortune and the shareholders will come back for more. There is hardly any humanity in it, yet Paul keeps playing the game, pretending everyone's content with their meaningful work.

He has received all the promotions he's sought. Paul started out as contributing editor, moved up to development editor, and now he can flaunt his high-ranking title as Executive Editorial Director—which includes attending events (his favorite part of the job) and overseeing production. Paul, however, doesn't expect kindness from his employer, not after what happened during his fifth year with the company. It was the Purge, as this phase came to be known, when LB fired its veteran personnel and brought in new people to fill positions in all departments. No mercy for seasoned editors on the wrong side of forty! The memo regarding this evisceration stated that the company needed new views and ideas, an infusion of fresh blood. Fucking vampires!

And what about LB authors? Fuck, some of them drive Paul up the wall, especially tenured profs on an ego trip, a type that abounds in academia. And there are those who whine about things they have no control over, like cover art and page design. Yet he does admire authors who work hard on their programs. And he pities those who feel rightfully betrayed by the company, who must watch their first-rate texts being butchered by interns fresh out of college, then repackaged as colorful booklets that shun sound methodologies and trade them for dazzling illustrations. The company doesn't always care about pedagogy, not if providing a quality product means a decrease in profits. But Paul cares. He cares too much for his own good. All he's gotten from it is many a sleepless night. Fuck. What a downer!

He wishes he could delete, like a godlike editor, the memories of work-related experiences that haunt him. Fortunately, there are pleasant or at least interesting memories: his interview for his job at Lorthew Books, for example, when he met Mr. Kenneth Michaels, the legendary founder and president of the company. Paul couldn't believe that this famous fellow was taking the time to interview a lowly prospective editor. It could mean that his chances were good, Paul thought, for only candidates with high potential would move on to this last round. He'd heard that Mr. Michaels oversaw all new hires, and nothing was done without his approval. Paul knew he was in his fifties, divorced three times, and currently single. Most likely on the prowl? But Paul had no idea what he looked like. Was he handsome? Cute? Nerdy? Fat?

Such a pleasant surprise, finally shaking hands with the Big Boss that momentous day! Mr. Michaels turned out to be tall, of pallid complexion, gentle-mannered, and clad in exquisitely formal suit and tie. He brought to mind a mid-career Cary Grant. Hard to believe that this dapper gentleman had been responsible for creating one of the most youth-oriented companies in the world. After some chit-chat, Mr. Michaels praised the multilingual thrust of Paul's résumé: a bachelor's degree in Romance Languages, fluency in Spanish and French, a master's in Applied Linguistics from the University of Texas. He had also become familiar with twentieth-century American literature in grad school, and he'd learned to write well.

"Writing comes easy to me," Paul told Kenneth. "But I don't feel inclined to make a living from it. And I don't have the mind of a scholar, either. Although I do enjoy imparting knowledge, academia wouldn't be the right fit for me. My aptitude is for editing. I love the challenge of *fixing* a text, of detecting its pitfalls and bringing forth its beauty..."

What a pompous monologue! At least he was sensible enough to leave out the doozy of a phrase he'd come up with, having to do with bad writing... *The editor's job is to breathe life into a necrotic narrative...* He'd actually meant to use the word *necrotic*. What was he thinking?!

"Yours is a carefully planned academic package," stated Mr. Michaels. "I believe you'd fare well as an editor." And now Paul braced himself for the usual *but*. Sure enough: "But I'd like to hear more about your strengths and weaknesses, Mr. Edwards. In simple words, tell me what would make you great at editing and what has the potential for ruining your work."

Another answer Paul just couldn't convey in simple words: "I'm always ready to cut. My major strength is related to this editorial aptitude. I'm a perfectionist, and my main weakness is manifest in my vocation for editing as well: a need for structure. I strive for flawlessness, refusing to accept that nothing, not even the most brilliant writing, is entirely flawless."

Kenneth burst out laughing. "Be forewarned, Mr. Edwards!" he pronounced. "You won't come across much brilliant writing in this business! Flawlessness is not something we can afford." Paul said he understood, as he tried not to feel ridiculed and self-conscious. "At any rate," Mr. Michaels went on, handing him a manuscript, "here's the test you have to take. If you ace it, we'll give your application serious consideration."

Paul wasn't feeling optimistic by now. He was convinced, in fact, that Kenneth had read him as gay and had decided not to offer him the job for that reason. He'd picked up on the man's sardonic, homophobic smile, his obvious discomfort when Paul would utter certain words with a feminine lilt or express himself vigorously with his hands in a manner that could be interpreted as affected. Paul had learned to perform as straight in professional settings, disguising his queerness, hiding his feathers. But sometimes he just couldn't help being himself...

Nevertheless, he was going to give this test his all. He was to edit fifty pages of a first-year textbook. Plunging into the task right then and there, he simplified the grammar explanations, spiced up the exercises with cultural references, and corrected the spelling errors that plagued the sample. There was a short reading on the culture of "America," too complex a subject for so little space and with such limited vocabulary. Americans were described as industrious and generous people—all of them!—who loved football, burgers, shopping, and fireworks on Independence Day. Oh, and they valued their personal freedom. *All* of them! The style was uninspired, the narrative voice lackluster. Paul would come to conclude, after collaborating with many academic authors, that professors of literature didn't make exciting writers. With rare exceptions, lit profs preferred to expound truths about the luminaries of their canons (Shakespeare, Eliot, Woolf, Twain, Fitzgerald, Hemingway, Morrison, and so on) rather than consider and discuss introductory language programs. Even those academics who saw themselves primarily as novelists tended to be lofty, verbose, unconcerned about student readers. Or worse: basic, skimpy. No doubt, they regarded writing textbooks as a demeaning chore.

This reading on "America" was to be the first of many pieces Paul would have to *whip into shape*: Kenneth's way of describing an editor's task. He infused the piece with high-frequency vocabulary, deleted complex grammar, and added transitions. The content couldn't be altered, said Mr. Michaels, because culture had to be delivered as an attractive package, focusing on sports, festivities, holidays, cuisine, and celebrities in pop music, television and film. Subjects with complex historical layers—such as the plight of Black people and Native Americans—tended to sink a textbook, so out with the grim stats and in with the sure bets!

When Paul turned in the sample, Mr. Michaels informed him that he'd hear back in a couple of days. Sure, Paul thought, *don't call us, we'll call you*. But his phone rang late that night. He was both elated and scared shitless when he heard the Cary Grant doppelgänger greeting him. "Today is your lucky day," said his future boss. "I'd like for you to join our team as a contributing editor. What's your answer, Paul?" Of course, it was, "Yes, thank you!"

Paul would end up learning a great deal from that man. The Big Boss took him on as a project, it seemed, sharing with him the tricks and secrets of his trade, grooming Paul as if the future of the company depended on him. And Paul was a quick study, always eager to go the extra mile to please his mentor. He was indebted to Mr. Michaels, yes, so much so that he began acting like a clone of the president. He would turn a blind eye to the company's dirty deals, to the abuses and mistreatment of its editorial teams, the demeaning remarks that were par for the course at the production meetings where Mr. Michaels presided. To his credit, the president did have positive, even flattering things to say to his staff on occasion. But not often enough!

He would come to have seriously mixed feelings about Mr. Michaels, both admiring the man and hating his fucking guts. Feelings he's never expressed to anyone, not even to Vincent. Because he doesn't want to have to admit that some days, he detests the person he's become.

Given the nature of his job, it's understandable that Paul wouldn't have made many trustworthy friends at Lorthew. There's only one person there he trusts: Alyssa, his assistant. Not an ideal office worker by a long shot. Alyssa doesn't "get" the textbook publishing industry. She's a young woman with no drive who just coasts along, waiting for Mr. Right to sweep her off her feet and marry her. Amicable, sociable Alyssa, still plodding along as a glorified secretary, unmoved by the prospect of a more demanding position or a promotion.

Paul shouldn't have let that friendship happen; he should never have let himself feel so close to Alyssa. Now he'd find it hard to fire her if he needed to. Because you just don't do that to a friend. Conveniently, the young woman is good at dealing with authors, including the most problematic ones. It's her forte, buttering them up, and a part of the job Paul abhors. So, despite her professional apathy, Alyssa is still an asset to him.

One of their recent conversations mortifies Paul because he acted like an ass, like a fucking mouthpiece for the company. They were having lunch at Café Misionero in the Mission District. The dining area on

Valencia Street was too crowded, but they decided to sit outside anyway. Their sexy waiter was solicitous and gallant, putting on an act that was wasted on Paul; meticulously groomed white men don't attract him. But Alyssa seemed impressed with the guy's overworked biceps. She flirted back, unaware that he was gay and simply hoping for a good tip.

"So, Paul, is Lorthew Books as bad as it looks to me?" Alyssa asked out of the blue once the waiter had brought their salads. Paul knew exactly what she was referring to.

"You only see part of the picture," he replied. And this was true; Alyssa wasn't privy to the machinations that went on behind closed doors. But seeing the whole picture would've only confirmed her view of LB. "Our MO may not be the most humane, but the bottom line is that thanks to our company, hundreds of educators and thousands of students are able to use the best teaching materials on the market, all well-researched and classroom tested. The process..."

Alyssa cut in, "Yes, Paul, but..."

He didn't let her finish, "The process is grueling at times, yet it has to be, or we wouldn't be able to beat the competition."

"You think it's worth it, then?" she asked. "Even if it makes everyone so unhappy?"

"Yes," Paul answered immediately. "The headaches, the stress, it's all worth it in the end, when we see our latest project in print. Such a great feeling!"

Alyssa was unusually pensive. "That must be what I'm missing, the personal reward," she remarked. "Something I don't get to have, since it really makes no difference to me whether a book gets published or adopted or whatever. I just do what I'm told. And all I see," she admitted, "is a bunch of nutsy people who hate their jobs."

Paul pontificated: "Any job that involves creativity and research requires some degree of madness to be done well, Alyssa. In our line of work, nutsy comes with the territory."

She laughed and said, "I guess that's why I'm the sanest person in our office, though sanity hasn't gotten me very far, has it?" Paul told her he appreciated her expedient work and the effective way she handled the company's authors. Then he lied to her, said he believed in her potential. She expressed her gratitude, "I'm sure they would've kicked me out long ago if it weren't for you, Paul, and I'll make it up to you, okay? From now on I'll give it my all." He reminded her that she'd made that promise before, and she assured him things would be different this time: "I'll work longer hours and skip my breaks and go nuts like, like..."

Paul finished her sentence: "Like me?"

She seemed flustered now. "No, no, I didn't mean to imply..."

He cut her off, "No one's forcing me to work as much as I do, Alyssa. I love my job."

She asked him: "But what about Vincent?"

"Yes, what about him?"

"Doesn't he mind that you get home late, that you have to work many weekends and...?"

She had finally managed to piss him off. Still, Paul tried to contain his irritation. He told her: "Vincent supports my professional goals and understands the demands of my career."

Her inane comment: "Yeah, that man's a keeper for sure!"

By now, Paul just wanted to lock himself up in his office, away from Alyssa. Or better yet, he would do something completely out of character and take the rest of the day off.

"We should be heading back," he said to his assistant.

"But you hardly touched your salad!"

He curtly explained he wasn't hungry and offered to get the check.

Why did he side with the damn company? Why did he speak of "our MO," of beating the competition? He should've told Alyssa what he really thought: that a textbook publisher shouldn't be in cahoots with tycoons, that it shouldn't be allowed to exploit its employees so that a handful of avaricious assholes can keep getting filthy rich. He should've told his loyal assistant the truth: that Lorthew Books was not as bad as it looked to her. No, it was fucking worse!

Elena

She should be honest with herself. Yes, Mass gives her comfort and focus, but she doesn't abide by everything her religion dictates. Elena can't accept some of its precepts, especially when it comes to women and pregnancy. She knows too many cases of young Catholic wives who've ended up with a bunch of kids before they turn thirty, mainly because they're forbidden to use contraceptives. They're supposed to follow the rhythm method, the only form of family planning sanctioned by the church, which typically fails and keeps women having babies their whole lives. And most husbands are okay with this because impregnating their wives asserts their manhood. Never mind that they're not able to support such a big family.

Pregnancy takes such a toll on a woman's body! The discomfort of carrying a baby for nine months, the pain of childbirth, the exhausting work that is expected, no, *required* of women. None of it seems fair at all. It infuriates Elena that abortion is illegal in the Dominican Republic in all circumstances, and it's been so for more than a century. She knows of this case, a neighbor who got pregnant and found out early on that the fetus had some rare disease; it would be born missing one lung and both kidneys. The baby had no chance of survival, so my neighbor and her husband decided it was best to terminate the pregnancy. But the woman's doctor told her she had to carry it to full term, which she did, only to watch her child die seconds after birth. It's so cruel, so inhumane.

Elena gets that the Catholic Church forbids abortion because only God can give life or take it; that in cases of advanced pregnancy, you'd be destroying a human being, not a fetus. Yet, fundamentally, this is an issue of women's inferior position in patriarchal societies. Men assume that they have control over a woman's body, that they can dictate what she can and cannot do in that regard. Elena is convinced it's all about fear. Men are terrified of the female of the species because they know she's superior to the male. Because women can do anything a man can do if they set their minds to it, but they also hold the key to the miracle of life. No wonder they keep being put down, oppressed and belittled. No wonder there are so many machista societies in the world, her own country included. How can anyone claim that a godly spirit guides those societies? No, that's not part of God's plan. He must be wiser and more empathetic than that.

God understands why Elena made sure she'd have only one child. It was because she longed to be a parent but didn't want to bring many more people to this overcrowded planet. And there was a personal reason as well: childbirth hurts too much. It rips your entrails apart. Elena couldn't imagine greater physical pain. Why would she want to repeat that experience?

Ay, she needs a break from all this heavy thinking! She tends not to dwell on tough topics unless it's for a specific reason. If only she could watch an episode of *Lost Love of My Youth* right now. That would relax her and make her laugh. But the telenovela won't be on for several hours, and she doesn't want to watch any other show. Maybe she could tell herself her own telenovela saga to pass the time. Yes! She'd enjoy doing that, concocting an outrageous plot, a convoluted story with melodramatic scenes to take her mind off reality. Something to do with Alessandro and Elena, perhaps? Yes, something like... like... Okay! She's got it...

Alessandro marries a lovely Florentine lady, and they have two daughters. One of them, the youngest, travels to Santo Domingo for a vacation. She meets Luis at the beach. They fall in love at first sight. Then, in a scene with lots of crying, overacted emotions, and bombastic music, Elena (the main character of this telenovela) realizes that the lovebirds are half-siblings. And how does she come to know this? Ah, because Alessandro decides to join his daughter in Santo Domingo without his wife, since they're separated. How convenient. Destiny wants him to run into Elena, and so he sees her walking down her street. A dramatic reunion! They go to Parque Colón. He shows her photos of his children, and she notes that one of the pictures is of Luis's current girlfriend, whom she's met a couple of times. Ay, ay, ay! Elena is suddenly trembling, her legs are giving out on her. Alessandro has to hold her so she doesn't fall. And now, being in such close proximity, they both realize they're still in love. They kiss passionately. But Elena must tell him the truth (there's always some big truth in most telenovelas), that they have a son together, Luis, and that he's dating Alessandro's daughter! How will Alessandro be able to take all this in at once? He had a child with Elena! He's still in love with her! Their son is dating his daughter! Ultimately, all of this happened because fate, *el Destino*, willed it so...

She's feeling relaxed at last. Thank goodness it's raining. Elena is tempted to get some shuteye. Luis is sound asleep himself, getting the rest he needs. A nap would do her good, yes, although sleeping in the middle of the day has triggered the most bizarre dreams lately. It's because of her arm, which is hurting again. Her mind must be dealing with the pain by creating the wildest scenarios—wilder, even, than any telenovela she's ever watched—harking back to her youth.

The spring storm rages outside, and her bed is summoning her. Maybe today she won't dream about running, about feeling detached from the world, from time. And she won't have to wear a mask, one of those porcelain masks people wear at carnivals. Everyone here always wears them. She's been in this dance hall before, long ago, with masked strangers in costumes, all frenziedly dancing. If only she didn't feel so sad... Why is she crying? There's a tightness in her chest. She's so exposed! A man in a harlequin costume is making love to her while everybody watches. He has a long, thick needle instead of a penis, and every night the needle goes in deeper, further, too close to her heart. Ay, his painful thrusts! And now it's his voice that cuts through her flesh. *I had the right to know my son. Why didn't you tell me about him?!*

Elena runs, leaps from body to body. The lights are blinding. And the harlequin-man keeps holding her down, forcing her to listen. She can smell the minty warmth of his breath. Who is he?! What does he want from her? *A woman who shuns marriage, who wants a baby, not a husband. Bah! How about a woman who uses another human being to fulfill her genetic impulse? A woman who will break a heart, if that's what it takes.* Why is he screaming at her? *Vergogna!* Why does he talk to her in a language she can't understand? *Vergognati!*

She no longer hears the harlequin-man's voice, only sinister laughter. And now all the strangers are screaming, too, accusing her. Their voices are deafening! They're telling her she's going to be punished—not for having a baby out of wedlock, which is no sin at all, but for using a young man and then tossing him like garbage. For this, she deserves to be sacrificed to the gods!

Home. If she were there now, she wouldn't be in danger, and her lovely Cinderella dress wouldn't be getting ripped to pieces. Elena begs her beloved God to free her from this nightmare, from that man's voice and his needle... *I had a right to know my son!!*

God will make her parents come to get her. They'll cover her with a blanket and give her a cup of warm milk. And they'll forgive her for running off in the middle of the night and committing yet another act of sheer folly. She'll promise them she'll be a good Catholic girl from now on. No more escapades. But her parents aren't really here to save her. And there's that needle piercing her heart. She can't cry for help. Is she taking her last breath? There's no air...

"Mamita!" Someone's calling her, saving her at last. She feels his fingers tenderly stroking her head, her face. It's not the harlequin-man, thank God! "Wake up, Mamita, please." She gradually emerges from her slumber and is greeted by a voice she loves, "Are you okay?"

"Hello, baby," she says to her son. "Yes, I'm fine."

"You were screaming..."

"I was having a bad dream. Sorry if I woke you up."

"No worries. I was tired of sleeping, anyway. I need to stretch my legs a little." He helps her out of bed. "What were you dreaming about?"

"I forgot already."

"It must've been scary..." Silence. "You want some coffee?"

"Sure. I love the way you make it!"

He heads for the kitchen, and she joins him there after a visit to the bathroom. Finding her son busy at work, she sits at the table.

"I'm in the mood for some espresso," he says while filling up the cup with fresh grounds.

"Good. Me, too." As she watches him, "Make sure you measure the grounds, okay? And don't fill the cup to the brim, or it'll overflow."

"Relax, I got this. I showed you how to use this machine, remember?"

"Yes, of course I remember. It took me a while to get the hang of it…"

Luisi was so excited when they received the box all the way from Italy. That's where the best coffee makers were made, he claimed. This one was manufactured by La Pavoni, one of the first Italian espresso machine companies. Kind of complicated, with a lot of parts to it!

That fancy gadget evoked so many memories in her… because it had come from Alessandro's homeland. She had to stop herself from thinking about Luis's father every time she used it. What had become of Alessandro? He was probably a family man by now (although not like the telenovela character she'd imagined!), married to a lovely Florentine lady, and with four gorgeous kids, two girls and two boys…

"See?" says Luis, in total command of his chore. "Now I wait for the green light to tell me it's ready and, minutes later… done!" He serves Mamita a porcelain demitasse filled to the brim with Dark Roast. "Strong and super-sweet for my sweet lady!"

"Thank you, mijo!" she exclaims, savoring the beverage. "This is delicious, much better than the coffee I brew." He makes a funny face. "I mean it!"

"If you say so." He sits next to her with a full mug. "Hey, you got me thinking about Richard. I've been missing him…"

"I know. His visits always make you happy."

"Yeah, 'cause he's my best friend."

She smiles, kisses his forehead. "And what about me? I thought I was your best friend."

"You? No, you're just my mom."

Laughing, "Well, thanks a lot, son!"

"Anyway, Mamita, let's have Richard over for dinner next Sunday, okay?"

"Yes! I'll make something special for him."

"And I'll help you make it."

"That would be fun!"

Luisi could become a chef if he wanted to. He has a knack for cooking and doesn't need a lot of instructions, especially if they're making sancocho, his favorite dish, and also Richard's. He's learned his way around the kitchen. Luisi knows how to cut the plantains and the yuca, how long to boil the stew, and many other details. This is yet another way Luis has surprised her. Surely, he takes after his grandfather Jacinto, a gifted cook who had some signature dishes no one at home could replicate. So it shouldn't be a surprise at all.

"I'll talk to Richard," he says, "when I see him tomorrow at the Cristóbal."

"Tomorrow? No way, young man! You're sick and in no shape for..."

Interrupting, "I have to be there, Mamita! The manager is letting me sing at the bar."

"Well, you can sing some other time."

"No. Señor Zamora says there'll be some important tourists there tomorrow, checking out the place. I must perform even if I lose my voice."

"But you're losing it already. You sound hoarse, baby."

"I'll sing low, without belting."

"What would be the point, then?"

"I don't want to disappoint Mister Paul. He believes in my talent and pulled strings for me with Señor Zamora. It's the opportunity I've been waiting for, Mamita."

Displeased but resigned, "Fine, Luisi, we'll see how you're feeling by then."

"I'll dedicate my show to Elena Miranda Ramos, the coolest mom in the whole world!"

"Thank you, baby. Sing for them your song about true love. I'm sure they'll like it."

He laughs. "Okay. I'll be back before Cinderella!"

"She at least had a prince."

Kissing his mother, "I'm better off 'cause I have a queen."

In jest, "Get away from me! I don't want your cold."

"It's what you deserve, for treating me like a kid."

She opens the fridge to gather ingredients. "How about I make you a little soup?"

"No, that's okay, Mamita. I'm not hungry. This coffee's fine for now."

Pretending she didn't hear him, "I'll put some chicken in it, the way you like it."

"Didn't you hear what I said?"

"Maybe potatoes, too. Or would you rather have noodles?"

In a loud, angry voice, "I told you I'm not hungry!"

She shouts back, "But you have to regain your strength, you damn brat!"

Shocked, "Mamita!"

"See? I can cuss, too."

She slams the fridge door shut and sits back at the table. "Okay, suit yourself. I won't make you eat." Pensive, seeming defeated, "Life on this island gets so tiring some days..." Silence. "We must struggle with everything, the scorching hot weather, the torrential rains, the hard work, the government, the tourists, even the nourishment of a sick son!" Silence. "And to make matters worse, we're surrounded by water. We can't just take off running."

"We could swim away."

"What a dumb idea!"

Laughing, "Yeah, but it made you smile... just a little." Silence. "And speaking of water, Mamita, it's sure coming down hard right now."

"You used to love the rain when you were little."

"I still do!"

Absorbed in the memory, "You'd run out there and stand barefoot, drinking in the thick raindrops." Laughing, "Ay, the crazy things you used to think up!"

"Yeah, like my idea of making a Spanish omelette with lizard eggs."

"It turns my stomach just to think about it."

"Our bathroom was always full of those tiny eggs."

"Maybe that's where you got your interest in cooking, baby."

Jokingly, "Sure, Mamita, that's where it all started..."

"You'd say to me, 'It'll be a yummy dish, just wait and see.' And then you'd take over the kitchen, and we would make the disgusting concoction together."

"But you'd never let me eat it. You'd always tell me the sad story of a little boy who died from eating chameleon eggs."

"That story was true. He dropped right in front of his mother, like a dead baby pigeon."

"I never ate our concoction, not even behind your back."

Feeling nostalgic, "That's the way it used to be, Luisi. You'd always do what I said."

"And what do you want me to do now? I await your orders, ma'am!"

"I just want you to get better."

Firmly, "I *will*. I promise you!"

Paul

No more thinking about fear! He ain't got nothing to be afraid of... Oh, dear, he just sounded like his brother, that bonehead! But, yes, life is beautiful. He's in paradise, and he can afford the most gorgeous islanders in the world, like the stud who accompanied him here today to Boca Chica, or the ones who walk by him, proudly strutting their stuff. And he has a loving partner waiting for him in SanFran, keeping their bed warm in the fabulous, remodeled Victorian they own on Haight Street. How lucky he is to have found Vincent, a wonderful man who won't ask any questions and won't join him on his escapades. It's healthy to have a long break from each other once in a while, says Vincent as he tries to accept Paul's absences and his stints in the Caribbean. Always welcomes him back with a rose bouquet, that romantic man. And they have a tight-knit circle of friends with whom they enjoy dinner parties and boys-in-the-band bitch sessions.

Hey, but that's too rosy a picture... There's also the fact, the grim truth, that his beloved circle is getting smaller, decimated by AIDS. Whenever they get together lately, there's someone missing from the group. Someone in the hospital. Someone on a ventilator. Someone with Kaposi sarcoma. A searing absence Paul and his friends feel in their hearts and their guts.

Oh, what the fuck—he should just count his blessings. He's still alive and kicking, and he managed to escape the Texas hell, creating his own kind of heaven in the most heavenly gay city in the world. He can also see Tony once a year, reunions he always looks forward to, though he'd never admit this to the conceited Spaniard.

There is Señor Don Antonio Fernando Luján Saavedra (ay, those endless Spanish names!), seated in a chaise lounge under a beach umbrella by the bar, waiting for Paul as agreed. He's bare-chested and in a bikini, sexy in his own way. Tony obviously works out. Obvious, too, that he's hung, judging from the shape of his basket. As usual, the Gallego is writing. And Paul decides to disturb the peace, dressed for the occasion—tight, sea-blue trunks, a white terrycloth shirt tied at the waist, and his ever-present "image-maker" hanging from his neck.

He goes up to Tony impetuously and snaps a picture of him.

"No more photos of me, Paul!"

"You don't have to scream, darling. I get the message." He places his camera on the table and sits in a chaise lounge by his friend. He strikes a cabaret-singer pose, legs crossed, hands daintily placed on his knees. "Ay!" he cries out, "I'm going to miss this place!"

"I always do," says Antonio without looking up from the page.

"What a name for a beach! Boca Chica, a small mouth that has nothing *chica* about it."

Antonio, still reviewing his notes, "Are you ready for the fair?"

"I'd better be! It's almost time for me to don my professional hat." Paul makes himself comfortable in his chair, takes a deep breath. "Where's your little friend?"

Antonio faces Paul. "Are you referring to Richard?"

"Who else? You've claimed exclusive rights to him."

"He said he needed to stay home today to do his homework."

"And you believed him?"

Shrugging his shoulders, "So, where's Luis?"

"Hell if I know, though I could venture a guess. I needed a break from him today."

"You mean you're here alone?"

"No, babe, I brought a new hunk. I told him to take a hike while you and I chat."

Antonio fixes his eyes on Paul. Suddenly, unexpectedly, Paul feels uneasy. "Why are you looking at me that way, Tony? That's not an expression I'm familiar with!"

"I was just thinking..."

"Fuck, I sense one of your downers coming on."

"No, no, I was thinking that you're a good photographer."

"Thank you, Tony! As long as I don't take photos of you, right?"

Smiling, "Yes, well, that's a temptation you must resist. I don't want my image to be part of anyone's collection."

"Hey, I'm confused. Aren't you supposed to be Mr. Narcissus?" Silence. "Anyway, that's too bad. You're a sexy subject."

Antonio points to his crotch. "Thanks, but don't get any ideas."

Paul laughs. "Not to worry. You know you're not my type. Too ambiguous..."

Sighing with relief, "Good. I'll make sure to keep it that way."

"Thanks for your compliment about my photos, darling. So nice of you."

"I mean it, Paul. I like your black and white shots, the contours you capture. The depth. You have a talent for perceiving and expressing movement. I love the print you gave me of the Cristóbal's façade. Did I tell you I had it framed professionally? It hangs in my study."

"Wow, I'm speechless. No, I didn't know. Thank you thank you thank you!"

"Why don't you ever talk about your photography, Paul? You have no qualms about discussing every detail of your sex life and boasting about your professional accomplishments. But not a word about your creative work. Too personal, perhaps? Too close to the heart?"

"It's not that at all. I just don't think I'm as good as you claim. I don't even have a dark room. And I'm not that knowledgeable about cameras, either. Lucky for me, Vincent is. He's up on the latest models, the best brands." Handing his camera to Antonio. "He gave me this one, a Canon T-50, which is used by professionals. My favorite of all the ones he's given me."

"You might want to consider taking up photography full time."

"No, it's just a relaxing hobby for me. Snap snap snap! And I'm busy enough already."

"When you retire, maybe?"

"No. Whenever I retire, I'll move to this island and do nothing but veg out all day."

Laughing, "And fuck all night!"

"You got it, Toñita!" Paul takes his shirt off, tucks it under his head like a pillow. "There, that feels better. Let's catch some rays!"

Antonio puts his notebook away in his bag. "Let's!"

"Were you working on your novel?"

"Just taking some notes." Silence. "By the way, if I ever finish this book, I'm going to dedicate it to you, since you pitched me the idea. A very promising idea."

"That's so sweet! Happy to help." Silence. "Just make sure the island sounds real, okay? Like the passages you wrote about Massiel."

"I plan to. My goal is authenticity, realism without excessive embellishments."

Paul is excited. "Hey, babe, it just occurred to me that I could translate your novel into English for you. What do you think? I'll be your official American translator, the most qualified for the job. Who else would know more than me about this place, about the story you'll be telling? It'd be a new area for me, but it could be fun. And I like challenges."

"Thanks, Paul. You're right that there's no one better fit for that job. I suppose it'd be a challenge to translate my very Spanish interior monologues into a Germanic language." Silence. "Perhaps that's the reason my work hasn't been published in English..."

"Darling, if it could be done with the *Quijote*, it can certainly work with your fiction. The best translations of Cervantes' oeuvre sound as authentic as if they'd been written in early seventeenth-century English originally." Silence. "The real challenge wouldn't be your monologues, in fact, but the colloquial expressions the Cristóbal guys use, their colorful Caribbean idioms. But of course I'd try to find the closest equivalents."

"Okay, it's a deal!"

"Great! I can't wait." Silence. "Read me some of your notes, please."

"Fine. But no mocking." Antonio brings out the notebook, flips through it, finds the page he wants. "This is part of a dialogue." He reads, "You've done it with a lot of guys here, but you don't know what you're missing. With me, you'd get to know pleasure like never before..."

"Hot though unoriginal. Go on."

Antonio, reading, "These young men fuck other men yet still consider themselves straight. How's that for a powerful yet misguided assertion of male heterosexuality?"

"It's not that complicated, Tony. Sex is a natural thing for these people. It's always there, in every thought and interaction. Dominicans have a fluid sexuality."

Antonio, exasperated, "Yes, of course, every single person on this island is sexually fluid." Sarcastic, "Thanks for your keen observations. Now, do you want me to continue?"

"By all means!"

Reading, "Young hunks. Their bodies, primal objects of desire. We talk about their cocks (length, width, color, texture) as if we were describing trees."

"Because they are! Upright and thick palm stems. But do take note, Tony: that's not a felicitous metaphor. In fact, it's quite facile. Dicks as trees? Please!"

Antonio, pretending to be upset but smiling, "That's it. I'm not reading another word."

"Sorry, sorry. Didn't mean to upset you. Please continue."

Reading, "Once again, the phallus reigns supreme. It permeates every thought, fantasy, interaction; defines who we are, shapes our identities. It is a damnation, an inescapable curse."

"There you go again, sounding like one of your characters."

Reading, "The phallus, an omnipresent symbol that invests our lives with meaning. The linguistic matrix of gay discourse but also the moving force—a tsunami!—of straight culture everywhere on this planet. Even when we reject it, we're still defining ourselves against it."

"Indeed. So we might as well embrace it wholeheartedly. Why fight it?"

"Because that would be a self-serving, hedonistic stance, Paul."

"Yeah, well, I wonder who you'd be without your big dick."

"Can you be serious for a minute at least? Listen..."

Tony is now deep in thought, or pretending to be. Which means he's searching for a way to sound erudite and intellectual in order to impress Paul. Fat chance, Gallego!

"According to Lacan..." Tony starts to say, then pauses for effect, "the phallus is the transcendent signifier of desire, a simulation but also signification itself, omnipotent yet impotent like the fake Wizard of Oz. The prime meaning, what men wish to *have* and women wish to *be*."

"Impressive... Lacan, wow. But you and Lacan are leaving us queers out of the picture, as always." Laughing, "And there ain't nothing fake about the phallic wizard of this island!"

"I disagree. This island, its beaches, our hotel may all be one big simulation."

"I wouldn't call it that." Pensive. "A performance, yes, maybe—a very convincing and enjoyable one." Silence. "Anyhoo, going back to your novel, I suggest you write about us tourists, too. Just be careful how you treat us. No heavy-handed condemnations, okay?"

"Well, here is my definition." He reads, "Self-worshippers. Hedonists who seek pleasure like the ancient Greeks, but burdened with guilt, unwilling to admit their innate masochism..."

"Ay, ay, ay! Speak for yourself!" Paul stares at a group of young men who pass by. "Maybe you should focus on the beauty of these people instead."

Antonio, smiling at the passers-by. "Too easy. Or facile, as you'd say."

"Then find a romantic angle."

"Is there anything romantic in any of this, Paul?"

"Obviously yes, in your case." Laughing, "A dapper leading man in love!"

"Not funny."

"Just give us your own version of the Cristóbal scene. Write about the hotel, starting with its name, which has nothing and everything to do with Columbus."

"I'm surprised someone hasn't done it already."

"Me, too!" Giving Antonio a gentle pat on the head, "Work fast and furious, darling. And publish your novel before some gutsy Dominican writer beats you to it. Expose the abuse and while you're at it, crank out a bestseller that'll make you rich and famous."

"Fame and money. All that matters, huh, Paul?"

"No, Toñita. That's just an added bonus."

"And what good would it do to denounce what's going on at the Cristóbal? A book could never change the fate of those young men. It wouldn't bring an end to their prostitution."

"Ay, girl, you can be such a downer."

There he goes again: Antonio locked up in his head. What could he be thinking about? This silence is unbearable. Speak up, girlfriend! Even if it's just to deride your Texan buddy!

"Fine, Paul," the moody Spaniard says at last, "so how about a happy, very *gay* portrayal of the Dominican Republic? What would you say if you were writing about this island?"

"Well, let me think... Okay, so, I wouldn't start out the way you would for sure." Standing, Paul pretends to put on a monocle and holds a thin branch as a pointer. "Welcome to my exciting novelistic universe, Dear Reader! We're here to learn about a country called the Dominican Republic, where our story takes place. Let's get some basic info out of the way first, shall we?" His pointer on an invisible slide-projector screen, "Location: the Dominican Republic shares the island of Hispaniola with Haiti to the west. But don't worry about how that freaky situation occurred. Not relevant for our tale." Silence. "Capital: Santo Domingo (the former name of the country.) Size: nineteen thousand square miles. Population: six million people, with one million living in the capital." Silence. "Main natural resources: minerals, though tourism (a very "natural" resource, you could claim) beats it by far! Ethnic makeup: mostly multiracial..."

"What about the political sphere? Are you leaving that out?"

"Politics. Okay, Tony, suffice it to say that the island endured a ruthless dictatorship for a fuckload of years, but its government has evolved to become a just regime that protects everyone equally, including the busy sex workers employed in the tourist industry, who make a major contribution to the country's economy. Indeed, thanks to the enlightened new president, those workers now have health insurance and a hefty retirement pension, which they can claim as soon as they turn thirty, by which age they will have exhausted their professional potential..."

"If only those guys had that kind of support for real!"

Paul tosses his pointer, sits back in his chair. "And now, Dear Reader, forget all those historical facts, which have surely put you to sleep by now. Let's focus on Quisqueya, an enchanted island with a rich Indigenous past, so we can learn about the beautiful art Tainos created; about their dances, like the Areito, and some of their fun games, such as the Batu."

"Yes, art, dances, and games that my remote ancestors didn't give a shit about!"

"Fortunately, it all survived despite colonization."

"Sure, but very few Indigenous Tainos did. They were exploited, mistreated, thought to have no soul and deemed undeserving of mercy, unworthy of entering the Catholic God's kingdom." Silence. "You can't bring up their art and festivities without mentioning that they were all savagely exterminated, victims of exhausting work and European diseases."

"Oh my God, just what I was trying to avoid, a depressing history lesson. Yes, Tony, the Spanish colonizers were ruthless, ignorant, violent, greedy, and only interested in finding gold. They did all their massacring in the name of God and the Catholic Church. Yes, religion strikes again. So, there, we got the sad historical truth out of the way. May I continue?"

"Of course, but only if you'd be willing to talk about foreign dominance, revolutionary struggles, deranged dictators..."

"No way, darling. I'm not messing with any of that stuff. No discussion of La Trinitaria and Trujillo and the Civil War of 1965, much less of the new president and his socialist ideas."

"Why not him? Finally, a progressive leader on the island."

"That would be much too easy. A president named Salvador—a savior!—and with the last name Blanco... What could go wrong with that? Long live the Revolutionary Party!"

"I suppose you'd rather have a puppet of the United States."

"No, Tony. It's just that I'd prefer not to write about politics at all. I'd rather focus on other things. I'd describe Luis's singing, for instance, his voice that seems to thunder out of his very soul. His adonic body bathed by the mellow sun of a Santo Domingo evening."

"Nice! I'm sure you'd want to describe his cock, too."

"No. Again: too easy. I'd rather highlight the island's natural beauty, which would include some of its gorgeous inhabitants, no doubt. Its beaches first: their crystalline waters, with palm trees reaching for the sky along the endless shore, the lingering sunset, the warm midnight breeze; and the sweet, succulent fruit, nípero, mamey, guanábana..."

"Surprise, surprise! The textbook editor has a poet's heart!"

"Too kind. But correction: I'm not just an editor." Self-mockingly, "My position is of the highest rank. I supervise the production process of all our books and represent the company at its promotional events. Like book fairs, where I proudly display our great, innovative publications."

"Seriously, Paul, does LB really have the best books on the market?"

"Well, let's just say that we know how to compete."

Antonio walks to the shore and looks out at the ocean. Paul joins him minutes later.

"Let's stop using these young men, Paul. Let's never come here again."

"It's a nice wish, dear. But how do we stop all the others from coming?"

"The government would have to intervene, crack down on places like the Cristóbal."

"And you know that's not happening." Pensive. "Hey, here's an ideal scenario: the government teams up with the Ministry of Public Health and the Ministry of Education to provide health education, contraceptives, and scholarships to the country's sex workers. What do you think of that initiative? Any chance Señor Blanco would have the balls to pull it off?"

"I think he would." Daydreaming, "Our young friends would finally have someone powerful looking out for them."

"Yes, Tony. But then, as soon as the plan became known to the public, literally hours after it was featured on the evening news, the shit would hit the fan."

"What do you mean?"

"Thousands of people on the island would pull together to form a coalition." Thinking, "Let's call it the Dominican Coalition for Morality, or the fucked-up DCM, which will oppose the government's initiative because providing condoms and assistance to prostitutes would only encourage their abhorrent behavior and condone their sinful lifestyle."

"How sad. That could very possibly happen."

"And not only that, Tony. Then a Dominican bishop would go on a rampage against the president, accusing him of promoting sex tourism instead of trying to eradicate it, thus tainting the soul of the country with support for deviants and sinners. How Christian of him!"

"Yes, yes, religion would strike again."

Paul leans his head against his friend's shoulder in a loving gesture. "In your book," he tells him somberly, "you could say that this tiny paradise is a morsel in the mouth of a big bad wolf." Silence. "You may say that your Gringo friend and partner in crime is an editor from Texas; and that you, well, you happen to be a bisexual novelist who hails from old Castile. But we could all the same be lawyers, businessmen, or professors from everywhere in the world. We all abuse and exploit these people because we can afford it. And we keep coming back."

Antonio tries to offer Paul a smile, says, "Now who's being a fucking downer?"

Back in his chair, Antonio fetches his notepad and searches for a passage. Paul sits by him. "Here," he tells Paul, handing him the notebook. "I'd like you to read this. I believe it encapsulates what you just said. Tell me what you think."

Paul reads the passage aloud, "In the burning hot mornings of the tropics, when the young male whores of this island think of the night's work ahead, they see in all of us tourists one single, profitable, unappetizing body to be pleasured for a price: the means to a life without poverty, to a future of freedom." Silence. Paul tries to think of what to say...

"So now I know what it takes to shut you up!"

"Just give me a second, Tony." Pensive. "The tone is heavy but sincere and heartfelt. Just make sure your narrative isn't this deep throughout." Silence. "And the trope is effective, I think. All the bodies becoming one single body. Synecdoche, right?" He daintily hands Antonio the notebook. "Not bad for just notes, darling. Can't wait to read the finished project!"

"Really? You think it might work?"

"Yes, dear, really. But remember to provide enough Santo Domingo markers so it doesn't sound like some fantasy island, unfortunately without sexy and debonair Montalbán. Who the fuck needs him, anyway? You can make your own kind of magic without him."

Antonio, cracking up, "Ricardo Montalbán?! I knew it. You *are* bullshitting me!"

"Ay, writers are so sensitive!"

Antonio tosses his notepad. "Forget my damn novel!" he pronounces. "Let's do something real for these guys, Paul." Deep in thought. "How about setting up a scholarship or an educational trust fund for sex workers? You know, an incentive for them to go to school and..."

"Hey, yeah! The white saviors come to the rescue!" Silence. "All joking aside, I think it's a great idea. And since this scholarship would be privately *and* secretly funded, no one could oppose it. We'd make sure to keep it under wraps, just in case."

Excited, "Now you're talking, Paulita!"

"Let me take care of the details. I'll talk to the Autónoma folks. I'm sure I can drum up a lot of support from the university. I know people in high places there who'd go out of their way to humor me." Silence. "The fund could be accessible to college-age sex workers, on the condition that they pursue a course of study and stick with it. What do you think?"

"I love it! How can I help?"

"I'll keep you posted. I'm sure there'll be a lot of paperwork at first. You know, setting up the fund, defining conditions for qualification, types of academic advising that will be needed, recruitment efforts. And, most importantly, we should get ready to write a big yearly check."

"You got it. So, what name are we going to give this fund?"

"How about... the Quisqueya Scholarship Fund?"

"Fantastic!" Antonio leans over to embrace Paul, kneels by him and holds him tight. "Thank you for being onboard with this idea, Paul..."

"Oh my, I'm not sure I can handle this outburst of emotion!" Stroking his friend's head, "Actually I like it, babe. And you're welcome. It's about time we took some kind of action. You know, put your money where your mouth is. Anyway, it's a start. A flicker of hope, as you'd say. The sky's the limit!" Laughing, "Shit, I'm so full of idioms. Once an editor..."

Antonio, still embracing his friend, "... Always a fucking editor."

Luis

The turning point. Is that what this scene would be called? It's when something important happens that changes the protagonist's life forever. Which is what's about to take place tonight, something *important*, as Luis faces his audience and prepares to regale them with his songs. A concert—his first!—at the National Theater, the most prestigious venue in Santo Domingo. If he succeeds here, he'll be famous for sure. He'll hire a savvy manager and get a recording contract so he can sell his music, his voice traveling everywhere thanks to his records.

There they are, his fans, thousands of them, waiting impatiently for him to start the show. And there's a huge orchestra ready to accompany him. A string section because you need violins to sing ballads, but also trumpets, a sax, two conga drums, an electric piano, and a flute. Yeah, he's ready to grab his guitar. He's been rehearsing his repertoire (cool Paul word) for months.

Luis Miranda Ramos looks hot in a sky-blue silk shirt like the ones singers wear in those MTV videos he watches at the hotel, with a thin leather tie, black jeans, Cuban-heeled boots, and his hair fluffed up in the style of famous bands like Duran Duran and Tears for Fears. It feels good to be this person. He imagines himself as his idol, singing one of Luis Miguel's first hits, "Decídete," a song Mamita loves. She says her son resembles the Mexican singer but is more handsome and has a stronger tenor voice. Yeah, he's a *pechú* performer! He has never told anyone (and never will) that sometimes he imagines he's Luis Miguel's lover and lives with him in a grand Mexico City penthouse. But it's only a fantasy he beats off to once in a while 'cause there's no chance of that ever happening.

Now if only he could be totally original as he launches his career, not a copy of his idol but the real deal. And with a name that would stand out, *El Gran Luis*. Yeah, that would work.

Ladies and gentlemen! No, not yet... Before the show begins, he has to give an interview. Part of the job! There's a reporter backstage who's writing an article about him for *Dominicano en Vivo*, the most popular magazine in the country. She's been following him everywhere, hoping to capture a variety of angles on his life for the piece, aiming for an intimate portrayal.

Luis finds the reporter standing by his dressing room, ready with pad and pen. She's young, pretty, confident. He shakes her hand, thanks her for her patience, and invites her in. They sit. Right off, he tells her there isn't much time. His audience awaits! She gets to it. "Let's begin by talking about your style of music," she says. "How do you describe it?"

"I'd describe it as a mixture of Dominican folklore and contemporary pop. I especially like our home-grown bachata, which can be upbeat and happy but also mellow and sweet."

"Tell us about the performers you most admire, the ones who've inspired you."

"There's only one, Luis Miguel. I like his voice and his elegant, classy look."

"Yes, I agree that Luis Miguel is quite gifted. I happen to like his songs a great deal."

"Although he tends to be much more theatrical than I'd ever want to be."

"Interesting. That reminds me... You've been quoted as saying that you often perceive your life as if it were a play, as a *theatrical* performance..."

"Yes, but for me there's a difference between the life you live and your art. When it comes to my music and my concerts, I prefer a more intimate, personal style. I don't like to act out my songs with lots of hand gestures and dramatic moves, like Luis Miguel. And, again, my performance on stage is different from my day-to-day life, which sometimes seems to unfold as if the people I know and myself were characters created by some god-like playwright."

"That's fascinating, Luis. Can I call you Luis?"

"Of course, that's what my friends call me."

"Thank you. So, yes, that's such a novel idea, life lived as a play. No one had ever related their experiences to me that way. You obviously love the theater. We can talk about your favorite plays and playwrights later, if there's time. Before we get to that, however, I'm sure your fans would like to know more about the people who've influenced you, other than Luis Miguel."

"My mother, Elena Miranda Ramos, is the source of all my inspiration. I owe her my musical talent, too; she's a great singer. My mother made great sacrifices so I could have a successful career. I wouldn't be here, giving an interview, if it weren't for her..." Shouldn't he mention Mister Paul? The Gringo deserves some credit for all he's taught him. No, better not make any reference to his previous life or name one of his best clients. Just in case. "And the other important person is my best friend, Richard, who's always encouraged me to pursue my dream. Richard is a gifted poet. He knows all about creative moods and understands that sometimes I need to withdraw from everything and everyone to work on my songs."

"A good, supportive friend indeed, one who knows when to stay out of the way. And speaking of songs, Luis, tells us about your repertoire for this evening's event."

"I'll be performing twenty of my original compositions. I chose that number because it happens to be my age." He pauses, laughs. "But also because I've only written twenty so far!"

"Now let's talk about a rumor that has been circulating in the media, that before you became a singer-songwriter, you made a living as a sex worker. Is this true?"

Shit, he didn't expect that question! How to answer it? If he says yes, the admission could ruin his career. If he says no, then someone might dig up some hard evidence, dirt, and then he'd be considered not just a hustler but a liar. How about a half-truth, then? He should try to sound honest and intelligent, using big Paul words. Yeah, he should channel the Gringo...

"Well, actually," he states confidently, "I prefer to use the word *escort* to describe the work I used to do. You see, my job entailed showing tourists around our city, taking them to the best restaurants and clubs and beaches; overall, just making sure they had a fun time." Awkward silence. "You can't reproach me for wanting to make people happy, right?"

"No, no, I didn't mean to imply that."

Yes, she did. Bitch! But he showed her. He came up with the best answer ever. And now she's getting on his nerves. Luis must suppress his wrath! (More cool words, thanks to Paul.)

"Do you have any other questions for me?"

"Just one, Luis. Are you musically trained?"

"I never took music or voice lessons, but I've worked hard at teaching myself and perfecting my art. And speaking of which, now I need to go and make my magic."

"By all means. Thanks for your time. I look forward to your show. Break a leg!"

The booming voice of the show's presenter resounds in the packed auditorium. God, he loves that ovation! Luis plays a few guitar chords. The orchestra comes in, then his voice, softly, while the stage is lit brightly and fully. He walks out, bringing his guitar, takes a bow and sits on the stool center-stage, in front of the mike. Soft strumming. Melodious picking. Applause!

He looks up, hoping to see his mother in the highest balcony, across from the stage. That's the place reserved for the president and other high-level people. Dignitaries, he thinks they're called. Heck, yeah, that's what Mamita is, the dignitary of his home. She's in a dress worthy of her beauty, clad as a magnificent Afro-Caribbean queen. The spirits of Emilia and Jacinto are sitting beside her. Luis can sense their supportive, loving presence.

Hard to see Mamita's face from here, but he'd bet she's smiling proudly. He'd love to be up there with her, feeling her reassuring warmth, to obey his impulse to climb from balcony to balcony like a naughty kid to reach her and kiss her. Unfortunately, there's no chance of that happening. So, he'll just ask for a spotlight on Mamita and say:

"Ladies and gentlemen, allow me to introduce my mother, Elena Miranda Ramos. I love you, Mamita! This concert is for you!"

Luis looks below at the audience and sees Paul in the front row, winking at him. And Richard stands in the wings, giving him his sweetest smile and a thumbs up. Richard would've climbed up the balconies with him to kiss Mamita if Luis had asked him. Because he loves her. A funny thought: In his mind, Richard would've been a creature in one of those sci-fi stories he likes, an alien with tentacles for feet which would stick to walls to propel him. What a crazy stunt that would've been, the two of them making everyone laugh. The show before the show!

His first number, finally. While he performs it, he realizes that it's sounding even better than it did in rehearsal. He gets the audience to sing the refrain with him; they've learned it by heart on the spot! This song leads to a powerful crescendo that brings his fans to their feet—moving them to clap for long minutes. And when El Gran Luis has sung all his songs, he'll take a bow again, and the crowd will ask for one more number. They'll be screaming, *Encore! Encore!* And, of course, Luis will humor them. He'll give them his heart and soul in a grand finale.

Wait. But if this is his greatest performance, why do his throat and chest hurt so much? He can't see Mamita's balcony! And why is he standing alone with his guitar on the Cristóbal stage, trembling because he's so nervous? Where are his cheering fans?! He can see Paul, Antonio, and Richard seated at a table to the side, trying to focus on him but distracted by the hubbub of men hooking up. Señor Zamora is having his usual shot of whiskey at the counter, looking annoyed. No one here cares about El Gran Luis. They haven't even noticed him.

This is all wrong. He must fix it! He'll close his eyes and wish that this shitty reality will vanish. In its place, he'll dream up a show worthy of his talent and his effort. He must sing! That's the incantation for this miserable scenario to become the turning point.

He'll sing a siren's song, with the power in his voice to lure horny sailors and trap them in his bed of algae. Or better yet, he'll be a hot merman singing for a room packed full of johns. It was one of those johns who told him about sirens, hideous monsters, and mermaids, who sing like angels. This guy was a professor, a scholar of legends, and...what was the other thing? Myths! Yeah, that was it. He was an expert on mythology, and he told Luis all about the tales of sirens and mermaids, who aren't real beings, but people need to believe in them anyway. Just like Luis Miranda Ramos needs to believe in El Gran Luis, who *does exist*.

He catches his reflection in the mirror behind the bar counter, looking sexy in the outfit Paul bought for him in a downtown boutique. He takes a sip of water, clears his throat, and psyches himself up for the most crucial moment of this play about his life. So far, his audience has enjoyed several intimate scenes in his house and at the Hotel Cristóbal. And now, at last, the scene of Luis performing a song he wrote about true love. Here he goes...

Dammit, he's coughing his lungs out as he tries to sing the first line. No, the horrific sound must be coming from someone in the audience. How rude is that?! He tries again, and now he sneezes, and then his singing gets drowned out by a loud, painful cough. Shit, maybe his mother was right; maybe he has a bronchial infection. He sees Señor Zamora approaching him with a handkerchief on his mouth. The boss is whispering hurtful words in his ear...

Fuck, what kind of play is this?! Not a comedy nor a tragicomedy for sure 'cause there ain't nothing funny about any of it. So, is this a tragedy?! Maybe. But in tragedies, someone must die, and Luis is not ready for that denouement (great Paul word.) He's still too young! He keeps telling himself that things will work out in the end because his god, a powerful playwright, is looking out for him and will save him. Luis has so many questions for that deity. Like, who is the antagonist in this play? Could it be a bronchial infection that's making him think dark thoughts? Yeah, a fucking illness is his worst enemy, his adversary. And if it turns out that he caught the faggot virus, then the Gay Plague would be his antagonist. But not just that virus but also the john who infected him and the other tourists he's fucked. Which would include the Cristóbal and the whole city of Santo Domingo. Because it all has conspired to make sure that Luis remains a broken man who won't be able to provide for his mother and rent a beautiful house for her. And who won't fulfill his dream of becoming a superstar.

There are no answers, no comforting message from his playwright-creator. That mighty being won't tell him if he's going to get a happy ending, and that's because playwright-creators don't exist. Luis knows that now. He also knows that the only conflict in this drama is the one he has with himself, for putting his life at risk, and for not listening to his mother's advice. If this were the denouement of his story, then the last scene would show the protagonist repenting for all his stupid actions. Luis, imploring his imaginary deity not to let this story end as a tragedy, not to let its message be that hustlers like himself have no future.

He should cut his losses and split, get far away from this stage. Problem is, he can't move. It feels as if a wicked siren has taken over his body, stealing his voice, his will. That siren is turning the audience against him, making them boo and hiss. She's also polluting the airwaves with blasting techno-pop music and transforming the bar into a dance floor where couples are moving to the frenzied rhythm, happy, horny, drunk, unaware that El Gran Luis is still standing there, feeling embarrassed and hurt and disappointed, his heart breaking. They push him aside. They laugh at him as they invade the stage to do their awkward, idiotic dancing.

And now Luis can finally run out, dropping his guitar on Richard's lap. As he leaves, he can see Mister Paul talking to the manager. Maybe Paul is telling Señor Zamora that Luis is sick, not in top form, and asking him to give him another chance some other night. Please?

The lights dim, and a transparent curtain falls on the Cristóbal stage. Suddenly, absolute silence. Everyone in that room stops, frozen like frightening statues. The absence of light and sound overwhelms him. Is Luis deaf, too? No, he does hear a friendly voice breaking through the eerie quiet and the darkness, calling him, asking him to please wait...

Richard

It broke his heart to see Luis on the Cristóbal stage, so defeated, looking miserable because he couldn't sing. His guitar playing was beautiful, though, and that should've been enough for those creepy tourists to be pleased and to clap. But no, instead, they booed him when Luis didn't hit the right notes, and when he had to stop because of a coughing attack. Those shitheads! Those assholes! Except for Mister Paul and Señor Antonio, who were clapping excitedly, they should all be sent back to whatever country they came from. Or better yet, to Hell!!

Even the manager was mean to Luis, and that's unusual because Señor Zamora always has kind words to say to his "brood of chicks." But not this time. This time he went up to Luis, evidently pissed off, and whispered something in his ear. And right after that, Luis dropped the guitar on Richard's lap and ran out of the hotel. Richard tried to follow him and finally caught up with Luis when his friend sat on a bench at the malecón, gasping for air.

He sat beside him and said, "Hey, buddy, didn't you hear me calling you?"

"What do you want?" asked Luis.

Richard, holding up the guitar, "You forgot this!"

"Thank you," Luis said, coughing, and he placed the instrument on the side of the bench.

"You need medicine, Luis. Some cough syrup would do you good. Mamita should give you a spoonful as soon as you get home. And you should get into bed immediately and rest as much as you can. And take lots of vitamin C, which fortifies your immune system. That's what my dad says, and Papi knows his stuff. I do take vitamins every day. They've helped me a lot 'cause I haven't gotten a cold in a long time. If you want, I can ask my dad for strong cough medication. You might even need antibiotics. I think you're supposed to have a doctor's prescription for those, but Papi could make an exception in your case. Let me ask him, okay?"

"Sure, thanks." Luis sneezed and wiped his nose with his shirt sleeve. "Don't worry about me, okay? I'll be fine."

"I do worry about you. And I'll be checking up on you until you get better."

Luis, annoyed, "Great, so now I'll have to put up with two Mamitas!"

Richard gave Luis a pat on the thigh, just like Luis had done to him the day they met. "Hey, I was wondering," he said, "were you nervous on stage?"

"No, I just couldn't sing because of this nasty cold."

"You'll be able to try again when you feel better."

"Yeah, if I get another chance."

"I'm sure you will. Señor Zamora understands that you're..."

"No, he doesn't," said Luis, interrupting. "He just told me to get the fuck off his stage and never come back. Told me I'd made him look bad with his special guests."

"Forget that crazy-hair bastard! We'll find you another bar, maybe even a theater."

"Thanks for your support, little brother."

Luis had never called him 'little brother.' That was so sweet!

"You'll always have my support, Big Bro," Richard decided to say.

"It's just that... I wanted to show off for Paul, put on a great performance for him."

"But you've performed for him a lot already, in his room..."

"Yeah... I have to get over my disappointment, that's all." Luis grabbed his guitar and stood up. "I need to go, and you should get back to the bar. Don't make Antonio wait!"

Luis was pursing his lips; it's what he does when he's angry.

"Are you mad at me?" Richard asked him. "Did I say something wrong?"

"No," Luis replied, walking away. "Just get back to work, okay?"

Richard, trailing behind, "Are you jealous of Señor Antonio?"

Luis stopped, turned to his friend. "Why would I be jealous of a john?"

"He's more than a john, Luis."

"Oh yeah? And how so?"

"To begin with, thanks to him my brothers now have all the school supplies they need, and new shoes and uniforms. I got my brother Johnny the Walkman he wanted so bad, and for my mom I bought a bunch of kitchen stuff." He forced a smile. "Maybe now she'll get excited about cooking and start making yummy meals like Mamita." Silence. "And I've started to save to get my dad a nice bike, so he doesn't have to ride the bus to work. And for me..."

"Shut up! I know what our money can buy."

"Sorry. I was just trying to explain."

"Doesn't your family wonder where you get all the dough?"

"I told them I'm waiting tables at a fancy downtown restaurant, with lots of tips."

"And they pretended to believe you, right? I'd bet they didn't even ask you the name of the place." Silence. "They *know*, Richard, but they choose not to know. Same old story."

"Okay, so? You're just pissed 'cause I make more money than you."

Luis, suddenly curious, "How much more?"

"Double what all you guys charge."

Luis lovingly cupped Richard's face in his hand. "Just look at my puppy showing his little fangs!" Silence. "And what did you have to do to get double out of the Gallego?"

Richard tensed up. "Nothing weird or kinky."

"You're lying!" Luis held Richard gently by the shoulders. "Tell me the truth, you piece of shit. Did you break Rule Number Two? What did he do to you?!"

Richard pried himself away from Luis and said, much too defensively. "I trust Señor Antonio, okay? He cares for me, he really does. He changed his return flight so we could spend a few extra days together. And he's coming back to take me traveling all over the world with him."

"You're such an idiot." Luis clutched Richard's crotch with both hands. "This is all they want, you fucking fool. If you give it to them, they'll promise you the world!" He slapped Richard's butt. "And more so if they can have your ass, too."

"I didn't give him my ass..."

Long, painful silence. Luis sat, strummed his guitar. Richard sat by him.

"You did. You can't lie to me," said Luis, calmly at last, and he tried to sing. His voice trailed softly over the strumming, overwhelmed by the sound of the boisterous surf, of the traffic and the people who passed by, chatting. "I know you better than you know yourself."

Richard felt cold and frightened. "Can this be our secret, Luis? Please?"

"Don't worry..." Luis suffered a coughing attack. "Just don't let anyone else use you that way again. Never ever. You promise?"

Richard, with index fingers as a cross over his lips, "I promise!"

Luis offered Richard a hug, said, "All's good, then," and he got back to his playing. Soon he stopped, feeling nauseous, and leaned his head on Richard's shoulder. "None of them will give us a hand for real," he told his friend. "Believe me, kid. They just won't."

"But Mister Paul has been really good to you."

"Yes, but he'll never take me to the States with him. And if I made my way there somehow and called him up, he'd probably invent all kinds of excuses not to see me."

"Are you sure? How do you know that?"

"It's happened to some of the guys at the Cristóbal. They get in touch with their johns who promised them all kinds of things, and the creeps pretend they're too busy to see them."

"I guess you're right. No one's willing to help us."

"You're on your own, little brother."

Silence. Minutes later, Richard said, "But... we've got each other, no?"

"Yes, and let's not forget that."

"We should just get the fuck out of here together, Luis, go to the States and maybe do the same kind of sex stuff at first, which would pay better there, wouldn't it?"

"The two of us leaving together?" Uncertain, "Yeah, why not." Excited, "All I know for sure is that I'm going to launch my career as a singer in America. I'll be famous there, more than Luis Miguel. And I'll make our bachatas the most popular music in the world."

"That sounds fantastic, Luis!"

"And as soon as I start earning big money, I'll stop selling my dick. No more johns. I'm going to make records. And I'll tour, giving lots of concerts everywhere."

"What about Mamita? Will she stay here or go touring with you?"

"She'll definitely be with me wherever I go. In fact, she's going to design all my cool stage clothes, you know, the Gran Luis look."

Richard, feeling forsaken, "Whereas I have no idea what I'll be doing..."

"You'll be working with me, of course. You're going to be my manager."

"Really? And what does a manager do exactly?"

"Managers negotiate contracts, book concerts, deal with the press..."

"You think I could do all that?"

"For sure you could. You're good with people, and you have a knack for negotiating, obviously. But first you'll have to learn English. We can practice it together, okay?"

"No problem. I speak a little already. And when will this great thing be happening?"

"Soon!" Silence. "By the way, since you'll have lots of free time working with me, you can take classes and write poetry, which is your passion, right?" Overcoming his physical discomfort, revived by his creative energy, "Hey, Richard, I just had a great idea! What if I composed melodies for some of your poems? We'd be collaborators, a songwriting team!"

"Sure, Luis. But you've never read my stuff. How do you know I'm any good?"

"I just do... 'cause I know you."

"Thanks!" Deep in thought, then cheerful, "Okay, let's write songs together."

"Big hits, Richard!"

"Yeah!" Suddenly glum, "And until then... we're stuck at the Cristóbal."

"Not stuck, buddy. We can leave that dump any time we want."

"True. But we shouldn't just yet..."

Richard stood up, walked a few feet away from his friend and stared out at the ocean, which was unusually serene. He breathed in the salty air, listened to the waves, and at that precise moment, it seemed as if time had stopped racing toward the future, as if it didn't exist.

Luis stood beside him, said, "I like your face in profile. Looks really nice against the sunset. Like one of the pictures Paul takes."

Richard, at a loss for words, "Thanks, Big Bro." Silence. "How are you feeling?"

Luis tried to laugh but coughed instead. "Like shit."

"Let's get you home, okay?"

"Yes, I'm ready."

"Here, let me carry the guitar for you. My first job as your manager!"

"My *songwriting* manager. Just make sure you don't catch this fucking bug."

"I won't. I take vitamins." Silence. "And thanks for everything, Luis."

"You don't have to thank me."

"Yes, I do. For showing me the ropes and looking out for me and..."

"Okay, okay, you're welcome!"

"And also... for all your love."

"What did you just say?"

"It's the truth... I know you love me, Luis. And I love you."

"Buddies don't say that to each other, Richard."

"I can't help feeling what I feel."

Luis, pretending not to care, "Whatever." Then, tenderly, "Hey, why don't you visit with us tomorrow? Mamita would be happy to see you. She wants to make sancocho for you."

"Thanks! She knows how much I like it. What time?"

"Doesn't matter. Spend the whole day with us. It's Sunday."

"But... what about Mister Paul and Señor Antonio?"

Luis could finally laugh wholeheartedly. "They can go to fucking hell!"

Richard, shouting, "And burn there forever, yeah!"

"We don't need them anymore, right?"

"Right!" Richard noted how spectacular the obelisk looked against the starry sky, as they walked down the malecón. He was daydreaming. "Because we're going to be a team..."

"You betcha, my friend!"

"Are you sure about that, Luis?"

"One hundred percent sure."

"Good!"

Richard hoped he could replay this moment in his mind like a time loop. Forever.

Acknowledgments

This novel was initially imagined as a play, hence the theatrical elements it incorporates. Before it found its final form, the story went through several drafts that my dear friend and theater scholar Polly Hodge brilliantly edited. Thank you, Polly, for your invaluable feedback!

I would like to take this opportunity to thank the scholars and playwrights who've inspired me to write for the stage and to create theatrical fiction: Juan Villegas, Lillian Manzor, Pedro Monge Rafuls, Manuel Martín; and the critics who have generously studied and taught my creative work: Rudyard J. Alcocer, Ylce Irizarry, Lázaro Lima, Andrea O'Reilly Herrera, John Ribó, Eliana Rivero, Kristy Ulibarri, and Alan West-Durán. A big thanks to Matthew David Goodwin, organizer of the Latinx Visions conference in New Mexico, who provided me with an ideal venue for my very first reading of *Encore! Encore!*

As always, I wish to acknowledge the ongoing support of my family: Karen, my soulmate and most demanding critic. Annika, gracias por toda tu valiosa ayuda, Baby. *Aprisiesion mosh!* Aidan, gracias por nuestro diálogo, siempre estimulante. Chewie, you are the best canine assistant a writer could have!

I owe a debt of gratitude to my editor Ian Henzel at Rattling Good Yarns Press for his insightful suggestions. Before working with Ian, I had no idea that editing a work of fiction could be such a fun and rewarding experience. *Merci, mon cher ami!*

To my dear friends Tracy David Terrell and John Miller, in memoriam, so deserving of the dedication of this book. To the young Dominican men whose lives are voiced by two of my characters; may this novel shed at least some light on their plight. And to Manuel Puig, whose playful spirit hovered around me as I wrote this story.

About the Author

Elías Miguel Muñoz is proud to have contributed to forging the Latinx literary canon. He has published seven novels and two poetry collections that explore his Cuban immigrant roots and themes of exile, sexuality, and friendship. Muñoz's critically acclaimed books include *En estas tierras / In This Land* (1989), *The Greatest Performance* (1991), *Brand New Memory* (1998), *Vida mía* (2006), and *Diary of Fire* (2016). His theatrical work has been produced off-Broadway, and his writing has appeared in numerous anthologies: *Best Gay Stories 2012* (2012), *Ambientes: New Queer Latino Writing* (2011), *The Scribner Writers Series: Latino and Latina Writers* (2004), *Herencia: The Anthology of Hispanic Literature of the United States* (2002), *The Encyclopedia of American Literature* (1999), and W.W. Norton's *New Worlds of Literature* (1994) among others.

Muñoz envisions *Encore! Encore!* as his first novel in a series featuring the histories and cultures of Hispanic Caribbean countries. He is presently developing a science-fiction project that delves into three pivotal time periods of the Caribbean region. Muñoz resides in California and welcomes visitors at eliasmiguelmunoz.com.

Printed in the USA
CPSIA information can be obtained
at www.ICGtesting.com
LVHW091329021123
762340LV00004B/166